# The Last Hope

## Book Four of the Sevordine Chronicles

by

Shawn P. B. Robinson

BrainSwell Publishing
Ingersoll, Ontario

ISBN 978-1-989296-62-2

Cover design and artwork copyright © Shawn Robinson
Interior Page Dividers designed from images downloaded from Freepick.com.

BrainSwell Publishing
Ingersoll, ON

# Dedication and Thanks

This book is dedicated to Scott Cahan (an author of a couple series, one a Christian Humor MG Superhero series and also a Christian Sci-Fi series). Scott, you've been a great friend and support to me throughout the years. Despite the fact that we've never actually met in person, I have appreciated your help, direction, advice, and critique so much!

This book is a work of fiction.
So, here it is.
I'm coming to grips with the fact that I should probably just accept that I must concede that I have to tell people this book is fiction. I find that strange. I find that somewhat disturbing. I find that… concerning, on many levels. But, I accept it. Now, for you, I ask that you accept the difficult to believe truth that this book is not true. I mean to say… it's fiction. All of it.
If you can believe that, you will do well in life. I hope.

# Preface

Oh, I love this book!

I wish I had more to say, but this was a fun one to write. However, as much as I love this book, book 5 is absolutely awesome! So, get cracking on this book and then dive into book five!

Shawn P. B. Robinson

# CHECK OUT THESE BOOKS BY
## Shawn P. B. Robinson

## Adult Fiction (Sci-fi & Fantasy)

The Ridge Series (3 books)
ADA: An Anthology of Short Stories

## YA Fiction (Fantasy)

The Sevordine Chronicles (5 Books)

## Books for Younger Readers

Annalynn the Canadian Spy Series (6 Books)
Jerry the Squirrel (4 Books)
Arestana Series (3 Books)
Activity Books (2 Books)

www.shawnpbrobinson.com/books

# Table of Contents

*1*

⎯·⎯·⎯●⎯·⎯·⎯

# The Beginning of the End

I calm my breathing as I stare out at the waves. The bitter wind bites into my skin, but my clothes are warm. Besides, my time here has taught me how to handle the cold.

After spending months working on a boat out at sea, shivering and doing everything I can to stay warm, the wind now feels good on my face. It helps keep me focused.

In my right hand is a piece of paper. I've read it a dozen times or more. Ellcia is right. It's our marching orders—I'm sure of it. But it's not as clear as I would like.

Hemot is traumatized by the note. No, not traumatized. Angry. Upset. Scared. Just a whack of not-good emotions coming from that guy right now.

It's no wonder, considering…

The great thing about the wind coming off the ocean is I can no longer hear Hemot back in the village. I expect he's still yelling.

I close my eyes and take a deep breath. Someone's approaching from behind, but everyone in this village can be trusted. They are loyal and kind.

Whoever it is sits down beside me. I hope it's Ellcia. I'd like to spend time with her. We haven't had a chance to talk. Now that I've told her how I feel, I only want to talk about that.

The smell, however, tells me it's not Ellcia. That's the smell of a large man who works on a boat.

Without opening my eyes, I acknowledge my visitor. "Nordin."

"Prince Draydon."

I open my eyes and smile. I don't really like the name "Draydon." I prefer Caric, but Draydon is my given name and likely the one I will have to rule with. In fact, it's time. It's time to give up being Caric, and take up who I truly am.

"You're calling me by my royal name. That must mean you believe the secrecy is gone."

Nordin chuckles to himself. "For now, at least. I don't know what's on that little piece of paper in yar hands, but I suspect it's what's gotten young Hemot all worked up and what's caused Ellcia to retreat into the kitchen to work. She won't talk, she just scrubs pots like each one needs to be taught a lesson." He takes a deep breath and lets it's out slowly. "It's time for ya to return to the castle, isn't it?"

I nod. "We have to reach the castle sometime in the next month. I just don't know if we have a week, two weeks, or the full thirty days."

"Do ya want to show me what's on the paper?"

I hand it to him, and he unfolds it. He clears his throat and then reads, "On behalf of the Kingdom of Sevord and on behalf of the Lord Yune and the Lady Aldora, the…" Nordin shakes his head. "I'm sorry, my Prince, but I'm not good at reading this formal print. It's like they try their best to make it confusing."

I smile again and take the note back. "That's okay, Nordin. I've spent a lot of time reading it. It's a wedding announcement and invitation. Prince Roran and Lady Marleet, Lord Yune's daughter, are to be wed in thirty days."

Nordin nods slowly, and the two of us stare out at the sea. After a while, he says, "That seems like just regular information about a couple Nobles to me. Not marching orders. So, there must be something about the wedding that's a problem."

I chuckle. "You could say that."

"What is it?"

"That's what I'm trying to figure out." I try to piece together my thoughts and lay them out for my friend and mentor. "Marleet would not willingly marry Roran—that much I know for sure. So, that means either we have to rescue Marleet to get her out of the situation, or the wedding is just a ploy by Parthun to kill both Marleet and Roran. Either way, we must get to the castle and get her out."

"Why ya?"

I shake my head. "What do you mean?"

"Why ya? Why not Captain Tilbur? Why can't someone else get her out of the castle?"

That's one of the things I like about Nordin. He asks the most obvious questions, but ones I miss all the time. "I don't know. But I'm pretty sure this is what we're supposed to do."

"We have well over a hundred that can fight," Nordin explains. "A hundred and seventy, to be exact. We can be ready to move at yar command."

My mouth drops open. "A hundred and seventy… to fight?"

He nods. "Well, we have more, but to protect the children, some need to remain behind. The women of our village do not typically go to war, but over the last couple months, we've been training them as we've known we need as many hands as possible. I've counted up those who can fight, considering how many we need to care for the children, the sick, and the elderly as they will be left behind. That gives us one hundred and seventy. Understand that in our village, no one under the age of sixteen goes to battle, so there are a few who might be able to fight, but they are too young—although do not doubt their loyalty to ya, Prince Draydon."

Gratitude floods my heart. I know I can count on my friends here. But I also can't risk them just yet.

"Nordin, this mission won't be won with numbers, but with stealth. We will not be able to storm the castle or force our way in without… well… many will die. But if we can sneak in, we might rescue Marleet without any blood spilled at all."

Nordin puts his big hand on my shoulder. He's done that a few times over the months, and it always makes me feel like he's proud of me. And it makes me feel really small. That's one meaty hand!

"Then, my dear Prince, we will continue to train. If ya so desire, we will also send word to Shizzer, just to the north of us. They are loyal to ya, although they don't know about ya yet. I will visit them and speak with a man there whom I often have dealings with. They will stand by ya as well. They are a larger village than we are. I expect they'll be able to train well over two hundred. Many of their men have fought under yar father." Nordin drops his hand back to his lap and stares out at the sea. His voice comes out a little quieter as he says, "I never wanted to fight in another war, but I believe it's coming. And we will stand by ya, Prince Draydon."

I want to tell him that I don't want to risk his life or people, but I also know that we cannot sit and do nothing. If I've learned one thing over the last while, it's that a King must lead with all he has. There's always risk, but risk must be taken for the sake of the Kingdom.

"Thank you, Nordin. I see why General Lirnal spoke so highly of your people." I pause for a bit and add, "As for Shizzer, yes, please send word. We might need them soon."

Nordin smiles back at me. "When do ya leave, Yar Majesty?"

I step down from the rock and turn to face him. I feel the resolve flood through me. "As soon as we can."

"Ahhh!"

I spin around in time to see Hemot's pack fly across the room. It slams into the wall, and lands on our bed. Some of the stuff inside spills out and drops onto the floor.

"Hemot, calm down."

"But she's getting married!"

I'm feeling frustrated as well, but not with the wedding. I'm upset with Hemot. He just won't focus.

"Look, I get that you're upset. But that's what we're doing! We're going to rescue her."

He turns to me, and I step back. The look in his eyes is not just anger, it's hatred.

"You don't get it, do you, Caric."

"I'm Draydon now." I say, earning me a surprised look, but then I ask, "Get what, Hemot?"

"What if she wants to marry him?"

I grumble and shake my head. "We've been over this, Hemot. She won't marry him. That's all there is to it."

He grinds his teeth and clenches his fists. "And what if that's all changed? What if she isn't interested in me anymore? What if Roran's it?"

I do something I've never done before. I don't normally act this way, but this is just driving me nuts. I punch Hemot in the chest, and he stumbles back.

"Enough with the drama! Get a grip, Hemot. I don't want to spend our entire trip back to Sevord City listening to you complain. We're going to rescue Marleet. That's a good thing. Focus on that."

Hemot looks at me in shock. I guess it's been a lot of years since we've wrestled, and I'm not really one to punch people—especially when I'm angry.

"Can I punch you back?"

"What? Punch me back? That's what you took from what just happened? You think this is just a fight?"

"Yeah. I just figured we were now punching each other."

"Okay, maybe hitting you wasn't the best move. I'm sorry. It's just I want this angry moping to stop."

Hemot frowns and moves over to his bag. He goes back to packing but goes at it like he's mad at the stuff he's taking with him.

When we're finished, we're both wearing our traveling clothes, our armor, and our packs. Hemot also has Marleet's sword and pack.

We head downstairs and are met by Nordin's wife, Hella. She has her typical sweet smile and gives each of us a hug. I don't remember my mom all that well, but if she was anything like Hella, I was the luckiest little boy in the world.

She points Hemot toward the common room, and he moves off in that direction. For the last couple months, everyone's been pretending that we're just a few extra workers in town, but judging from the cheer I hear when Hemot enters the common room, I think they're starting to treat us as something more.

"You, young man, have a Lady to speak to."

I raise my eyebrows and am about to ask what she means, when she shoves me into the kitchen, closing the door behind me.

No one else is in the room, aside from Ellcia. Nordin was right. She's really going at those pots. I think the one she's working on is already clean. But it's clearly going to get cleaner.

I move over to her side. "Ellcia."

She doesn't stop. Doesn't slow down. Doesn't even look at me. "Yes, Ric?"

Ric is the nickname they gave me over the last couple months, just to help disguise me. Ellcia was Cia, and Hemot was Mot. Not very creative, but it worked.

"Are you okay?"

"Fine."

"Are you mad at me?"

"Nope."

"Are you lying?"

"Nope."

I'm not really sure what to do with all that.

I reach over and put my hand on hers. She stops her attempt to scrub through the bottom of the current pot. I suspect that piece of iron has never been so clean.

"What's wrong, Ellcia."

She just stares at the pot. I think if I let go of her hand, she's going to go at it again.

"Is it because of what you said when Tilbur was here?"

Her face goes beet red, and she presses her lips together. That's it.

I pull her around to face me. She just stares at my chest. I guess that's better than nothing.

"I don't know about you, but I'm glad it happened."

She takes a sharp breath, but she's not mad. "You are?"

"I am." I glance back toward the door to make sure we're alone. "I've been keeping that inside for far too long. Now that you know how I feel, I feel free. I feel like we have something special—more than what we had before."

The side of her mouth twists up in what appears to be a smile that she can't keep inside.

"But…" I say.

The smile disappears. She looks me in the eye. "But what?"

I close my eyes. I know what I have to say. But it's likely going to cost me what I want most. I take a deep breath, open my eyes, and dive in. "We both know I don't really have a choice now. I'm pretty sure that I have to be King. I think since Roran abdicated the throne, we won't be able to get him on it—even if we break him of his spell."

She nods.

"That means, then, that…" I clear my throat. I know I'm just stalling. "Ellcia, I want to marry you one day. But I know you don't want to be royalty. You *really* don't. Neither do I, but that's the path I'm on now. It's just a matter of time before I have to lay my claim for the throne. I'm… what I'm asking is… well…"

She smiles. That puts me at ease. "Are you asking me if I would be your…" Her face goes pale, and she stops. Apparently, it's just as awkward for her.

I blurt it out. "I want you to be my Queen. But I know what that will cost you. When the day comes, will you still want me?"

She smiles again. "I will. I know you don't want to be King, and you know I don't want to be Queen. We'll both take what we don't want, the throne, to get what we do want, each other."

"Then you'll be my Queen?"

"If you'll be my King."

Both of us are grinning, and I find myself starting to laugh when Ellcia's detail-mind kicks in. "Oh no! I haven't packed! We're supposed to be leaving soon, right?"

"No worries, my dear!" Hella says as she opens the door. "I already packed everything for you."

I frown. "You were listening at the door?"

She gives me a dismissive wave. "Of course I was, Your Majesty. I'm not going to miss something like this."

She hefts Ellcia's pack onto a counter and starts stuffing food inside. "I left Hemot's food supplies in the other room so he could pack and give the two of you some privacy."

"But you didn't think we needed privacy from you?" I ask.

"Oh, I don't count." She smiles sweetly at me as she slides a bag of food my way.

I shake my head but start stuffing the food into my pack. We're going to need a lot as it's quite a hike to get to the castle.

Out in the street, the entire town has assembled to see us off. I'm a little nervous about that as it was only yesterday that Tilbur and his men were here. If one of his men is traveling through this way right now, they'll see us and see the way the townspeople are acting...

Nordin and Relin come up to me and Hella steps up to Ellcia. The woman wraps her arms around Ellcia and gives her a big hug. Nordin, then Relin do the same to me.

When they're done, Hemot growls, "And me?"

"We wouldn't forget ya, Relin cries out with tears in his eyes, and then wraps his arms around Hemot. He hugs for a long time. Long enough that Hemot appears to be rethinking his desire for a hug. When he finishes, Nordin hugs him as well, lifting Hemot right off the ground.

Once he drops Hemot, Nordin comes back to me. Speaking loud enough for everyone in the crowd to hear, he hollers, "Prince Draydon! Ya have the loyalty of every man, woman, and child in Nimville. Godspeed to ya as you head back to Sevord. I don't know what awaits ya there, but if ya need us, ya have only to call."

Everyone goes silent, and I nod. They remain silent. I nod again. They're still not saying anything. I feel awkward.

Ellcia hisses in my ear, "Say something!"

"Oh, right!" Turning to Nordin, I loudly call out, "Thank you, Nordin, son of..." I shouldn't have started down this road. I have no idea what his dad's name was.

Nordin's eyes shift around, and he whispers, "Pickle. My pa's name was Pickle."

"Pickle?" I whisper back. "Are you serious?" When he looks at me with confusion, I continue. "Thank you, Nordin, son of..." I shake my head, "Pickle. I know that if I take the throne, I have your loyalty. And as Nimville is there for me, the throne will be there for you. If you are in need, all you will ever have to do is call."

Nordin smiles back at me, and Hella gives me a nod as if to say, "Good job." I can't help but smile back.

Once we've said goodbye to a few more people, we head out.

It's time to head back home. I don't know what awaits us there, but we have to do all we can to rescue Marleet.

# 2

## The Hope Grows

The next day, we make our way through Deliver.

On the way through a couple months ago, we avoided all the port towns, but this time, we're planning to walk through them.

It's more curiosity than anything. I want to see what other towns are like and how they're handling the news of Parthun's rise to the throne and demand for everyone's allegiance.

But there's more to it than that. I feel… responsible.

These are my people. Really MY people. I'm going to be their King one day, if I can claim the throne without getting killed, that is. I need to know what they're like and what they're going through. I have to know my people if I'm to be a better ruler than Parthun.

When we enter the town, I'm surprised to see…

Hmm… it's just not what I expected.

"Everyone looks angry at us," Ellcia whispers.

"Like they wish we'd never come," Hemot adds.

I examine all the people within sight. "It's not anger."

"What do you mean?" Hemot asks.

"It's suspicion." I shake my head. "Look at them! They don't trust us. They see us as a threat."

Ellcia leans in close. "What do we do?"

I scan the area. The village is about the same size as Nimville. Maybe fewer people, but it's spread out over a larger area. "We stop in for a meal."

Ellcia grips my arm tightly. "I don't think that's a good idea."

"It's necessary," I say. I know there's risk, but I have to know my people. I have to know what's got them all spooked.

We head to the common room of the inn. Just like Nimville, this common room is bright and cheery. Unlike Nimville, the people inside aren't laughing. While those outside seemed suspicious, the ones inside are downright angry.

It's only mid-day, so most of the men are gone. I assume they're out on the boats. Only about eight or ten men sit at three tables on the far side of the room.

A woman, about the same age as Hella, but far less happy, approaches. In a voice that sounds like she's trying really hard to be cheerful, she asks, "Welcome to Deliver. It's always good to have visitors. What can I get you to eat?"

"We'd like something warm," I say. "It's a chilly day out there."

She smiles at me, but it doesn't reach her eyes. "I'll get you all fixed up, young man," she says and bustles off toward the kitchen.

"Wait!" I call out, and she comes back. I motion for her to come a bit closer, and she leans in. If she's anything like Hella, this woman is likely the most influential woman in the entire town and the most well-informed. "We just came from Nimville. Why is everyone here in Deliver so…"

I look around at the men. They've stopped talking with one another, and they're watching me like a hawk. I turn back to the woman. "Why is everyone here so angry and suspicious?"

She comes in even closer, and her eyes fill with hate. "We just had our world torn apart, young man, and then were forced to swear allegiance to a traitor. If you're from Nimville as you say, then you should know exactly what's spoiled our pudding!"

I've never heard that pudding saying before, but I get the idea. "What's your name?"

"My name's Merka. Short for Merkabellawonterin."

I see why she shortened it. "Merka," I whisper, "My name's Caric. We've been in Nimville for a while. We weren't born there. But we were there when the soldiers came through, led by Captain Tilbur. The people of Nimville have gone through the same thing, but they are happy and cheerful. What's happened here?"

She looks at me with suspicion, but I know what it is. There is a big difference between these two villages. One had us. One had the future King in their midst. Nimville had hope.

But Deliver has none.

The woman shakes her head, gives no answer, and storms off. I turn to the men on the side of the room. Two of them grip their knives. They really hate us.

"Stay here," I whisper to Ellcia and Hemot.

Ellcia's eyes go wide, and she shakes her head. I put my hand on her arm and tell her it'll be okay before grabbing my chair and dragging it over to the men.

They look like they're about to stand up to meet me, but the chair changes things. They know I'm coming to chat.

I drop it down in front of them and sit. And wait.

The eyes of all the men are on me, and I examine each one in turn. Not one drops his gaze from me as I return it.

When I've looked over each of the men, I decide to take the risk.

"My name is Caric," I say with confidence. "My loyalty is to the throne of Sevord and to the proper line, the line of King Hartor and his son first. Since Prince Roran has abdicated the throne, the next in line is called to rule. That..." I pause... this is where it gets awkward. "That is... my loyalty is not with Parthun. The next in line to the throne is General Geran's son, Draydon."

I've taken a terrible risk. If the men are loyal to Parthun, and they attack, I'm finished. I'll never get my sword out in time, and Hemot and Ellcia will not overpower ten men used to hard work in harsh conditions.

The men continue to stare at me, but their expressions have changed. There's still anger there among some of them, but there's confusion mixed with a... softening.

"Those are traitor's words," one of the men in the back says. "We could kill you right now for saying that."

I nod and give a smile. "But you won't."

"And why won't we?" the man asks, before picking up his drink and taking a sip.

"We've just spent the last two months working in Nimville with Nordin and Hella." At the mention of their names, the men perk up, and I see some more suspicion slide away. "They've gone through all you've gone through, but they are happy."

The men frown, and I put up my hands.

"There's a reason why they are happy."

"Why's that?"

"Because... they are not only loyal to the throne like Deliver is loyal to the throne, but they also have hope. I think if you were loyal to Parthun here in this village, you would be happy as he's taken the throne. The fact that you're angry and full of suspicion and look at us like we're invaders tells me that your entire world has turned upside down. You feel betrayed, correct?"

A few of the men slowly nod, but they don't give any more of a response. I wait, until finally one of the men asks, "Why do they have hope?"

"Because," I begin, and let my smile grow, "the son of Geran lives."

The man closes to me grips the handle of his knife. "You're a liar!"

I shake my head. "Nope." I feel like I should have given a better response, but it was all that came to mind. I can't imagine the look on Ellcia's face right now. I don't dare glance back. She won't be pleased.

The man who called me a liar leans forward. "Give me your hand."

That… makes me nervous. I am about to ask why, when the men grab me and throw me to the floor. Next thing I know, I'm pinned to the ground, and my right arm is stretched out to the side. They're prying my fingers open, and I see a flash of a blade.

Panic fills my heart. I think they're going to cut off my hand!

I hear Ellcia and Hemot struggle. Past the men holding me down, I catch sight of them. One man has his arms tightly wrapped around Ellcia, and two men hold down Hemot. He's given them quite a fight. Two months on a fishing boat changes a guy.

"Wait!" I holler. "What are you doing?"

I feel the blade on the tips of my fingers. I struggle, but I fear if I struggle too much, the knife will cut.

"Let him up," one of the men says. "He's telling the truth."

The men climb off me, and I retreat to Ellcia and Hemot. I don't know what's going on now, but then again, I rarely do.

The man who called me a liar comes up to me. He nods at each of us before saying, "You have been working on a boat, that much is true. Your hands look like you're about two months in."

I nod back at him. I'm sure my face is sending a clear message of how scared I am.

"If you're telling the truth about working on a boat, maybe you're telling the truth about all of it."

I wait, expecting more. But… that's it. There's no more coming from him.

"I am telling the truth about Geran's son, Draydon. He survived."

"How?"

"He survived in the castle. The Regent kept him on as a servant, and Draydon had no idea he was anything more than a servant for eleven years. Now he's learned the truth, escaped the castle, and he'll soon be ready to claim the throne. He will soon remove the traitor Parthun."

The men growl. "Where is he? If he lives, he has our loyalty, but where is he?"

I examine the men. Off to my left, Merka and a few ladies have entered the room. The expressions on their faces match their crossed arms.

"Did the men of this village not fight in the Battle of Reber's Gate?"

"Of course we did!" one of the men yells.

"Then do you not remember General Geran?"

The largest of the men growls. "Yes, we remember him. We have grieved his death every day since his murder."

"Then if you remember him," I say, "would you not recognize his armor and his sword? Would you not recognize the family resemblance?"

The men examine my armor, sword, and face. After a moment, one of them gasps, then another, then another.

"But…" one of the men in the back begins, "You said your name was Caric."

I nod. "The name given to me by the Regent to hide my identity from even me. I had no idea who I was. I could only remember little flashes of memories from my childhood—memories that didn't fit with the lifestyle I had been given in the castle. But despite the lies told to me, I have grown attached to the name and use it now to protect my true identity. But I am Prince Draydon, son of General Geran, and next in line to the throne!"

The man who called me a liar drops to his knees first, followed by a guy in the back, followed by the entire group. A quick glance toward the kitchen and I see Merka and the women with her on their knees as well.

"Forgive us, Your Highness. We… we didn't know. I'm sorry I called you a liar. I'm sorry we forced you down on the ground. I'm sorry, my King."

"First, I am not your King, yet. Second, all is forgiven. Please do not even consider the matter ever again. What is your name?"

"Twerp, my Prince."

"Please stand… um… Twerp." I try to make a point not to smile. What kind of parent calls their son "Twerp"? It's like they're trying to ruin his life. "Everyone, please stand." I'm struggling with my words. I feel like that name just threw me right off. I can't think of how to move forward.

When they're on their feet, I manage to come up with a good question. "Where are your loyalties? Is it to the throne and the proper heir?"

They all bow to me, and each one gives me his or her vow of loyalty.

"What is your command, my Prince?"

My mind goes blank again. I'm sure I had some reason I revealed myself to these people. I just can't remember what it is.

I stare at them for a moment, then two. I feel uncomfortable at first, but then I realize they are ready to wait as long as it takes for me to say what I need.

I calm my mind, doing my best to focus. Finally, it comes to me. "I wanted to give you hope and to make a request."

Twerp bows low before me again. "My Prince, hope is always appreciated. But requests are never necessary. Your command is what we look for."

"For now, Twerp, I do not wish to command, but to request. I have your loyalty, that I see clearly, but what I wish is to prove that your loyalty is not unfounded. It is well placed, and you can trust me."

Twerp and the other men smile. Merka does as well.

"I wish to give you hope. The people of Nimville are not downcast like you because they have known of me for a while. Word is being sent to Shizzer as well, and soon they will have hope. I also want you to have hope. Know that what we live under right now is only temporary. As I am able, I will serve the people with all my heart."

Twerp smiles again. "And your request, my Prince?"

"I wish for you to keep the knowledge of my existence secret for now from anyone who might have questionable loyalties or anyone who might tell someone they should not."

"It will be done, my Prince."

"And, I wish for you to train. Be ready. There may come a time when your Prince needs you. I want to know that I can count on the people of Deliver to rise up and fight when the time comes."

Twerp and the other men smile. But not just a normal smile. The smiles are huge. I now see how many teeth are missing among them. "Don't you worry, my Prince. The moment we hear your call, you will have every man, woman, and child able to carry a weapon."

I laugh. "Thank you, Twerp, but I would rather the children stay out of the fight, along with anyone who is needed to care for them and the elderly. We cannot risk the future of our nation on me."

Twerp shakes his head. "No, my Prince, we would risk the future of the nation for the nation. We will give our all for you to be on the throne. But, we will honor your request. No children. And we will protect the vulnerable."

I nod and give a quick smile. "Thank you, Twerp." I feel like I'm insulting him every time I speak to him. "We are heading to Sevord. I don't expect to lay a claim for the throne just yet. There are matters I must address first, but I wish for the fishing villages to be prepared to come to the aid of the kingdom."

Twerp shifts on his feet and gives a worried look to the others. "Your Majesty, have you spoken with others yet, or just us? Do others know who you are?"

"Just you… and the people of Nimville."

Twerp visibly relaxes. "My Prince, you took a risk in speaking with us. We are grateful." The other men along with Merka and the women nod their heads. "But Sire, I would recommend that you keep your identity secret to the men of Port and Grimmer. The closer you get to the capital, the loyalties are more…" He looks around as if he's after the right word. His eyes land on Merka, and I turn to her.

She stares at me thoughtfully. "I think Twerp is trying to say that the closer you get to Sevord, the more the people are like a fruit salad."

I nod… then shake my head. "I'm sorry, Merka. I don't know what that means."

"Well," she begins, "here you've got peaches and apples. We're all different, but we're all fruit, and we're loyal.

It's the same with Nimville and Shizzer, along with the small villages and clusters of houses north of there. Peaches and apples. All loyal."

I nod, hoping for more.

"But," she says, "when you get down south to Grimmer, then to Port, sure they're fruit salad, they have peaches and apples, but they also put tomatoes in."

"They put tomatoes in their fruit salad?" I ask in shock. "Who would do such a thing? They're barbarians!"

"No," Merka says, giving me a disappointed look. "I don't mean they actually put tomatoes in their fruit salad. I mean, tomatoes are a fruit, but they have no place with peaches and apples."

"I am more confused now," I say, "than when you all began. I think perhaps saying it plainly will help."

Merka frowns at me. "I mean, they're a mixed bag. Some are loyal to the throne and are like peaches and apples. Some are more like tomatoes. They're not loyal, and they have no place in a salad." I give another confused look, and she says bluntly, "Not all the people in Grimmer and Port will be loyal to you."

I blink a few times. I'm about to tell her that she should have led with that, but I feel Ellcia's hand on my arm. She pipes in, "Thank you, Merka. We will keep our identity secret in those villages."

Merka smiles at Ellcia and then asks, "Will you need a place to stay tonight?"

I smile at the thought. It'll be nice to be warm tonight. It's still winter, and sleeping outside in that cold is horrible—even with a fire.

We accept, and it's not long before she brings a meal out to us.

I hope to spend the rest of the day relaxing and maybe even take a hot bath, but before I can settle in, I find two of the men in the village come to me and ask me to render judgment on a dispute.

At first, I just can't imagine why they would want me to speak into the matter, but then I remember all of Nordin and Hella's training. This is part of my future role.

I agree, and they set up a chair like a throne in the common room, and people gather to hear my verdict. It turns out the case is about nothing more than who owns a particular chicken. Just a chicken. But the worst part about it is that after all the evidence is provided, I'm convinced that one man owns the chicken without question, but the other man clearly owns all the eggs. I find it unbelievable, yet, the evidence is all there.

I hope, in the future, when I'm deciding matters such as this, that they are both more important and... simpler.

The next morning, we leave early. The people are up before dawn, just like in Nimville, but we're used to it. We join them for breakfast and head out just as the men make their way down to the water for the day's fishing.

Late morning, we catch sight of Grimmer. It's a little smaller than Deliver or Nimville, but after what Twerp and Merka told us in a most confusing manner, we decide to avoid the village altogether.

Just to the east of the main path, up on a hill, runs a smaller path. When traveling along here a couple months ago, we used that path just about the entire time.

When we find a good spot to climb, we make our way up the hill. It's harder traveling along here, but it'll be good to avoid contact as much as possible.

We skim past Grimmer and move along from there. By late in the day, we pass Port, also keeping to the high path and avoiding the people.

It's disappointing to me that the two southerly fishing villages are not loyal to the throne, but to Parthun—or at least some are—but I have to remind myself that they likely don't know all the details. They would only know what Parthun lets them know.

That night, we settle down to the east of the path in a little dip in the ground. With the trees blocking some of the wind and the higher ground around us, we're able to stay a bit warmer. The fire Hemot builds burns bright and hot—just what we need after a long day of hiking in the cold winter air.

# 3

## The Pip Head

It took us around six days to get to Nimville from Sevord two months ago, but we're now on the eighth day, and I think we still have most of the day's traveling left to get to the city.

When we came through this area before, we were running for our lives. This time, we're kind of hesitant to go back for fear of what we're about to face. Only Hemot wants to push on quickly. It's probably best. He's keeping us moving.

Ellcia had been just behind me when we started this morning, but about an hour into our hike, she pulls up next to me. "So, Draydon, where are we heading first?"

I open my mouth to answer, but then shut it. Panic floods my heart. I don't have the slightest plan worked out. It's as if I had no idea that I might have to figure out how to get into the castle and get Marleet out.

"You didn't think that one through, did you?" she asks with a laugh.

I'm about to react, but then I stop myself. I know she's just joking around with me. She's not trying to be mean.

I shake my head and let out a small chuckle. "Give me a moment," I say. She's definitely better at setting up plans, but I've been working on that kind of thing lately with Nordin. I need to be able to do this well and think through all the options.

A moment later, I say, "We need to find Berin. We have to get into the city, but we need someone we can trust like him to help us with contacts and more. He might have a way inside that we don't know about." I take a deep breath. I think Hemot's listening, but he hasn't slowed down. His focus is on one thing and one thing alone—getting Marleet away from Roran.

"We don't know what the gates of the city are like right now. It used to be that entering the city was restricted. It might still be that way. It might also be that the army is still camped out around the city, and Captain Frindor might be patrolling. They won't be looking for me—because they think I'm dead—but that doesn't mean they won't catch us in a random patrol. And then we're definitely going to die. Berin is our way through all that."

"Do you remember how to get to his house?" Ellcia asks.

I smile. "No, but I don't think that's a problem. He's not far from the cliffs—about a few hours this side of Switcher Pass. I think if we move up that way, we'll find it." I glance ahead at Hemot. He's not going to like the next part. "In fact, I think we need to move off the path soon and start making our way up toward the cliffs."

Hemot comes to a halt and quickly turns around. "Caric!" he hisses, using my old name. "If we move off the path, it'll slow us down. It's already been a week since we found out about Marleet. She's getting married in less than three weeks from now. You really think we have time to go for a stroll through the woods."

I'm not feeling very patient with him. He's been grumpy a lot of the trip. "Hemot, tell you what. I'll let you make this decision. You know we're getting close to the castle. And you know soldiers like to harass people when they have nothing to do. So, consider for a moment what Captain Granel and Captain Frindor are going to do to keep the soldiers in line?"

Hemot's eyes shift back and forth, and he grinds his teeth. "How am I supposed to know?"

I close my eyes for a moment. "Hemot, they're going to send them out on patrols. All through this area. All along the paths. They might even come as far north as this point—maybe farther. How much do you think it'll set us back if we get caught by Frindor's men?"

I see comprehension in Hemot's eyes, but he's still angry. I put up my hands and take a step forward. "Hemot. I'm not suggesting we leave the path because I don't care. I'm suggesting that we leave the path so that we can make it there safely. I'm thinking of Marleet and of the Kingdom. If we get caught, this could all be over in a minute." I come in close and put my hands on his arms. "Hemot, what's your decision? Leave the path or stay on it?"

I'm shocked to see a tear stream down his face. I haven't seen Hemot cry much over the years. He's always covering any pain with jokes or new adventures. I'm a little uncomfortable with it, but he comes in and wraps his arms around me and starts to sob on my shoulder.

I really had no idea how much Hemot was hurting over Marleet. I hold him close, and he seems to need it. Ellcia comes in as well and wraps her arms around both of us. A moment later, she starts to cry, and I try to hold her as well.

I don't know what to do with crying people. They make me uncomfortable. I just... I just...

The tears flow down my face, and I sob along with them. I can't believe it's been almost three months since we lost Marleet. I can't believe all the horrible stuff that's happened. I can't believe this all started because we just walked out of the castle one day.

Even so, I would never take it back.

We make our way through the woods. The cliffs are not far from the path in this area—maybe a two hour's hike. We try to stick to the low ground to avoid standing out. By mid-afternoon, we've caught sight of two patrols already. I think if we were still on the path, we'd have seen dozens, maybe more.

We likely won't reach Berin's place until late this evening. We stop for a bit of a meal since we skipped lunch, then push on.

As the sun begins to set, I see a well-worn, but small, path. I'm hoping that's the one that runs by Berin's house. We move in the same direction as it, but we stay well off the path, and it's not long before we see a small cottage.

When we draw near, I hear noise, swords clanging, so we crouch down. At first, I think there's a fight going on. I hear men yell and holler, but something's not quite battle-like.

We scramble through the underbrush and, when we get close, I see Berin in front of his house. He has about a half-dozen soldiers with him, and he's teaching them. They all have swords, and he moves among them, adjusting the way they stand, the way they move. At first, I think maybe he's teaching basics, but I quickly see that each of the men are extremely competent.

And then one turns around, and my heart goes cold.

It's Captain Frindor.

He wears his typical scowl, and his eyes shift back and forth as if he's expecting an attack at any moment. While his sword remains in its sheath, his hand never leaves the hilt.

"Is this really the best the great Berin can do?" Frindor shouts. "I have heard stories, not only of your prowess in battle, but your ability to teach anyone. These men are sloppy, but I see no improvement. Perhaps you've lost your touch, eh?"

I watch Berin closely. Since spending time learning from Nordin, I've learned that I need to pay attention to every situation, every interaction. How Berin reacts will tell me a lot about him.

Berin's face shows no anger, upset, or even hurt. Instead, he bows to Captain Frindor and says, "Thank you, Captain, for reminding me of the heights of which I have achieved. It is true. I even once received the Medal of Bravery from King Hartor himself for facing off against a dozen men with only a fork and a spoon. I can show it to you, if you wish. I mean, the medal, of course. Not the fork and spoon. They're probably mixed up with the other cutlery in my drawer."

Frindor's eye twitches just a little, and he clenches his jaw.

As best as I can tell, Berin just threatened Frindor, making it clear the Captain is out of his league, but I really don't know.

"Carry on," Frindor barks.

Berin comes around to face the soldiers, and in another moment, all of Frindor's men, including Frindor himself, have their backs to me. I take the opportunity to stand up from my hiding spot and make eye contact with Berin. He gives the slightest nod and then goes back to what he's doing.

We retreat back into the forest a little ways, and within half an hour, Berin dismisses the soldiers and sends Captain Frindor away. Once they're out of sight, he waves for us to come, and we rush up and through his front door.

Berin's cottage hasn't changed at all in the last two months, aside from a few extra swords stacked in the corner. It's small—one room—and there's no bed. Last time we were here, we just slept in chairs. That's not a problem, since they're fairly comfortable, but it's a little hard on the neck after a bit.

He closes the door behind us and, in typical Berin style, just walks past us without a word. He's not rude, nor is he overly quiet, he just only speaks if there's a need.

When he reaches the area with the small stove, he sets to work on making a stew. Hemot has some rabbit left over from his last catch and offers that. Not long after, it's all in the pot, and Berin comes and sits down in his favorite chair.

He examines each of us while we sit there in silence. It's great to see him again, and I find I just can't stop smiling.

His eyes land on me, and I just wait while he examines me.

"I think you're about ready to go by Draydon, instead of Caric."

My smile grows larger. I nod. "I still don't like the name, but you're right, I've decided that I need to claim the throne."

Now Berin smiles. "That's good to hear, Prince Draydon. I assume…" He pauses for a moment, and his eyes drift up to the ceiling. When he speaks again, his words come out slowly. "I assume the wedding is part of what draws you back. I also assume that you aren't planning on putting forward a claim just yet, but you're going to wait a bit. Is that correct?"

I nod.

"Then, the first thing you need is to rest up. Then you need to get into the castle."

I nod again.

"Okay…" Berin stares at the ceiling again. "Then here's what I suggest, Your Majesty. Stay here for the night. You'll enjoy the sleep in the cottage a lot more than on the trail. Then tomorrow, you'll need to hide in the forest while I go to the castle and speak to a few people. I think I've managed to find a way through the gates—not for you, but for me. Once inside, I might be able to arrange another way in. When I come back, we'll head to the city together."

"That sounds good, Berin." I smile again. "It's good to see you."

Berin gives me his large, toothy grin. "And you too, my Prince. A lot has happened while you've been gone."

"For us, too," I say.

"Then bring me up to speed now, and during dinner, I will tell you of what has happened here."

I lay out our experience up the coast, including what we did, what we learned, how Nordin and Hella treated us and more. He tells me he remembers Nordin from the wars, but just in passing. He didn't even know the man was from Nimville. The only thing he remembered was that Nordin was not only extremely intelligent but also fiercely loyal.

When we tell him about our journey back, he looks relieved when we say we didn't tell anyone in Port or Grimmer about who we were. He nods and affirms what we learned in Deliver. The two villages close to Sevord are a mixed bunch when it comes to loyalty.

When I'm finished, the stew isn't quite ready yet. He adds a few more spices and salt before coming back to us.

Before he begins, he leans back and says, "I believe I met this Marleet of yours."

Hemot leans forward, almost toppling off his chair. "Where is she?!"

Berin shakes his head. "Oh, this was a while back. She's in the castle right now. If I understand the situation correctly, she's under close watch as the Regent, sorry, the King, suspects she and Prince Roran might run."

That catches me by surprise. "Why would they run?" Hemot looks at me like it's obvious, but there's something I'm missing. I don't think Marleet would want to marry Roran, but I'm not sure why Roran wants to run. It also makes it sound like she's wanting to run with Roran.

"Good question," Berin says. "The King's suspicion raises many questions. It is clear to everyone that the King has manipulated the Lady Marleet into marrying the Prince. The Prince is obviously infatuated with her—from what I remember, she's quite a pretty young girl—but I don't think she's as interested in marrying the Prince. I'm also confident that the Lord Yune and the Lady Aldora are not in favor of this union. The fact that the King suspects the two young ones will run suggests he's not only forcing the marriage upon them, but there's also a possibility that the wedding will not take place."

Hemot flops back in his chair when he hears this. I glance his way to see a very relieved smile plastered across his face.

Berin shakes his head. "No, Hemot, I'm sorry. That's not good news. The ways of nobility are complicated, but they are also sly and deceitful. If the wedding, at this point, doesn't happen, it'll be due to one of a few things. First, if there is some scandal—but that is unlikely in his situation. Second, if one or both flees the castle—also unlikely in most situations, but more likely in this one. Finally, it could come as the result of death. That's what I suspect. I think the King is going to have one or both killed before the wedding takes place."

I feel the blood drain from my face. That's why Tilbur was so intent on bringing us out of hiding. They are targets, and he's not able to protect them.

We all sit in silence for a long time. I want to cry and yell and throw up, but none of that will help. It won't even make me feel better. The sound of the fire burning in the stove pulls me back, and the crackling of the wood calms me. I nod. "Then, it's a good thing we're here."

I glance at the others, and smiles break out on their faces. That's what we needed. We needed to be reminded of not only what needed to be done, but the important part we played in this story.

I turn back to Berin. "When did you see Marleet?"

He smiles. "Well, that's an awkward one, actually. I wish I'd known who she was and who you were looking for at the time, because I could have brought her back to you."

I shake my head. I don't understand.

"While you were here two months ago, I was out one day checking my snares, and I came across a young woman in the woods. She didn't tell me her name, but upon some reflection and speaking with a number of people, I believe she was your Marleet." He shakes his head. "If I had known, I could have brought her to you here. But I didn't. I didn't know anything about her, and she didn't tell me. I actually thought I was showing kindness to her because she was clearly trying to hide. So, I didn't tell anyone about her—aside from mentioning to the three of you that I met someone in need—until now."

I'm kind of irritated at that. I glance over at Hemot, then at Ellcia. They both appear to be just as irritated. I don't think any of us are mad at Berin—it's not his fault. But we came so close to having her back. I have no idea how she got out there in the first place. I'd love to hear that story, but for now it'll likely have to wait until we find her.

"I'm sorry we didn't tell you more about her when we were here, Berin," Ellcia says. "That might have saved us a lot of trouble."

Berin nods. "It might have, but I think it would have created another problem."

"What's that?" Hemot asks. He's still upset, but it's hard to be upset at Berin. It's just a terrible situation.

Berin takes a deep breath and frowns. "I suspect that the Lady Marleet's presence is the only thing that's keeping Prince Roran alive. I think the King has planned this marriage from almost the moment he found out Prince Roran had his eye on your friend—perhaps earlier. This is a way to excite the people, take their focus off what's just happened, and more. Then, to kill the Prince and Lady Marleet will shift everyone's focus away from what's happened and toward finding the murderer. If Lady Marleet had not been around, the King would likely just have killed the Prince and then blamed someone else just as he did after the rebellion."

"But then won't people suspect the King killed them?" Hemot asks.

Berin shakes his head. "No, that'll all be worked out already. They will have someone to blame. Someone who's involvement and death will further unite the nation around King Parthun."

I slump back in my chair, and I close my eyes. I didn't see it all before, but Nordin's training has been quite helpful. It… makes sense to me now.

"You know who will be targeted, don't you, my Prince?" Berin asks.

"Who?" Ellcia asks me.

I close my eyes. I don't want to tell her, but I think she should know. "Granel. It's your brother, Granel. He's the target."

Ellcia grabs my hand and squeezes like she's actually trying to break my fingers. "Granel? But why?"

I glance at Berin, but he signals for me to explain it. I'm glad I can understand these things a bit better now, but I almost feel I'd rather not know. "Granel is the greatest threat in the kingdom right now—since Parthun thinks I'm dead. Roran has abdicated and is about to die. Lirnal is in prison. No one, as far as the King knows, stands in his way. The marriage and murder will gain the loyalty of the Nobles as they will all stand with him as he searches for the murderer. He's only missing one thing."

Ellcia shakes her head. "What?"

"He's missing the loyalty of the Free Armies of Sevord. Their loyalty stands with Granel. He could likely call them to storm the castle, and most would follow. But, if he turns on Prince Roran and Lady Marleet and is hung for murder, their faith in him will fail." I sigh and shake my head again. "And the Free Armies of Sevord will disband, the soldiers losing their will to fight."

At first, no one says anything. I guess there's not much to say.

Finally, Berin breaks the silence. "You have learned much. The ways of the Nobility and the politics of the palace are complicated and warped things at times, but you will do well." He looks at each of us, then snaps his fingers a few times. "Hey! Stop it! Stop moping. This isn't bad news."

"It isn't?" Ellcia asks. "How can it not be?"

"Because," Berin says with a smile, "If we know what we face, we can defeat it." He looks at me. "What's the plan, my Prince?"

I smile. It seems so obvious to me. "We need to speak with Granel. He needs to know the threat, and he needs to have a solid alibi. So, when we rescue Marleet and Roran, he cannot be blamed for kidnapping or be put under suspicion of murder due to their disappearance. Once that is in place, we can enter the city, then the castle, and rescue Marleet and Roran."

Hemot laughs. "You make it sound simple."

The rest of us laugh as well. "It's not," I say. "But there's much we can't figure out until we get in there."

I turn back to Berin. "Can you tell us what's been going on since we left for Nimville?"

Berin leans back in his chair and steeples his fingers. His eyes drift to the cieling as he begins to tell us.

It turns out, the army is still mostly around. They're camped about a one-hour hike from Berin's cottage. There are a lot of them, though, so the supply runs are coming in from the southern villages along the coast, most of which have a certain amount of farmland, and from the city through the port, and through Switcher Pass.

He tells us the soldiers have grown restless, and many have returned to their homes. The biggest group to leave was just after Roran abdicated. About four or five thousand dropped their weapons and simply turned around, returning through Switcher Pass. The rest have remained under Captain Frindor and Captain Granel.

Apparently Frindor is spending a lot of time in the city these days. And Berin lets us know that he suspects Frindor's been Parthun's man for many years. Granel goes in occasionally, but is often treated with contempt.

Berin, we find out, has offered his services to train troops as that is part of what he did years ago. He's been doing that to gain an opportunity to enter the city to see his brother. He believes he now has enough pull to get that permission from Frindor.

In the end, only bits and pieces of information come out of the city. It's more a matter of piecing together the bits that are shared. Things behind the walls seem peaceful, just tense.

"So, here's what I suggest, Prince Draydon," Berin says. "I recommend that I head to the encampment tomorrow morning and meet with Granel. I'll explain to him the situation and ensure that he understands what he needs to do. I will then go into the city under the guise of meeting with my brother—which I will certainly do—but I'll also seek out some manner to get the rest of you into the city."

"And us?" I ask.

"You, I think, should stay in the forest, not in my house. It's always possible that a soldier will come looking for me and enter the house—not out of ill intent but wondering if I'm asleep."

"May I come with you?"

I turn suddenly to Ellcia. I have no idea why she would want to go. It sounds dangerous. I know I can't go. I'll be recognized. I expect Ellcia will as well, but she likely has more chance of going undetected than I do.

Berin rubs his chin as he stares at her, his eyes boring into her as if he's searching for a reason not to agree. "Why would you want to go?"

Ellcia glances at me, then back at Berin. "My brother. I… would like to see him."

Ah, that makes sense. I didn't think about that—although it's pretty obvious now that she mentions it.

Berin shakes his head. "I don't know if this is a good idea. I would have to explain you as my apprentice, but I haven't had an apprentice in years. It's also unusual for a man to take a young woman as an apprentice. Typically, you would apprentice under a woman." He shakes his head again as if he's trying to figure out how to make it work. He leans forward and asks, "Will they recognize you?"

Ellcia frowns. "I don't think many of them would. My brother would, of course, but not many people paid much attention to me while we were in the mountain. I've only met Captain Frindor once, and he barely glanced at me."

"Stand up," Berin orders.

Ellcia rises to her feet, a little unsure.

Berin stands, pulls her into the kitchen area where there's a little more room and circles her once, then twice. He stands next to her and holds his hand out to check her height next to his shoulder. Then he starts to play with her hair.

She looks at me in a panic, and I move over to them. "Berin, I think this is a little too… personal."

He turns to me in shock, letting go for Ellcia's hair. "Oh, I'm… sorry, my Lady. I… uh… didn't think."

"What are you trying to do?"

"I wondered if she could pass as a boy of around thirteen. You have the height and small build, but you'd have to leave the armor behind. It would give you away, and without it you will look that much smaller. Your face is a bit of a problem—you're… very… um…"

He looks at me like I might help, but I can't imagine where that sentence might go and be anything other than terrible. I shrug and shake my head.

"What's wrong with my face?" Ellcia asks.

"What? No, nothing's wrong with your face. You're just…"

"What?"

"Um… you just do not look like a boy at all."

Ellcia's shoulder's drop like she's quite relieved. "Oh, well, I'm glad about that." She laughs and gives an awkward look at me. "But what do we do about my face?"

Berin backs away and leans against the wall. "The issue might just go away when we shave your head."

Ellcia shakes her head slowly. "We are NOT shaving my head."

Berin smiles. "If we don't, we're going to have to hide it. Boy apprentices never have hair that long—never. They usually have their heads shaved. So, it'll be very strange for you to have long hair. Perhaps quite difficult to pass you off as an apprentice." He shakes his head. "It's tradition, actually, for boys apprenticing under a sword master. We might get away with it, but it's just as likely someone there will insist on shaving your head—I've seen that happen, and they won't be gentle. If I refuse, it'll raise more questions than you want to answer." He closes his eyes and shakes his head. "If we're going to do this, my Lady…" He shakes his head again, and stares directly into her eyes. "The best way to keep you safe is to shave it right off."

Ellcia seems to grow shorter beside me. I glance down to see if the floor is sinking, but I think she's doing it somehow. She glances up at me, but doesn't meet my eyes. I don't think I know what's going on, but I'm pretty sure it's not good.

When she speaks, her voice comes out small and quiet. "Can I think about it?"

Berin nods. "Of course, my Lady. I will leave just before dawn."

Berin moves to one of his cupboards and starts to pull out traveling food and an old waterskin.

I turn back to Ellcia, but she's gone. When I spin around, she's already at the other side of the cottage—which is not really far, actually, but she did move fast. She's not in her normal chair that she uses at Berin's house. Instead, she's sitting on a stool in the corner with her knees up against her chest.

I almost go join Hemot. I think that conversation will be easier. Whatever's going on with Ellcia, it's big.

Taking a deep breath, I head over. There's nowhere to sit, so I just lean against the wall. "What's up, Ellcia?"

She shrugs.

A quick glance at Hemot for support lets me know I won't get anything from him. He's fake-sleeping to avoid an awkward conversation. Not the first time he's done this.

"Do you want to be alone?"

She shrugs again. I feel irritated.

"Can you tell me what's going on?"

She shrugs yet again, and I almost walk away.

Before I do, she whispers, "What do you think about me going to see my brother?"

To be honest, I hate the idea. The thought of her going back where Frindor can catch her is one of the last things I want her to do. The shaved head will be a little hard as well. I like her hair. I'm not sure what I'll think if she doesn't have it. But instead of all that, I say, "What do you want to do?"

"I want to go see him."

I nod.

"Does that bother you?"

I nod again, and she frowns.

Her eyes drop to the floor for a moment, then come back up to meet my own. "Do you think it'll make me ugly?"

I frown. "Going to see your brother?" I shake my head. "Face scars aren't contagious."

She punches me in the arm. I'm really not sure what I've said that's wrong. "I mean if I shave my head."

A small laugh comes out. "Oh, that. Well, I'm not really on board with that idea, but…" I glance over at Berin, then back at Ellcia. "It'll grow back. I don't know how long it'll take, but you can grow it out again. I know you like it long."

"You do too, don't you?"

I smile. "I do, but I like you more."

She blushes. "How would you feel if I shaved my head?"

I shake my head. "I don't want you to shave your head. I'm nervous about you going as well, but if you have to go, it sounds like this is what you have to do. So… I'm behind you."

She nods, stands up, and gives me a big hug. "Thank you," she whispers. "I really want to see him, but I don't want you to find me… you know…"

I don't, actually. In fact, this whole thing is confusing for me. I just hug her back, and she seems happy.

She heads over to Berin and lets him know. He nods and pulls out a razor, sits her down in the middle of the kitchen area—which I find a little gross, considering, you know… food prep and all—and starts to work.

I turn away quickly. I now know that I'm finding this harder than I would have thought. But when I hear her crying, I turn back and stand by her. I guess this is a pretty big deal for her.

When Berin's finished, I do my best to control myself. It turns out her head under all that hair was really, really tiny. She has a few nicks and cuts from Berin's razor, but altogether he did a good job.

She turns to look at me. I think she's slouching a bit. She seems like she's trying to make herself small again. I'm not sure how to respond to it. She looks so different. She's still beautiful, but I already miss the hair.

I know I'm supposed to say something. I know this is a crucial moment. I know it… I just don't know what to say. Finally, it comes to me. "You still look great to me."

She smiles, but before she can respond, Hemot screams out, "You have a pip head!"

I turn around in shock. "What's a pip head?"

"That!" Hemot says, pointing at Ellcia. "That's a pip head! Your head is so tiny under that mop of hair!" He runs over to her. "Can I rub your head and make a wish?"

"No, Hemot!" she growls as she shoves him away.

The next morning, Berin wakes us early.

Since Hemot and I are going to spend the day in the forest, we head out at the same time as the other two. For Ellcia, Berin found a ratty garment that he said would look like something an apprentice would wear.

Berin leads us to a small dip in the ground that he says will give us some cover from the wind, if it picks up. He also tells us we should be able to light a fire down there, if we keep it from smoking too much.

We settle in as they head off, and Hemot starts to work on setting a fire before going out to set some traps. He tells me the traps are in case Berin and Ellcia don't make it back soon, but I know him. He's just trying to keep his mind off of Marleet.

# 4

## The Apprentice

I'm not really sure why I'm doing this.

I mean, I know why I'm doing this. I'm doing this to see my brother. It's strange, in a way. I just met him, although, I remember him a bit from when I was young. But… still… he's really a stranger to me.

At the same time, I wouldn't have left his side if I didn't have to.

Then again, I don't regret it. I want to be with Caric—no, Draydon, I have to get used to that—and I wouldn't trade the last few months with him for anything.

But, right now, I want to see Granel. I want him to know I'm okay. I want to see that he's okay.

However, I don't know why I'm trusting Berin. As soon as I set out with him, leaving Draydon and Hemot in that little dip in the forest, I realized that as little as I know Granel, I don't know Berin at all. I don't know if I can trust him. I don't know if he's dangerous.

Dread floods my heart. What if Berin is actually insane like his brother? Wait… the Switcher Murderer. I'm not sure if they ever caught him. Could Berin be…

I stop myself. I know I shouldn't let my mind do that kind of thing. If I'm not careful, I can get myself worked up. I should stop.

The hood's uncomfortable on my scalp. It seems to stick to my head like there's glue up there, but I know it's just the tiny hairs grabbing the material. I hate the feeling. And the hood wraps around my head too tightly. It's like my head is seriously small right now. Maybe I do have a pip head.

I pull back the hood and instantly touch my scalp. It feels wet, but my fingers find it's dry. I rub my head again.

Berin laughs, and I glance at him nervously. "Let me take a guess. Do you like the feel of running your hand over your scalp, or does it feel wet?"

I smile. "It's kind of both, actually."

"It'll be like that for a bit. It's the same if I grow a beard and shave it. When I go outside for the first time after, my face feels wet. You'll get used to it. But, you should probably keep your hood up. You're not used to having no hair up there. You'll get a headache from the cold."

He pulls a branch out of the way so I can walk between two trees, then follows through after. He then steps out in front again and leads us east.

"How much farther is it?"

"Only about an hour. We should see a lot of soldiers from here on."

"I haven't seen any yet," I say.

He laughs. "You have to learn to look more closely, Trip."

I cringe at the name. We had to pick a boy's name. I don't really like that one, but it's just as good as any, I guess. There was an older man in the castle named Trip. He worked in the kitchen. He was rude, obnoxious, and always made me feel uncomfortable. I'd rather not use his name, but I certainly can't be Ellcia for today.

"What do you mean that I have to look more closely?" I scan the trees, trying to see what Berin's talking about.

"We've passed at least a dozen lookouts. In fact, I see one not far away and then another up on that rise ahead."

I look at the rise. A group of soldiers should be easy to see, but I can only make out trees. "Where are they?"

"Sorry, Trip," Berin says, glancing back at me with a smile. "Soldiers don't like it when you point out their hiding spots. I'll tell you as we walk, but you can't look too closely. I find if you appear to discover soldiers in situations like this, they come out and question you. Best to pretend they're hidden."

I nod. That makes sense.

"When I point out where some soldiers are, just glance casually in that direction. The one close to us is just to the right. We turned a little west a moment ago to avoid running right into them. They're by that large birch tree, the one with the white bark. If you look at the base, you'll see what looks like a small mound of dirt with bushes all over it. There's likely two to three soldiers in there."

I look in that direction, careful not to look too intently. I see it now. I glance up at the rise ahead, I see another. It's not the same, but it's clear now that it's not natural.

"You see 'em?"

"I do," I whisper back.

"I expect in another bit we'll see campfires with soldiers around them, then shortly after that, we'll enter the edge of the main camp. The camp itself will be huge, so it'll take us a while to find Frindor and Granel."

We walk until we're past these two lookouts, then Berin speaks up again. "When we get there, you don't say a word. First year apprentices aren't supposed to speak unless given permission by their mentor. You say anything, and anyone nearby might strike you across the mouth to teach you a lesson. I've seen apprentices who can't hold their tongues lose all their front teeth."

I nod slowly. I don't normally have a lot of trouble keeping my mouth closed, but I think it'll be easy today. I'd rather keep my teeth.

"You'll also need to stick close to me. If you wander off by yourself, you'll find yourself pulled into training with other apprentices. If that's the case, you won't be able to leave—unless I can find you and pull you out."

"What'll happen if you can't find me?"

He laughs quietly. "A few years back, a young woman decided she wanted to apprentice under a man—so she pretended to be a boy. That exact situation happened to her, and… well… she ended up having to spend the day with a bunch of other apprentices—boys and girls—but when she finished, she had to go with the boys. And… well… at the end of the day, they all had to bathe in the river." He glances over at me. "You see the problem?"

I nod.

"I liked her. She was my apprentice. She said she had heard I was the best swordsman around and wanted to be trained by me. Didn't tell me she was a girl, though."

"Were you mad?"

Berin laughs really loud. "Well, a little. I don't like being lied to. But then again, I liked how much spunk she had. It takes a lot of guts to try to enter a three-year apprenticeship, all the while hiding something like that."

"Okay, so I have to keep quiet and stick close to you."

"Yup. Don't leave my side for anything." He turns to look at me. "Anything."

"What if I have to…"

He frowns at me. "You'll have to hold it. No other option." He turns a little to the west. "Is that going to be a problem?"

"I hope not." I immediately decide to stop drinking any of my water for the time being. I think I'd rather dehydrate myself. Unfortunately, I feel like I already have to go.

"So, we'll look for Captain Frindor. When we find him, I'll ask for permission to enter the city. I'll also find out where Granel is. Hopefully he's nearby. I don't really have an excuse to go find him, and Frindor might take it as a bit of an insult since he's the one I deal with all the time. But we'll do our best. Then we'll head to the city, enter, assuming we have permission, then find Hob and figure out the rest."

"You don't have a plan for once we're in the city?"

He shakes his head. "Nope. Can't plan for something like that. I have no idea what the city is like these days."

I don't like the sound of that. I like things planned out. Not knowing what's coming up and not having a plan worked out stresses me a lot. But then again, having no plan has been my life for the last three months. All I know about my future is that I'll be Queen one day. I just don't know how to get to that place.

I think on that one for a moment as we pass by the first soldiers not hiding. They're gathered around a fire cooking something that doesn't look tasty. They wave at Berin, and Berin calls a few of the older men by name.

I can't believe I'll be Queen one day. I never wanted that. In fact, I still don't. But Draydon's right. It's what we have to do for our people. And that's two things I do want. I want to serve our nation. I love our people, and I know the best thing for them is for someone to stand up and take the throne from Parthun.

I also want Draydon. And I'll put up with the fancy dresses and boring meetings and huge responsibilities to have him. I know he has to do this—he has to be King. I also know now that he doesn't want to lose me. Now that I know that, I feel like the luckiest woman in the world.

The luckiest, bald, pip-headed woman in the world.

I'm still not entirely sure what "pip" means, but it does seem to fit.

We step out onto the main road leading to Sevord, and quickly cross. A steady stream of carts move along the road, and the drivers look nothing if not irritated. I almost ask Berin why there's so much traffic up and down the road, but I remember his warning and keep my mouth closed.

Berin flags down a soldier and calls out, "Where are the Captains?"

The man looks Berin up and down for a moment, then glances for a second at me, then back at Berin. "Who's asking?"

"A retired soldier," Berin growls. "Don't make me come out of retirement. I'll teach you some manners, and Frindor will thank me for it."

Anger flashes across the man's face for a moment, and he opens his mouth, but thinks better of it. "Captain Frindor was at his command tent, last I heard, and Captain Granel left earlier today."

Berin nods and starts on, but then hesitates. "Granel left? Where'd he go?"

"No idea," the man says. "I'd be careful about leaving off their rank, though. Most men around here would cut out your tongue for such disrespect."

Berin laughs. "Most men around here would know better than to try to cross me." He then grabs my arm and pulls me along.

In a quiet voice, he says, "Most interactions with soldiers are all about who's toughest. I find if I give enough veiled threats, I can avoid fights." I nod, but he continues. "The command tent, if I understand correctly, is not far south of our position. And…" He pauses for a moment. "That's odd about Granel not being here."

I grit my teeth over that one, and force back the tears. I wanted to see him so badly. Not only that, but I may have shaved my head for nothing.

We weave our way past small and large sleeping tents, various training grounds, food tents, and large open areas that I assume are for practice or marching or… I don't know, actually. Most of what I see doesn't make sense to me.

Ahead, a large tent—fancier than all the others—sits with a lot of empty space around it at the top of a slight rise. I assume that's the command tent. We reach the tent, and Berin leads me around to the entrance, facing west. Standing at the door are two, large, angry looking soldiers.

"Here to see Captain Frindor," Berin states.

"Name?"

"Berin."

"Reason?"

Berin merely shakes his head. "My name's Berin. The Captain knows me."

The one man frowns, but ducks inside while the other stares at us—well, he stares mainly at Berin. I seem not to warrant much notice. I'm happy about that. I don't want to be caught.

Truthfully, I normally prefer not to be noticed. So does Draydon. That's part of why neither of us want the throne.

The thought of the throne hits me again. I casually glance around at the soldiers. They're doing all sorts of different things. Some train. Some repair tents. Others are talk, walk, argue, take orders.

But I now see them in a different light. They're mine. I don't mean I own them. But… if I'm their future Queen, there's going to come a time when I will be responsible for them. I'll have to lead them. I'll have to care for them. I—along with Draydon—will be responsible for each one of them.

I feel… awe. But I also feel terror at the thought. And humbled. Terribly humbled. I'm not sure I'm up for it, nor do I deserve it. But I'll do what I can to take care of them.

I'm pulled back from my thoughts as the soldier reappears. He grunts at Berin. "You can go in. Your apprentice stays out here."

I tense up. This wasn't part of the plan. I was supposed to stick with Berin, but what happens if I'm forced to stay out here?

Berin pushes me back roughly just a step or two, then growls at the man. "My apprentice stays with me at all times, or…" Berin puts his hand on the hilt of his sword. "Or… I'll take off your head."

The man reaches for his sword, but Berin jumps forward, drawing his own. Before either man can do much more than get their swords half-way out of their sheaths, Berin has his sword at the soldier's throat, and his knife at the throat of the other man.

"Pay attention, soldier!" Berin says. "I'm not used to listening to grunts like you. I've been a soldier longer than you've been alive, and I've trained royalty. I was even on a first name basis with all the king's brothers—including the man who currently sits on the throne. You think you can push me around?"

The flap on the tent flies open, and Captain Frindor steps out. "What's going on out here? Berin! What are you up to?"

"These two men," Berin begins, "are being difficult. I don't like difficult men."

Frindor shakes his head. "You're a difficult man, Berin!"

Berin puts his sword and knife away. "Captain, you are, as always, insightful beyond measure." He glances back at me, then back to Frindor. "May we come in?"

Frindor shakes his head in disgust, but waves us to follow as he enters through the tent flap. Berin holds the flap open for me, and I walk in past the guards.

Inside, the tent has a strong smell of canvas, but otherwise, it's not bad. Along the tent walls—up near the roof—are dozens of openings, giving a bit of a breeze and letting in lots of natural light. A few lanterns sit around the area as well, giving just a bit more.

In the center of the tent sits a large table with a map of Sevord laid out. A few soldiers stand around, but I don't recognize any of them.

"What do you want, Berin? I'm busy."

"I want to go see my brother."

Frindor shakes his head. "What?" He looks at Berin like he's crazy. "What does that have to do with me? If you want to see your brother, go see your brother." He turns to the table and examines the map.

"He's in the city."

Frindor looks up. "So, you don't want to go see your brother. You want authorization to enter the city."

Berin merely nods.

"What all are you going to do in the city?"

I'm not sure what to expect from Berin. I'm never comfortable stretching the truth, but if he tells everything, we're finished. I don't really know how much you can leave out before it's considered a lie.

"What *all* am I going to do in the city?" Berin laughs. "Okay, let's see. Well, I obviously want to go see my brother. That's a biggie. I also plan on stopping in the market. There's a lady I know there who sells pies. I haven't had one of them in over ten years, and, quite frankly, I miss them. They're good pies. I plan on buying two. I'll likely eat one with my brother, and the other I'll take back home with me. But there's also another lady who works as a cobbler. I… well…" Berin looks around at the men in the room with a shy smile… "I kind of fancy her. I don't know if she's still single and all, but I'd like to stop in and… you know… see her again. If she's married, I'll have to let that dream die, but at least I'll know. Aaannd…"

Frindor puts his hands up. "All right, Berin. I don't care. I'll authorize your visit through the gates, just for today. You have to be out before sundown. You try to wait to leave the city until tomorrow, they'll arrest you."

"That works for me, Captain."

Frindor frowns as he leans over the table and scribbles a note on a piece of paper. Without looking up, he asks, "Will you be taking the kid with you?"

"Trip?" Berin asks. "Absolutely. Haven't had an apprentice for a while. Enjoyin' it! Trip needs to see that there's more to being a soldier than fighting with a sword."

Frindor finishes scribbling out his note and shoves it in Berin's chest. I don't think he's mad. I just think that's the normal way the Captain acts.

Berin calmly takes the note and reads through it, checking the back as well. When he's satisfied, he nods, thanks the Captain, then leads me through the flap.

On the outside of the tent, he doesn't even glance at the two soldiers, but the one Berin threatened earlier barks, "Hey! You and me gotta have a talk!"

My heart races, and I don't dare move, but Berin just grabs my arm and casually walks away. When we're out of sight of the command tent, I give Berin a questioning look. I'm not willing to speak even when I don't think anyone's listening.

"Don't worry about someone like that," Berin explains. "Some soldiers join the army because they have something to prove. They can be dangerous in the wrong setting, but guarding the command tent? Not at all. He'll act tough to try to impress the Captain, but all you have to do to get away from him is… walk away. If he leaves his post for anything other than a command from the officer over him, he'll be lucky if they don't hang him. He won't bother us."

I give him another questioning glance, and Berin smiles. Speaking loud enough for anyone nearby to hear, he announces, "I give you permission to speak, Trip."

I smile. In a quiet voice, I say, "That makes it easier."

"It does," Berin says, "but I can't do this too often. Your job is to observe and obey, not speak. Only once you've been an apprentice for a while do you earn your voice."

"Can we pretend I've been an apprentice for a while?"

Berin laughs and shakes his head. "Despite the fact that I live in the middle of nowhere, I'm actually quite well known among the people of Sevord and, more importantly, the army camped out around us. As of yesterday, I didn't have an apprentice. You won't have a voice yet, Trip."

I nod. That makes sense. "What about my brother?"

"Well," Berin whispers back, "We know he's not here. He could be out on patrol. He could be off on a mission in the Talic Region. He could even be in the city. But he'll be a hard one to find."

"Should we go back now?"

Berin turns to me and gives me a sharp look. "Listen, Trip, you may have come to see your brother, but I'm here to see mine. I'm on board with getting you into the city, and your friend has my completely loyalty, but I'm still needing to get into the city myself. Besides, this is not only my chance to see my brother, but this is our attempt to find a way over the wall for the three of you.”

“I’m sorry, Berin, you’re right.” I shake my head. I can’t believe I got so focused on seeing my brother, I forgot about everything else. That’s not very… Queen-like. I’ll have to be careful about that kind of thing.

We head west toward the city, dodging our way through crowds, around tents, and even cutting through the occasional training grounds, much to the irritation of the soldiers in training. Berin just laughs at their insults. I don’t know why he’s being so annoying to them, but I think he enjoys it. He’s a smart guy. My guess is he has a reason for it.

I almost ask him, but it’s been a while since I’ve spoken. I’m not sure if my permission to speak runs out. Enough soldiers mill about within hearing distance that I don’t want to risk taking a hit to the mouth.

About an hour later, I catch sight of the walls of the city as we come over a bit of a hill. We’re in a forest, so it’s hard to see past the tents and trees and more, but it’s there.

As we start down the hill, a large group of soldiers come from our right and march where we’re walking.

I jump back and dodge one or two. They don’t seem to care that a couple of people are in their way. One of them runs into me, and I hit the ground hard. There’s no way I’m staying down with so many men and women marching through, so I scramble to my feet as fast as I can and push my way out of the crowd.

I can’t see Berin anywhere, but I think I hear him call out, “Trip!”

Spinning around, I scan the area. I’m back a bit from the top of the hill and can no longer see the wall as the soldiers march between me and the city.

I decide to wait it out. The line of marching soldiers seems to go on forever, but I have no other choice.

That plan is lost as my whole body twists around, and I find the nose of some large man pressed up against my own. "Who's your master, boy?"

I don't dare respond. I'm pretty sure that's not permission to speak. Instead, I just try to get my feet under me. The guy's huge. He has me by the front of my cloak, and my toes barely touch the ground.

"I asked you a question, boy!"

I open my mouth to answer, but the look of sheer delight on his face causes me to close it again just as quick. From the look of disappointment on his face, I think he was hoping I'd speak so he could strike me.

"No matter. You're coming with me."

I glance back toward where I think Berin went. There's no sign of him, but I don't have much time to look. The man grabs the back of my cloak and gives me a shove toward the camp. "Move it, kid!"

I spend the next ten minutes half-dragged, half-pushed along. No one really pays any attention. Part way there, I see another apprentice in a similar situation. He doesn't look happy, but from the expression on his face, it's not the first time this has happened to him.

The man holding me gives me a big shove, and I find myself sprawling forward. I land hard on my face in the mud. Pushing myself up, my hands sink in, and I try my best to wipe it out of my eyes. It tastes terrible. It's all in my mouth.

I hear the sound of plenty of horses around. Oh, I hope this stuff is mud.

Pulling myself to my feet, I try to find a clean spot on my cloak to wipe my eyes. I can barely see.

"You two!" a soldier calls. "Stop playin' in the mud. Get over here!"

The boy the other soldier dragged along pulls himself to his feet and starts toward the man who called. I glance back, but the guy who dragged me here is already walking away. I suspect this is his job—grab apprentices and bring them here.

A flash of anger rushes through me, and I envision myself ordering his arrest while sitting next to Draydon in the throne room. I don't know if I'll do that, though, but the thought gives me a lot of satisfaction.

Before I can dwell on it, however, I remember what I have to do. I can't disobey. The punishment will be too great.

I move forward. That's when I realize how cold I am. The mud—or whatever it is—is pretty soft. I think there's just too much traffic for it to harden. It is winter, afterall.

By the time I get to the soldier who called for us, the cold, wet mud has seeped through my cloak, and I'm shivering.

The soldier laughs when he sees me. "Don't worry, lad. We'll get you movin'. Join in. You two! Spar against one another. Show me what ya got!"

The boy turns right away and draws his sword. My fingers are nearly numb, but I wipe off my hands as best I can and draw mine.

The soldier whistles when he sees my sword. "You must have a rich master, boy!"

I glance down. It's not an overly nice sword, but it sure is nicer than the one the boy in front of me has.

"Tell you what," the soldier says. "Let's make it interesting. The better of the two of you gets to keep the nice sword." He turns to me and smiles. "Hope your master can afford another one of those."

The boy across from me looks hungrily at my blade. He's much larger than I am. I'd say he's around the same age as me, which means he's likely a third-year apprentice. It doesn't seem fair to pit me against him, especially when it could cost me my sword, but I have no voice.

I don't like this situation. However, there's nothing I can do about it, so I squeeze the grip of my sword a few times, hoping to warm my fingers. I spit out some more mud. No, I'm pretty sure now that it's not mud.

I'm feeling a cross between anger and upset. I think I want to scream and cry all at the same time, but that'll have to wait as the boy lunges forward.

I parry the boy's sword off to the side and step back around, careful to keep my footing on the uneven and slippery ground. The boy spins back and comes at me again, but I easily knock his blade to the side.

I'm not sure what's happening, but I've never really had a sword fight like this before. For one thing, he looks like he's actually trying to kill me. He's using a real sword, and I think it's sharp, despite the fact that it's beaten up and really old. If he gets me, I'm likely going to be done.

But the other thing is… everyone else I've fought has been a challenge until this point. This boy is… well… I thought maybe he was playing around with me at first, but he's clearly not.

I realize in that moment that I'm not all that bad with a blade.

The boy lunges again, and I parry his blade to the side yet again, then attack. His face fills with panic as I come at him again and again. I'm going easy on him, but he still seems to barely hold his own.

A moment later, I knock the blade out of his hand and bring my sword up to his throat.

He doesn't make a sound—which is not a surprise—but instead he just raises his hands.

I sheath my sword, give him a nod, and turn around.

The soldier who appears to be in charge in this area stands there with a look of anger on his face. I'm really not sure what I did wrong, but whatever it was, the look on his face lets me know I did it really, really wrong.

"So, you think you're pretty handy with that sword, eh?" He smiles at me. "Well, I think I'm going to challenge you for it. Any objection?"

I don't dare speak, but I nod my head.

"Can't hear you," the man says with a sneer. "So, I'll take that as a no."

He draws his sword and comes at me. I step to the side to avoid his blade, and draw my own. This guy's bigger than the boy and since he trains others, I'm guessing he won't be easy to beat, so I don't bother waiting to see if I can defend myself.

I attack right away, swinging, jabbing, doing all I can to get through. The man struggles to keep me back, but he's definitely well trained. After a few moments, he gets his feet well under him and attacks back. It's all I can do to hold him off. Again, he looks like he's really trying to kill me. I feel like the terror inside not only makes me want to curl up in a ball and cry, but it also gives me focus, energy, and aggressiveness.

I attack as much as I can, careful to apply all my training. Nordin taught me well, but Relin was the guy who really helped me understand what swordplay is all about.

I push forward, but my foot slips in the mud, and I lose my balance. The man comes at me, and I just manage to parry, but I still fall back onto my butt. My hood comes right off, and my head feels frozen almost immediately.

"Looks like that sword now belongs to me, boy!"

I pull myself to my feet. I'm not sure if this is something I can push back on. I can't speak—not without getting hurt. Even if I could. I'm not sure it would make a difference.

I put it back in its sheath and reach for the buckle. The sword is not worth my life, nor is it worth taking a beating. Maybe Berin can help me get it back.

"Arrrgghhh!"

I spin around just in time to see two men go sprawling off to the side. "Out of my way!"

# 5

———•———

# The Giants

I've only seen her a few times, but Nareesa is a hard one to forget. Rulf's mom is supposed to be completely human, but no one actually believes it's true. She's thin, but taller than any man, and has the strength of an ox.

I don't know why she's so mad, but… it doesn't matter. The soldier overseeing the training here backs away, giving her lots of space.

Nareesa doesn't seem to be focused in on us. She just looks mad and ready to tear people apart. As she passes me, her eyes meet mine, and she stops.

"Nareesa…" the soldier begins, but is cut off by a growl.

"Did I speak to you, boy?" Nareesa says to the man.

The man doesn't respond. I've seen what Nareesa can do if she attacks. I'm not surprised that he holds his tongue.

The large woman bends down and examines my face. She then glances at the soldier and asks, "Who's apprentice is this?"

"Dunno," the man replies. "We just caught him wandering around without his master."

Nareesa's face fills with surprise for a moment, and mumbles, "Him?" but then stops. "I'll take him with me."

"Nareesa, he's in training. You can't just take him. Besides, that sword is mine."

"The sword? It's yours?" She glares at the man. "But… I thought you were giving that sword to me, right?"

The man stutters for a moment, then gives a resigned, "Yes."

"Good! And I give it to this apprentice."

She turns back to me and growls, "You're coming with me!"

Before I can do anything, she grabs me by the front of my cloak and lifts me right off the ground.

I have to admit, I'm terrified. I'm moving faster than I think I've ever moved before, and my whole body swings back and forth with the movement of her arms.

The light suddenly gets dimmer, and I feel a lot of warmth, then I find myself flying through the air, crashing into a pile of clothes, carpets, and stuff.

"Look what I found!" Nareesa hisses, her voice much quieter than normal.

I can barely focus my eyes. I think I'm going to be sick. The whole tent—yes, I'm in a tent, I think—spins around me.

A large shape—much larger than Nareesa—hovers over me. It comes close, and I do my best to blink my eyes back into focus.

The face… it's familiar… At first, I think it's Rulf, but then I know it's not. In fact, this face is about twice the size of Rulf's. It's Rulf's dad, Traltor.

"Huh," he grunts. "It's the Lady Ellcia." He frowns as he examines me. "But there's something different about her. I can't quite figure it out."

"Look harder, Traltor," Nareesa growls.

Traltor comes in closer. His eyeballs are huge, but they're dwarfed next to his nose! My eyes have settled down, and I can focus again, but I kind of wish I couldn't. I don't think I want to know that I'm this close to his face.

He raises his chin a bit, and, before I can close my eyes, I get a clear glimpse up his nose. I think I shall have nightmares for the rest of my life because of this one moment.

"Still not seeing it?" Nareesa asks.

Traltor frowns. "Is she missing her beard?"

Nareesa opens her mouth to answer, but then catches herself. She looks at me with a confused expression before quietly asking, "Did you have a beard before?"

"No!" I say in disgust, then catch myself. I'm guessing I can speak around these two, but maybe not. If they punch me in my mouth, I'll likely lose every one of my teeth.

They don't seem upset, so I take that as proof that I can talk.

But before I can, Nareesa says, "She's bald, Traltor."

He looks at my scalp, examining it carefully. Slowly shaking his head, with sadness in his eyes, he says in a quiet, tired voice, "Oh my. How much time has passed?"

"No!" Nareesa growls. "She didn't go bald because of age. Human men do that. Not women. She shaved her head!"

He frowns. "If I recall correctly, she had nice hair. It was green. Or blue. Or bright yellow."

"It was purple!" Nareesa shouts. "Humans don't have green hair! Don't be ridiculous! It was nice. Kind of swirly. Like a cat. Why would she shave it?"

"Well, you could ask me," I say, trying to ignore the comments about color and... that whole cat comment.

The two look at me with confusion and shake their heads. I truly believe neither one had even considered that asking me might be a possibility.

Nareesa grunts, then asks, "Why did you shave your head?"

I stand up. In a quiet, but strong voice, I say, "First, you tell me where your loyalties lie. Is it with King Parthun or with Prince Roran?"

Nareesa frowns, and Traltor straightens up to his full height. He's a terrifying man when he wants to be, and I nearly run out of the tent. The tent is huge—bigger even than Frindor's command tent—but it takes him not much more than one step to cross from his side to mine. He leans down close, and I see the rage in his eyes.

"Neither!"

I hadn't really thought "neither" was an option. I don't know what to say. Instead, I just reply in a shaky voice, "Neither?"

He shakes his head. "Parthun is a traitor. He murdered King Hartor and General Geran. Hartor was the wisest, most humble, most kind King this land has ever seen. And Geran was the only soldier—the only human—I have ever feared. I would have died in either of their places without hesitation."

I still want to run out of there, but instead, I force myself to move forward. "And Prince Roran?"

Traltor stands straight again. "Roran abdicated the throne. He holds no more of my loyalty."

"Nor mine," Nareesa adds.

"Then who are you loyal to?"

Traltor growls. "I am loyal to the loyal and rightful heir to the throne. Roran abdicated. Prince Draydon is dead. General Lirnal is the only one who stands between Parthun and uncontested rule. I will stand with him."

I smile and whisper, "But Draydon is not dead."

In a flash, Nareesa's hand is over my mouth. The look in her eyes is one of death. I actually think she might kill me if I step out of line—even just a little. She brings her mouth in close and hisses, "Draydon is dead! You would be wise to remember that, little one. The truth is irrelevant right now. He is dead, and that is all there is to it." She pauses a moment and adds, "Remember, no one looks for the dead. They are the only ones who are safe."

She steps back and growls at me.

I open my mouth to respond, but before I can, Traltor shakes his head. "I'm sorry to have to tell you this, child, but Captain Tilbur went out a short while ago to hunt down Draydon. He stabbed him, and Draydon is... Draydon is dead. Few know of what happened, and even fewer know of all the details. You will be wise to remember what we have told you."

I get it, and a smile breaks out on my face. "I will remember. Thank you for informing me of Draydon's death." I know I can trust them now. In a whisper, I say, "I shaved my head because I wished to see my brother. I am traveling with Berin, a man who lives..."

"We know Berin, child," Traltor says.

I don't really like being called a child, but then again, I think I heard somewhere that Traltor is really old. Like... hundreds of years old. So, I guess in a way, if anyone can call me a child, it's him. "We are trying to get into the city to rescue Marleet. She's being forced to marry Roran."

Nareesa nods, and Traltor just stares at me. After a moment, Nareesa shakes her head. She puts her hands on her hips and frowns. "Child! We want to know why you shaved your head! Telling us you shaved your head to see your brother makes no sense! Tell us now, or I'll take you back to the apprentice training grounds. The boys were just about to go bathe. If we leave now, I can get you back there in time to join them."

I put my hands up. "No, that's fine. I'm sorry. I meant to say that I had to disguise myself as an apprentice in order to travel with Berin. I had to shave my head, or they would know I was a girl, and I might be recognized. If they recognized me, I would be killed."

Traltor nods. "Was that so hard?"

I shake my head and nearly roll my eyes. "No, I guess not. I'm sorry to take so long to answer."

Traltor smiles at me, and Nareesa nods. Traltor turns to a small stove in the corner of the tent and grabs a pot—just with his hands—and brings it over to the center of the area, while Nareesa pulls out a large ladle and three bowls. A moment later, I'm seated in the tent with a bowl of soup in front of me. Well, it's a large bowl. More like a small cauldron than anything. It's more soup than I think I could eat in a week.

They dig in without a pause, and I do my best to concentrate on my own soup. The way they eat is kind of disgusting. I lean back a bit as globs of soup splatter all over the place.

When they finish—which is in about the time that it takes me to get three mouthfuls in—Traltor says, "Bring us up to speed. We haven't heard anything since Gerr and Terr saw you." He glances at Nareesa. "Well, other than what we heard from Tilbur about poor Draydon's death. Why don't you tell us everything, but since Draydon's death is weighing so heavily on our hearts, you should probably not mention him at all in anything you say."

I nod. I think that makes sense, but it'll be hard to tell everything without mentioning Draydon. But before I can launch in, Nareesa leans over and begins to eat out of my bowl.

I hand it to her, and she and Traltor both dive in. I was kind of hungry, but not for that soup anymore. I've never been one to share food like that.

Ten minutes later, I've finished my story, and Traltor lets out a burp that hurts my ears. Then Nareesa adds hers, and they both turn to me like it's my turn.

I shake my head and ask them to tell me what's been going on with them.

Traltor looks at me for a moment, frowns, then says, "That's not a happy story." He grinds his teeth, and it actually sounds like he has gravel in there. When he calms down a little, he tells me about the trip to the city and how excited they were to see Roran take the throne. They describe in detail the days following Roran's abdication, and then go on to tell me about how Rulf had been arrested.

I'm shocked by that. I had no idea. I'm about to suggest that we try to rescue Rulf at the same time as we rescue Marleet, but then Traltor explains that Tilbur and Granel have both advised them to put up with it for now.

"Why?" I ask. "Why do you have to leave him in prison?"

Traltor shakes his head. "Well, they're right, I think. No one can hurt Rulfor. They can try to whip him or beat him, but he could fight his way out of there at any time. But, if we go in and rescue him, we'll be outcasts along with Rulf and won't be able to support those loyal to the throne. We'll have to run. Rulf could also break out of prison himself, so he knows the best thing to do is just stay there—otherwise, he'd be out with us."

"So, you're just leaving him in there?" I ask. I find that hard to believe.

Nareesa shrugs. "This may come across as strange, but giant-folk are a little different from regular humans."

I slowly shake my head. "That doesn't come across as strange as you might think."

Nareesa squints her eyes, then nods. "No, perhaps it doesn't. What I mean is, not much can kill Rulf. I mean, it'll be boring in the prison, but Rulf likes the quiet. They've actually thrown him in a pit, which is this slew of mud and slime and moss…”

She seems to notice my look of horror but puts her large hand on my shoulder. “Don’t worry, little one. That’s not a problem. Giants actually enjoy that kind of thing. It’s good for our skin. He’s probably loving it. The quiet. The dark. The mud and slime. My guess is he’s pretty happy.”

Traltor nods his head, and the look of longing in his massive eyes suggests he wishes he were there in the pit with Rulf. “But,” he says, “we’ve been ordered to leave him there, and to act angry. Which, to be honest, we’re angry about enough stuff going on, so it’s pretty easy for us. For now, we leave him. The moment he’s pulled out is the moment it becomes clear that Parthun is not in complete control.”

That confuses me. “Don’t we want that?”

Nareesa shakes her head. “If that wretch thinks he’s in control, he’ll relax. If he thinks we can threaten his control, he’ll tighten things down even more. He might even drive us away—exile us. If he does that, Rulf will have quite the search ahead of him when it comes time to find us.”

Traltor nods. “We will leave things as they are.”

I don’t quite agree, but then again, I don’t really understand how this all works. Draydon seems to understand it a bit better than I do. I wish he were here with me. Wow… he sure would look funny with his head shaved.

“You look funny with your head shaved,” Traltor says to me.

I feel my face grow hot, and I pull my hood up. I was just starting to get used to being bald.

“Traltor!” Nareesa hollers. “That’s rude!”

“Oh… um… I’m sorry,” Traltor says, looking quite sincere. “What I should have said was, you look funny with your head shaved, my Lady.”

“That’s better,” Nareesa said. Turning back to me, she adds, “So, what do you need?”

"I need to find Berin."

Traltor nods. "I can help with that!"

Before I can respond, he grabs me by the front of my cloak, just like Nareesa had, and runs out of the tent. The experience with Nareesa when she did this to me was both terrifying and quite uncomfortable. With Traltor, on the other hand, it makes what happened with Nareesa feel like a walk through a lovely garden on a warm summer day.

I squeeze my eyes closed and do my best to curl my body around his massive fist to keep myself from swinging back and forth. It's hard to tell for sure, but it sounds like people are screaming all around me. Something like, "GET OUT OF THE WAY!" and "IT'S TRALTOR! RUN FOR YOUR LIVES!"

When he lets go, I don't really even know that I'm falling until I hit the ground. I lay there, curled in a little ball as I hear people yell all around me. I think they're angry at Traltor, but he just laughs. I don't really care, though.

I try to open my eyes, but the world spins, and I clamp them closed again. A hand is gently placed on my arm. I almost cry out for Draydon—for some reason I'm sure it's him—but I hold back.

"Come now, Trip, the best thing to do after something like that is force yourself to your feet."

It's Berin, and I feel his arms come around me, pulling me upward. When I think I'm somewhat upright, I wrap my arms around him and cling with all I've got. I still don't really know this guy, but he's kind, and after what I just went through, I need some kindness.

"You going to be okay?" he asks.

I nod. My balance seems to be coming back. My whole body shakes, but I think it'll pass soon.

A large shadow passes over me, and I shrink back.

"Are you okay now, boy... apprentice... boy... um... boy..." Traltor says. He looks around like he's concerned he's going to blow my cover. To make it worse, he adds, "Cause you're a boy. A boy apprentice. I mean, 'cause your head is shaved, so… you're obviously a boy." He looks around again at all the confused faces, then says, "Goodbye, boy," and then winks at me with a satisfied look on his face and whispers, "I really sold that one!" before running off as soldiers dive out of the way.

My knuckles are white as I grip Berin's cloak. He gently, but firmly, pulls my hands away and watches as I try to stand on my own. I'm afraid I'm going to be sick, but my stomach calms down after a few moments.

"Well… boy…" Berin says with a bit of a smile. "Time to head to the city."

We move on and soon I'm walking okay again. I feel a little unsteady, but the more we move, the better I feel.

After about an hour, we're outside the camp. Soldiers are still all over the place, but there's enough distance that if we speak quietly, we can chat without too much fear of being overheard.

"So, Trip," Berin says. "You want to tell me how you came to be in Traltor's hands? I spent a lot of time running around to different training camps to find you."

I lay it all out for him from the point when we got separated to when Traltor found Berin. He doesn't look impressed, but he also doesn't interrupt. I like that about Berin. He's a good listener. Draydon is too. That's one of the things that irritates me most about Hemot and Marleet. Neither of them can let anyone else speak. The amount of times the middle of my sentences have interrupted the beginning of their own… frustrating.

"Now, that's interesting about Rulfor." He shakes his head. "I hadn't heard that Traltor and Nareesa's boy had been arrested. I would think if Rulfor is Traltor's son, no prison cell could hold him. But they do say that giant-men prefer solitude. Perhaps he's quite happy where he is."

I don't think that makes an awful lot of sense to me. I suspect it's merely something everyone is telling themselves to make themselves feel better about Rulf's situation. But then again, Rulf is an odd one. Maybe he likes sitting in a pit.

By mid-afternoon, I'm no longer unsteady on my feet, and my appetite has returned. I chew on some smoked meat Berin had in his pack. I'm not entirely sure what kind of meat it is, and when I ask, Berin avoids telling me. I decide to let it go. It's tasty, whatever it is.

When we reach the city, a lineup of people stand outside the gate. Actually, I see two lineups. On the right, about twenty people try to enter the city. They're dressed as commoners, and some have packs, others have a donkey or a horse with them.

On the left, four people stand, speaking to a guard. After a moment, one is let through, then after another moment, another two, then the final one. On the right-hand side, however, no one gains entrance. I'd like to ask the difference between the two groups, but we're too close to people for an apprentice to speak without permission.

When we reach the gate, Berin leads the way to the left-hand side. The soldier gives him an angry look but takes the paper we received from Frindor. I glance at the people to my right. They're arguing, pleading, and begging the soldiers for entrance to the city.

I guess that's it. I'm in the lineup for people with permission. They are not.

The soldier in front of us grunts, and I turn back to him. He hands over Frindor's permission note, and waves us through. He frowns at Berin and glares at me.

It seems strange to me that when we have permission to enter the city, these guards still treat us poorly—or at least seem angry toward us.

As we walk through the gate, my mind drifts to the future. Things are going to change in Sevord when Draydon's on the throne. He's a good man. He'll be a good king. No more of this cruelty.

We enter the city, and I feel both nervous, and a sense of relief at finally being home. It's strange, because in a way, I'm not home. This city isn't where I live anymore. There's no place for me here at the moment. On top of that, I have no memory of even being in this area of the city. In fact, it's possible I've never been through the eastern gate before, but still… there's something about coming back here…

"Berin?" a woman calls out. "Is that you?"

"Agnus!" Berin hollers and runs to a small stand at the side of the road. I rush to keep up. I don't want to get separated from Berin again. "Agnus! It's so good to see you!"

"Oh, Berin," she says and wraps her arms around him. "Gripper talks about you all the time—brags about how he was trained by Berin Gratterslayer."

I haven't heard that nickname before. I have heard of a gratter, though. Nasty creatures. The little I know of them, I'm impressed that Berin could kill one. He must be fast.

"Ahh, I miss the young pup. How is he these days?"

"Young pup?" Agnus laughs. "It's been eleven years, Berin. That boy is married and has two kids!"

Berin shakes his head. His face falls, and I see deep sadness in his eyes. "It's been too long. And Prestor? Is he well?"

Agnus shakes her head. "No, Prestor died about two years back. He…" her eyes shift left and right. "He asked too many questions."

Berin nods and lowers his voice. "I'm sorry, Agnus. Your husband was a good man. I consider it an honor to have known him."

Agnus does her best to keep her face calm. "Thank you, Berin." It looks like she doesn't want to talk about any of this anymore. Instead, she says, "Will you be buying a pie today, my old friend?"

Berin smiles. "I'd like two. What do you have?"

"Only mincemeat right now. How many will you take? Twenty? Thirty?"

Berin lets out a loud laugh. "No, not that many today, but only because I can't carry them all. I just need two. I'm going to see Hob. Haven't seen him in eleven years."

Agnus's face falls. "I… I hope that goes well."

"Have you seen him?"

Agnus begins to wrap up two pies from the table in front of her. They sure do look good. The old woman seems to be struggling with her answer as she works.

Finally, she stops what she's doing and looks directly at Berin. "I'm sorry, Berin. I have seen him. I take him a pie now and then, although I'm not sure he recognizes me or even if he eats the pies. He's… not well."

"Sick?"

She shakes her head. "It's not his body. He's healthier than I think you or I ever will be again. It's his mind." She drops her voice to a whisper. "The… all that happened… it's destroyed him." Before Berin can respond, she adds, "He's not the same Hob you remember."

Berin nods. "Thanks, Agnus. Either way, it'll be good to see him again."

Agnus comes around the table and gives Berin another hug. "We've missed you, Berin. I'll tell Gripper I saw you. He'll be sad he didn't catch you this time, but hopefully, this will be the first of many visits."

"I hope so," Berin says with a smile.

He offers to pay for the pies, and Agnus refuses. Berin shakes his head and insists until she takes the money.

A few moments later, we're on our way through the city again.

# 6

## The Sane Meets the Insane

The road leading to the castle is pretty straight from the gate, but it takes us a while to get there. The street is packed full of people—many soldiers and a lot of regular city-folk.

I spent a lot of time in the streets around the castle—not going much farther than the main market just to the north of the castle itself or west toward the port, but no one looks happy. It feels like there's a weight in the air. Not even the children laugh much as they run through the streets.

When we get close to the castle, I start to recognize some people, and I make sure I have my hood pulled up well.

The wall which surrounds the castle itself is just as high as the wall around the city. It's designed as a second defense and functions as a keep for the city. When we reach this wall, Berin turns and heads north. I'm not surprised. My guess is he doesn't want to wander through the entire castle. The north gate leading into the castle grounds is closest to the Forgotten Armory where Hob works.

At the north gate, the soldiers put up their hands to stop us, but Berin smiles at them and hands them the permission note from Frindor. I know both soldiers at the gate—by name—but neither of them look at me. They're not bad men, but I certainly can't trust them to keep my presence a secret.

Inside, we wander past the kitchen. I keep my head low in case some of the workers look out through a window. I know them all. In fact, I've worked in the kitchen a fair amount. It's where Marleet worked most of the time, but I filled in when needed.

We move along to a small door that I don't think I've ever used. It takes us into an area of the castle near the soldier's barracks, and we find stairs leading up. The Forgotten Armory is on the third floor. It seems strange to me to put an armory in a place which requires the climbing of so many stairs, but then again, it is the "Forgotten" Armory.

When we reach the third floor, a small, shifty-looking man slinks around the corner, but stops when he sees us. He doesn't really look at me—I have come to appreciate my disguise for what it is—but his eyebrows shoot up at the sight of Berin. Before we can respond, he turns and rushes off.

"That can't be good," Berin says, but continues on.

I watch the small man disappear around a corner. "Should we go after him?"

Berin chuckles to himself. "If we were in the forest, I'd say yes. But here in the castle, imagine trying to explain that one. 'Yes, my Lord, we're running through the castle chasing this man. Why? Oh, he looked shifty. Who are we? Oh, we're nobodies—just visitors. What reason do we have to chase anyone? Well, you see… um…'"

I smile. Yes, that makes sense. But it still makes me nervous.

We reach the Forgotten Armory, and it's just like I remember it. Still really quiet, still filled with old, beat-up armor, and still in desperate need of a good cleaning. In the center of the room is Hob's chair, but he's not in it.

Berin walks right in and past the chair. At the back of the armory are a couple doors. The one leads into what looks like a small office. It appears as though someone ate cookies at the desk recently. A mouse scurries away from the crumbs, carrying a large chunk of what might be a chocolate chip. Papers are strewn all across the floor, covering just about everywhere I can see. I don't get the impression that Hob was just messy. I think those papers spilled there in some kind of struggle.

Berin shakes his head, and I hear a deep growl in his throat. I step out of the way. He's angry about something. Maybe I'm right about the struggle.

We check another room, and it's small—also empty of people. I'm guessing this is where Marleet changed before we left the castle a long time ago. As I look around, I see a sleeve of her old dress sticking out of a box. It's marked, "LM Dress." I'm thinking maybe LM stands for Lady Marleet.

"What do we do?" I can't imagine searching the whole castle for Hob. Eventually someone will question us. We also have to be out of the city by tonight, and I think it's already sometime around the supper hour.

Berin shakes his head and wanders toward the door leading back into the hallway. "I don't think we'll have to worry about it."

"How come?"

"That man. The empty armory. The mess. Hob would be here, but the struggle suggests he was taken away. The man who saw us, I don't know him, but the look on his face suggests he recognized me. The fact that he ran off says he's either afraid of me, or he's going to tell someone."

"Is all that good?"

He shakes his head again. "None of it's good. But what it does mean is that someone will be coming for us soon."

My heart begins to race, and my breathing speeds up. "Should we run?"

"Nope." He plops down in Hob's chair in the center of the room, sets his two pies down on the floor, puts a foot up on his knee, leans back and stretches. "If we try to get away, we'll be captured on the run. They'll suspect us of something or other, maybe even throw us in a cell. If we wait here, then we'll appear far more innocent, and it'll be easier to talk our way out of whatever's about to come."

I don't like the sound of all that, but I think he's right. It doesn't matter, though. First, I can't go off on my own. I'm guessing it would be just as dangerous for me as an apprentice to walk alone through the castle as it is out in the army camp. Second, I already hear the steady rhythm of soldiers approaching.

A moment later, four soldiers enter. I recognize each of the men, although I don't know any of them well.

"Stand up!" one of the soldiers hollers. I think his name is Gink. It's a strange name and sounds like an insult or like some kind of lizard or insect or something.

Berin gets to his feet, picks up his pies, and says, "I'm coming."

One of the soldiers grabs my arm and whips back my hood. I nearly cry out in fear, but he's not looking at my face. He's checking to see if my head's shaved. He doesn't really even look at me beyond that.

It's not long before we're marching down the corridor. Berin, holding his pies, walks casually in front of me with a soldier at his side. Two soldiers lead the way, and the soldier beside me drags me along, gripping my arm like iron. I'm guessing since Berin has two pies in his hands, they're assuming he won't run. That makes sense. Who ever saw a man flee four soldiers whilst carrying two pies?

At first, I'm not sure where we're going. I'm hoping they're taking us to Captain Tilbur. In the past, I always saw him as the enemy, but now I know he's one of the good guys.

Unfortunately, it's not long before I realize we're heading toward the throne room. This can't be good.

We come out into a large hallway. It's the one leading to the main entrance to the throne. I've been here many times before, and in the throne room quite a few times as well, but never in this kind of situation.

The doors stand wide open, and we enter to find a few dozen people. On the side are maybe fifteen or so nobles. They look… well… I'm not sure what to make of their expressions. They're scared. I think. And upset.

On the throne sits the Regent—no, he's King now. There's no question about the expression on his face. It's hatred mixed with pleasure. He's happy about something, and it's not good.

In the center of the room, however, a group of people stand. Captain Tilbur's there. Behind him is my brother—and I nearly holler out to him before I catch myself. Behind my brother is a large group of soldiers.

To the left of them is Prince Roran. He has a dreamy look on his face, and he's looking at a few Nobles off to my left. No, not at all the Nobles. He's looking at one in particular.

Marleet…

Before I can react in any way, good or bad, someone kicks me in the back of the knees, and I go down. I don't dare lift my head, but I can see that not only does Berin go down, but he manages to save the pies. He sets them gently on the floor in front of him.

"Berin!" Parthun hollers out. "It's been far too many years. I understand you've been living outside the city all this time. I wondered where you'd ended up. I thought for a while that you had joined the rebellion."

Berin bows low. "Ah, your Majesty. It has been far too many years. It seems only yesterday that I had the privilege of training you and your brothers. Those were good days."

"Yes, they were," Parthun says.

I think I can almost feel the tension in the room. The ways of the Nobility are complicated. I'm not sure what's going on right now. The words are friendly, but the tone is not. I wish I could talk to my brother or Marleet.

The King continues. "Berin, before we deal with anything else, I don't believe you've sworn allegiance to me yet."

Dread fills my heart. First, Berin can't do that—not to a usurper. Second, what if they demand I swear allegiance? Not only can I not do that, but my voice. I might be able to look like a boy with my head shaved, but in a room like this… I'm sure I'll sound like a seventeen-year-old girl. Besides, what if Marleet, Roran, Tilbur, or even Parthun recognize my voice?

"My apologies, your Majesty. The soldiers did not come to my home to receive my pledge. I am pleased that I can do this now." He straightens up, although still on his knees. "Your Majesty, King Parthun, I am grateful to be one of the honored few who can pledge their allegiance before you, rather than before one of your esteemed servants. I, Berin, on this day, pledge my undying allegiance to the throne and to the royal line. I stand by this oath and will hold to it till the day of my death."

I nearly smile. I wonder how many in the kingdom have avoided swearing allegiance directly to Parthun by giving it to the throne.

"And your apprentice?" Parthun doesn't sound happy, but I doubt there's much he can do about this.

"My apprentice will also swear allegiance," Berin says, turning and looking right at me. "As I did."

I do my best to disguise my voice. I figure rather than trying to sound totally different, I'll just change it a bit. It ends up coming out a little weird, but I stick with it. I'm not sure I remember the words exactly, but I say, "I, Trip, on this day, pledge my allegiance to the throne and to the royal line."

I feel like there's more that I should say, but it's all I can come up with. At that moment, I realize I just pledged my allegiance to Draydon. It feels weird, but nothing's changed. I'll stand by him no matter what. I take a quick glance at Marleet. She doesn't give any indication that she recognizes me. That's good. I don't think she'd be able to control her response if she did.

Berin gives me a nod of approval and turns back to the King. "King Parthun, while it is good to see you, I must admit that I find it strange to be summoned to the throne room. I've never been one to walk these particular halls. I'm a soldier, not a Noble."

"Well, that's an interesting issue, Berin. You see, I am concerned about a matter of security. This young Noblewoman," Parthun says as he points at Marleet, "has been under suspicion for some time now. While we are anxiously awaiting her marriage to our dear Prince Roran here, she keeps sneaking around the castle and causing a great deal of… concern."

Berin nods, turns to Marleet, bows his head and quietly says, "My Lady." He then turns back to Parthun. "Thank you, oh King, for this clarification. But I must admit, the ways of the Nobility are not for me. I'm not sure I understand why such a matter would lead your soldiers to bring me here."

"I am not sure that's true, Berin." Parthun leans forward, and his eyes fill with malice. "It's been noticed that she's gone to see Hob, your brother. I've often wondered if he can be trusted, but I've tolerated him as he's quite mad, and I never considered him a threat. But now, my suspicion has grown."

"I haven't seen my brother for over ten years, your Majesty."

Parthun leans forward even more on his throne. "And yet, the day we arrest your brother, you show up. Don't you think that's quite the timing?"

Berin remains silent for a long time, but then nods his head. "Yes, your Majesty, I do see the problem. That does seem suspicious."

"And what, my dear Berin," the King says with a deep frown, "do you think would be a proper way for me to understand all this?"

Berin shakes his head. "I have no response to that."

"What did you carry into my throne room?"

I'm kind of taken aback by that question. It seems a little unexpected, but then again, the man sitting on the throne is a murderous traitor. What else would I expect but absurdity?

"Pies, your Majesty."

"Pies?" The King now looks confused.

"Yes, your Majesty. Pies. I have wanted to come see my brother ever since I heard he was alive. I just received permission from Captain Frindor to enter the city, so when I came in, I picked up two pies from a baker. I planned to share one with Hob, and the other I planned on taking home to eat. I haven't had one of Agnus's pies in over ten years."

The King looks down at the bundles on the floor and mumbles, "Yes... pies... Agnus does make good..." His eyes come back up to Berin. He seems unsure of what to do. After a few moments, he hollers out, "Captain? Your thoughts?"

Captain Tilbur steps forward from his place by the soldiers. "Your Majesty. I admit, I don't like this. The timing is off. It seems quite the coincidence that Berin would show up on this day of all days. Then again, Berin and Hob were always unpredictable, but…"

Parthun frowns. "But what? Finish your thought, Captain."

Tilbur shakes his head. "Both men have always been loyal to a fault. I've never seen them give the slightest indication that they are anything but trustworthy."

"Have your questions revealed anything?" the King asks.

Tilbur shakes his head. "He is quite insane, your Majesty. I ask him all sorts of questions, and I get answers, but they're strange, confusing, and convoluted. If he did anything disloyal to the throne, I'm not sure he'd even know it—and I definitely don't think he did anything intentional."

Parthun's frown deepens. I think there's something else going on here… not sure what.

A man—a Noble—steps forward. I haven't seen his face yet, but the moment he speaks, I know who he is. "Parthunnnn. It seeeems to me that we have arresteeeed a loyal soldierrr, and we have placed my daughterrrr under suspiciooooon for simply going for a waaaalk."

I'm surprised to hear Marleet's dad address the king by his first name, but maybe her dad and the King are on a first-name basis. If so, her dad has far more influence than I had thought.

"Lord Yune…" the King replies.

That's kind of confusing for me. Maybe only Marleet's dad gets to refer to the King by his first name, but it doesn't go the other way. That's strange.

The King continues, "I still have a great deal of suspicion about your daughter's activities."

"Would youuuu, Parthunnnn, prefer that I keep herrrr inside our quarterrrrs?"

At that, Marleet's head drops, and Roran starts to grow agitated. I can see he's quite taken with her. I… I hate to say it, but I'm starting to wonder if maybe Marleet is actually interested in Roran. Maybe the wedding isn't something we need to rescue Marleet from.

The King growls, and he waves his hand. "Bah!" he hollers.

I've never understood what that word means, but the idea comes across clear. He's done with this issue.

"Should I release Hob from custody?" Tilbur asks the King.

The King leans back in the throne and gives a dismissive wave to Tilbur. It's kind of confusing to me, but Tilbur nods at a soldier who runs out a door near the back of the throne room.

I watch him go, but when I turn back, I'm shocked to see Tilbur is staring right at me. He's examining my face. I almost duck my head down, but then I think that I don't want to put him in a spot where he's actually suspicious. I hold his gaze for a moment, and then he gives me the slightest nod.

A moment later, two soldiers come in with Hob. His legs drag behind him, and the sounds he makes are a cross between wails and laughter. He's not struggling at all, but his body hangs limp. I can't help but think he's been beaten to the point where he can't find the strength to even raise his head. He looks like he has no life left in him.

"Ah, Hob," Tilbur shouts, "Cut it out! We're letting you go. Don't go boneless on us again."

"Oh, you're letting me go?" Hob shouts and leaps to his feet. He jumps and spins in the air with the grace of a dancer, and lands on his feet before breaking out in song.

"Hob!" Tilbur shouts again, grabbing him by the arm. He drags him toward us and gives him a shove.

Hob lands on his knees before his brother, but his eyes focus on the bundles. When he speaks, his voice comes out filled with wonder. "Those… those bundles… they look like pies… pies from Agnus." He covers his face with his hands and shouts, "BUT YOU CANNOT TEMPT ME! I VOWED I WILL NOT EAT OF THE PIE AGAIN UNLESS I EAT IT WITH MY BROTHER!"

"Hob," Berin whispers. His voice sounds like it's ready to break.

Hob opens his eyes and focuses on Berin, kneeling before him, but he looks more confused than anything. After a moment, he tries to straighten his hair, and then asks, "When did I change my clothes?"

"It's not a mirror, Hob!" Tilbur shouts.

Hob's eyes open really wide, and he lunges forward. "Berin! Berin! You found me! You came back!"

The two roll on the floor and wrestle together like two little boys. I lunge forward and rescue the pies before they get kicked. I'm rather hungry.

"Tilbur!" King Parthun shouts. "This is my throne room. It's not a playground.

Tilbur grabs each man by the scruff of their neck and drags them toward the door. Neither Hob nor Berin are large men, but that can't be easy. Tilbur's a big guy, but I hadn't realized he was as strong as that!

I scurry after them, but when I catch up, Tilbur's already shoved both men out of the throne room. As the Captain walks by me, he doesn't even make eye contact.

Either he doesn't actually recognize me, or he plays his part well.

I stand off to the side while Berin and Hob give each other another hug. The sight makes me miss my own brother even more.

A moment later, Tilbur walks out, grabs one of the pies out of my hands, and says, "The King felt the second pie should be examined for security reasons." The look on his face says it all. Parthun was hungry.

As we walk, Berin and Hob chat. It's funny watching them. Berin is so controlled and reserved—aside from that awkward wrestling match in the throne room. But Hob is wild and unpredictable and nonsensical. So, Berin asks questions, and Hob mutters about this and that and isn't clear, although I can piece together some answers to Berin's questions from what Hob says.

I know my way around the castle quite well, but I find we end up in an area I've never been. I always steered clear of the soldier's quarters, for the most part. It's not that it was dangerous or anything for me, it was more that there's no reason for me to be there, and it stinks.

Today is no exception.

We head into a small room. On the door, scratched into the wood, is Hob's name. Inside, the room is spotless, everything completely neat and tidy as if it's cleaned every day.

It's small, though. Very small. Just a bed, a wardrobe, a small table, and two chairs.

Hob plops down on the bed, and Berin and I take the chairs. Hob mutters quietly for a moment, then stops, staring at the floor with a look of pain in his eyes.

When he looks back up at his brother, tears stream down his cheeks. "Berin…"

"I'm here, Hob. I know it's been hard. I'm here now."

Hob shakes his head. "I'm… Berin, I'm… I…"

Berin just waits. Hob's struggling.

"I'm… in here… Berin."

Berin leans forward and puts his hand on Hob's shoulder. "I don't understand."

"I…" Hob appears to be in agony. It's like he's fighting something. "No, I'm in here, Berin." He pauses for another moment and grinds his teeth. "I know… I'm… not… right. I know I act… strange. Do strange things. I know I'm… my head is… messed up. I know. But… Berin. Hob. Me. I'm in here, still. I just… don't… know how to get out."

Berin's bottom lip begins to quiver, and he sits next to Hob, putting his arm around his brother. Hob just leans in and cries. As he weeps, he keeps mumbling something about how sorry he is and how he tried so hard to save the King.

"No one could save him, Hob. But you did what you could."

Hob nods. "I saved two."

"Pardon?" Berin asks.

"I saved two. I did, Berin. I saved two. I saved Geran's son. They were after him. He was brave. They had him in their arms, going for the window, but he fought hard. He has Geran's fire, but he doesn't know it yet. Farnum's brothers. Bad men. Four men to kill one child. I killed two, then ordered Geran's son to hide while I killed the others."

I'm left speechless. I don't really remember much from that day. That night. That nightmare. But I didn't know that about Draydon. He owes Hob his life.

"And," Hob adds, his face twisting like the very attempt to say more is agony. "I saved him. I saved Prince Roran. I saved my King's son. But I couldn't save my King."

"What?" Berin shakes his head. "Prince Roran?"

"I got him out, Berin. I got him out. I got him out of the castle. But Parthun's men attacked me. I had to fight them, and I told the Prince to run. Once I'd killed the traitors, I went looking for the little Prince, but I couldn't find him. I would have taken him out of the city to you. But I couldn't find him. I thought all this time that he was dead. I saw his ghost in the city many times, following Traltor's son, but he was dead. It was too late. When his ghost came to me, I wanted to protect his spirit, so I gave him the Armor of Agno. I thought if no one could see Prince Roran's ghost, he could be at peace. But now he's alive again and doesn't want to be King. That leaves only two who stand before Parthun. Prince Draydon and Prince Lirnal. But Prince Draydon is now dead, and Prince Lirnal is in prison."

I open my mouth to tell Hob the good news that Draydon is alive, but Berin shakes his head. He gives a look around at the walls, but I don't know what that means.

I keep my mouth closed. I guess in the end, Hob might think I shouldn't speak if I'm an apprentice.

Hob falls into silence, and after a few minutes, Berin gets up and slices into the pie. He finds some old dishes in a cupboard and serves out a slice for each of us.

Hob doesn't move, so Berin waves the pie under his nose, and a moment later, his brother comes to the table and eats while still on his feet. When I try to get up to give my seat to Hob, he shakes his head at me, but then stops. He examines my face and pulls back my hood. I feel like his eyes are boring into me, and he comes in really close—far closer than I'm comfortable with.

When he pulls back, a slight smile forms on his face and a look of peace enterss his eyes. Under his breath, I hear him say, "Another one survived." A tear forms in his eye before he gives me the slightest nod, then turns back to his pie.

The mincemeat certainly is good—there's no doubt about it. I've never liked that kind of pie before, but that lady must really know what she's doing.

We remain for about an hour—it's all the time we have. We have to get out of the city before nightfall, and we still have a long walk back to Berin's house. I'm not looking forward to that. I think it'll be the middle of the night before we can rest. Hmm… or maybe Berin's planning on camping out tonight. I don't think we actually spoke about that.

I still haven't found my brother, though.

When it comes time to leave, Hob is actually acting far more sane and controlled. Even this small amount of time with his brother seems to have helped.

Before we exit the room, Berin steps in close and gives his brother a big hug. They hold on for a long time. At first, I think it's just that they missed each other, but then I hear some quiet mumbling. They're talking.

I make a point not to listen. I don't know what it's about, but both men likely need their chance for privacy from me. I'd step outside the room so they could talk more freely if I didn't fear being out of sight of Berin as an apprentice.

We leave the castle, and Berin's grin stretches from ear to ear. It feels good to see him so happy. I suspect it's been far too long since he's smiled like that.

# 7

## The Enraged Captain

The crowds in the city are a little less than they were earlier in the day. The more I walk the streets, the more I realize how much I miss the city. I don't miss being a servant—although it was easy compared to the life I'm living now—but I miss the area, the people, the activity.

But I've also missed my brother. He wasn't in the camp. I saw him in the castle, but of course I couldn't speak to him. I don't know where he is now, and we can't start asking around for him, as we have no reason to need to know where he is. But even so, that's exactly what I want to do.

When we get to the gate, the soldier studies Frindor's note closely. It's as if they're trying to find a problem with it. When the man seems fully disappointed, he hands the paper back and waves us through. We walk out onto the drawbridge and then to the road. The sun looks like it's about an hour from setting. Since it's about a six-ish hour hike back to Berin's cottage, it's going to be a long walk, and it'll be late when we get back. We also still have no way back into the city, as far as I know.

On either side of the road leading east, the land is clear of trees. I suspect that's partly to avoid offering the cover of a forest to an approaching army, but it also worked out well to give us all a clear view of the Prince's return to the city a couple months ago.

And now, the open space seems to be perfect for whatever construction is underway.

None of what I see before me was going on this morning, but at present, the area is filled with soldiers. They're building… stuff. I'm not sure what. Platforms and… something else.

Berin glances my way. "You may speak, apprentice."

"What's going on? What are they building?"

He shakes his head. "I don't know for sure, but it's odd to see soldiers doing the work. I guess they have nothing else to do at the moment." He pauses for a moment as we walk on. "You know… I think they're building stages and platforms and bleachers."

"What do they need all that for?" I'm wondering if there might be some celebration coming up, but it's odd to do it in the middle of winter.

"Hmmm…" Berin says quietly. "The wedding. I suspect this is in preparation for the wedding."

The wedding… that confuses me. The wedding is still about three weeks away. I'm not sure how long it'll all take to build, but if they did this much just since we came into the city, it won't take long. "Aren't they doing this a bit early?"

Berin nods his head. "That they are, Trip." He doesn't sound impressed.

I don't know what it means at first, but then it all comes clear. The work will be finished early—at this rate, maybe within a few days. That means there might be little reason to wait the rest of the time for the wedding.

The King wants this wedding right away.

And that means we're in a rush.

I think Berin comes to the same conclusion as he picks up speed.

There's no one else around, so I whisper, "How are we going to get back into the city?"

"That's what I was talking to Hob about just before we left. He's going to have a chat with Tilbur."

"Can we…" I begin, but catch myself. I'm not sure how to ask this. "Can we… you know… count on Hob? He's quite mad, you know."

"Oh, Trip," Berin says with a laugh. "Hob is definitely mad, that's for sure. However, he's always leaned a little in that direction. But no matter how insane he gets, you can always count on him. He'll find a way."

I hope Berin's right.

But the other big thing on my mind is still my brother. I didn't get to see him. I shaved my head and came all this way for nothing.

I do find that I like the feel of my shaved head, though. Now and then I reach up and run my hand over it. It feels pretty weird. I hate having no hair, but that part kind of makes up for it.

"Berin!"

We turn around at the sound of a soldier hollering at us. I almost squeal with joy, but I catch myself. Coming toward us is my brother. He doesn't look happy.

"Berin!" he hollers. "What are you doing here? I had you training troops, then I see you wandering in the castle, getting in trouble. Now you're taking a stroll through a field! You think you can just abandon your orders?"

"I ain't in the army no more, Granel!" Berin growls.

I've never actually heard Berin speak with such poor grammar. I also didn't expect my brother to be so rude.

Granel comes right up close, nearly pushing his nose into Berin's. Still at a shout, he hollers, "I don't care if you're in the army or not! When I give you an order, I expect it to be followed!"

Berin stands straight for a moment, but then his shoulder's slump, and he takes a step back. "I'm sorry, Captain. I… wanted to visit my brother in the city."

Granel crosses his arms and stares at Berin. I notice Berin's eyes flash quickly to me, and Granel turns his head slowly to see me. I want to smile at him, but I'm kind of disappointed that he's yelling at Berin. I didn't think my brother was like this. But maybe all officers are.

My brother examines my face for a moment. His expression doesn't change, but something does. I can't put my finger on it, but he looks like he's… happy. However, he merely turns back to Berin and barks, "What am I going to do with you?"

All around us, soldiers move back and forth. Most just ignore what's going on.

"Well, Captain," Berin says, bowing his head slightly. "Perhaps I could be of service."

My brother gives Berin a look of absolute disdain, but then orders, "Follow me. Bring that apprentice of yours as well. I don't want some ignorant child wandering around with no idea of where to go, getting in trouble, upsetting my soldiers!" He then heads off through all the construction.

Berin waves for me to follow, and I rush to keep up. For an old guy, he sure can move when he wants to.

We weave our way through a group of soldiers. I don't dare lose sight of Berin. At one point, I even grab his cloak and hold on to it like a little child. I'm not ending up in another apprentice group.

We reach a command tent—much smaller than Frindor's—and Granel heads inside. No guards stand at the door.

It's nearly dark, and inside are a few lit lanterns. I wish they offered some warmth as well. The tent is empty of people, but in the corner sits a cot—I assume my brother's—and in the center of the room is a table with papers spread out.

I turn to see my brother, but he's come right up to me and pulls me into a big hug. "You're okay…" he whispers in my ear, his voice filled with relief. Then he asks, "You are okay, aren't you?"

I nod and just squeeze back. When I first met him, I barely knew him. But as the days and weeks have gone my, I've remembered more and more. I remember how close we were. I remember how much he loved me and how much I loved him.

He pulls back and says loudly, "What do you know about bleachers, Berin?"

Granel smiles at me and puts a hand on my cheek, then up to my head. In a whisper, he says, "You shaved it to disguise yourself? I almost didn't recognize you."

"Don't know much, but I can tell you a bit!" Berin replies, just as loud.

In a whisper, Granel says, "We only have a bit of time before someone is likely to come asking questions or needing orders." He turns to me. "I wish we had more time to spend together, but Frindor has me under constant watch. What do you need?"

"We are going to need a way into the city in another day or so," Berin whispers. "Hob is working on it on his end, but we need a way to communicate as to times and more."

"Your goal?"

"Rescue Lady Marleet."

Granel smiles in his way. "Good. As you likely know, this is all an elaborate setup. The King is seeking to put her to death. She and the Prince will be killed the night before their wedding."

"And the construction?" Berin asks.

"It'll be done within a few days. At that point, I expect the King will declare that there is no need to wait until the appointed time and the wedding will be scheduled soon—likely five days from now."

Berin nods. "As I feared. We will need to move quickly. Orders?"

I hadn't realized Berin was taking orders from my brother, but that's pretty exciting.

"Stay in my camp tonight. I'll have someone provide a tent." Granel glances at me. "I'm sorry, but the two of you will have to share." He then turns back to Berin. "I'll be reporting to Captain Tilbur tomorrow morning at first light. I'll communicate with him and then come back. You'll act like you slept in, and I'll chew you out for laziness, then give you the details."

Berin nods and says loudly, "That's all I have, Captain. I haven't built many of these in my time, so I can't really be of more help. But, it's late. You don't suppose you could spare a tent for me and my apprentice for the night? Then we'll get out of your hair tomorrow morning."

Granel gives a sound of disgust. "I'll order it. But don't you get in the way, Berin!"

I find it kind of hard to move back and forth between the trust and anger—it's jarring—but these two men seem to roll with it just fine.

We head outside, and it's not long before we have a tent. It's small, but there's enough room for both of us. Once it's set up, we head to a large tent and get a meal from the food provided for all the soldiers. The men seem to respect Berin, and like everyone else, they seem not to notice my existence.

A few other apprentices sit around here and there. One of them nods at me. The others ignore me.

The rest of the evening is spent listening to Berin regale the soldiers with stories of wars and adventures and more. I suspect some of what he says has been embellished a bit. Either that or he really has had some wild experiences.

Some of the other older men tell a few stories as well. Draydon's dad, General Geran, comes up often. He's considered quite the hero among most soldiers, although a few spit on the ground when they hear his name.

At one point, a few of the men try to pick a fight over whether he was a hero or a traitor, but Berin calms them down.

Just before King Hartor was assassinated, General Geran was seen meeting with Parthun. It's thought among some that Geran was involved in the plot to kill the King. There's no evidence for it, as I understand, but it's certainly a divisive issue. I'd think the fact that General Geran was killed in the rebellion might be a strong argument that he fought against it, but no one seems to consider that.

When things calm down, a few more stories are told. One even includes a quick mention of Nordin and Relin from Nimville. Nordin was quite a well-respected officer in the Battle of Reber's Gate. And Relin was… it sounds like he was… well… it's hard to piece it all together, exactly. I get the impression that when something dangerous needed to be done, they called Relin. And he never failed.

We listen to stories late into the night, and then Berin and I head to our tent. It seems smaller once we're both in there. Unfortunately, Berin snores. Not loud. It's like a gentle, high-pitched whine.

And it's just… enough… to drive… me crazy.

Now and then I hear a soldier call out the hour of the night, and I hear guard duty change over. It's well after three in the morning before I actually doze off.

When I awake, I hear a lot of soldiers on the move. Berin's eyes are open, but he just waves at me. We have to stay in the tent like we're sleeping.

I doze off for a bit, then wake up to the sound of a horse whinnying outside our tent. It's quite irritating and boring.

I decide I want a bit of a conversation.

"So, Berin, did you and my brother have that whole angry interaction thing worked out already?"

Berin smiles. "Well, sort of. It's not that we had it worked out. It's that way among many who are loyal." He pauses for a moment. "Most of the soldiers are loyal, actually, but a number of us are involved in trying to bring the rightful heir to the throne. We all treat each other that way when we might be observed."

That makes sense. I guess they have to have some arrangement. But I guess that also means they must all know who they can trust.

"Are you really all working to see Draydon take the throne?"

"We are, Trip. When Prince Roran abdicated, we thought at first we could deal with the enchantment and still remove Parthun, but then as the days wore on, it became clear that the people had lost their faith in Prince Roran, and we figured that Parthun would spin the issue. He's presented it not as an enchantment, but as indecision from an uncommitted royal." He takes a deep breath and lets it out slowly. "There's a story of a king a few hundred years back who didn't care for the kingdom. He threw parties, spent foolishly from the nation's treasury, killed anyone who stood in his way or who demanded he make a serious decision… He is seen by history as uncommitted. The people see Roran in the same light as they saw that King. They love Prince Roran and are excited about the wedding, but they'll never follow him now."

"But it's not his fault." I sit up and face him. He can't really sit up, as the tent's too short for him.

Berin slowly shakes his head. "People are fickle, Trip. They trust those they shouldn't, and they struggle to trust those they should. Parthun's good at what he does. He has men all through the nation not only reporting back to him but spreading his lies. Until the nation is presented with the truth, a lot of people won't even look beyond what they're told. Lies and rumors can hold the hearts of a nation."

I know he's right, but I hate it. It feels so overwhelming. "And Draydon… how are we going to get him on the throne?"

"Well, our plan was to keep him safe for now. I wasn't brought in on things until well after the three of you left my place two months ago. We're arranging to present him to the Nobles, but it's a matter of when. It's something we have to keep secret, or else Draydon will die long before he reaches the throne room. At present, being considered dead is the perfect cover. It leaves Parthun to focus in on General Lirnal."

I feel sick to my stomach at the thought of poor Lirnal. I bet he's suffering terribly. "Can we rescue him?"

Berin shakes his head. "Nope. He's where he needs to be. If you tried to rescue him, he'd refuse to come with you. I haven't spoken with him in years, but what I do know of him confirms that for me. He'll remain in that cell as long as it's helpful."

I frown at Berin. "I think that's just horrible."

Berin smiles and looks me right in the eye. "Trip, do you really think he's stuck in prison?"

That catches me off guard. "What do you mean?"

He props himself up on one arm, and his smile grows larger. "If he wanted out, he could get himself out anytime. He would just have to say the word, and the loyal soldiers would lead him out. If something happened to Draydon, he would walk out of that prison and immediately put forward his claim to the throne. He's staying there because he doesn't desire the throne. He loves the people. He's there because Draydon is now our future King. He's suffering for his King—and he'll do that without complaint, even if it costs him his life."

I realize my mouth is hanging open, and I close it. "But… why does…"

"Why does he need to stay in prison?" Berin asks with a smile.

"Yes! I don't get it!"

Berin's smile grows. "Tell me, Ellcia. I see the way you look at Draydon. You hope to marry him one day, don't you?"

I feel my face go red and immediately feel embarrassed about my shaved head. That's weird that I think of my hair at that moment.

He lays back down and says, "If you're going to be Queen one day, you're going to have to get used to figuring out the ways of the Nobility and the matters of politics. Ask yourself this question: 'What will happen if General Lirnal walks out of the prison?'"

I'm irritated with Berin. I don't like it when someone holds back information from me. But I decide to try to figure it out.

I picture General Lirnal getting out of prison. If he did, he'd either escape or go straight to the throne room.

If he goes to the throne room, the only thing he can do is put a claim forward to the throne. Otherwise, Parthun's word still stands. And if he puts forward a claim… then Draydon's claim for the throne…

Hmm… something seems off. I don't get it at first, but then it hits me. The people will probably be thrilled with General Lirnal, but when Draydon comes forward, they'll be frustrated with another change. I know I would, if all this was going on. The one who takes down Parthun will be a savior. Anyone else will get in the way.

I smile. I'm getting it… I think.

And if Lirnal escapes the city, then it will divide the kingdom, as some will expect him to come forward for a claim, while Parthun will try to spin it as proof of his guilt for starting the rebellion that led to King Hartor's death.

When Draydon comes forward, it'll be into a mess of political upheaval, but not one for Draydon to solve, but one which will muddy the waters of his claim.

"I think I get it," I say with a smile. "But, then why shouldn't Draydon come forward right now?"

"When Prince Roran came back," Berin explains, "he was long-expected, so he was welcomed back by the people. He disappointed the people, and their trust is shaken. Parthun has used this time well since he's taken the throne and has now created a team of people who are ready to kill anyone who is seen as a threat. If Draydon tries to reach the throne room, he'll be killed before he can get within a hundred steps of the throne."

"But then Parthun will be seen as a murderer!" I say, almost too loudly, considering how secretive we need to be.

"Parthun will pretend that the murderer acted alone. He'll likely hang the guy who kills Draydon—or someone who can be blamed for it. As Draydon figured out, your brother will be the obvious target. Then Parthun's hands will appear clean."

I'm so frustrated with all this. I want to scream out, but not only will that not help, but it'll cause new problems. I can't believe that my brother is in danger. I'm proud of him for his loyalty, but the risk is too great.

Speaking of my brother…

"Berin! Get out here, you lazy worm!"

Berin smiles at me. "Time to put on a show."

He pushes back the flap and crawls out, then pulls himself unsteadily to his feet. "Captain? What time is it?"

I stumble out after him and use his cloak to pull myself to my feet. I shake my head and pull my hood up over my head. The wind is cold, but I'm also still a little shy about having no hair.

"What time is it?" Granel hollers. "It's past the ninth hour! Are you seriously just waking up now?" He pauses for a moment, then says, "No, wait, I don't care. It's time for you to leave. My soldiers have work to do."

"Of course, Captain," Berin says.

He reaches out a hand, and my brother takes it, pulling him in close. I hear my brother growling something at Berin, but I can't make it out. When he's done, he gives a shove to Berin and says, "The next time you come to my camp, you make sure you have something to contribute." He then turns to me and barks, "Keep an eye on this guy. Pay attention to what he says and does and use it to learn what kind of person you're going to be! We learn by example, apprentice!"

He then turns away and storms off.

"Well, Trip," Berin says. "It looks like we'd better be off."

We grab our packs and get our boots on. In a few minutes, we're heading out.

We've left the tent where it is, but Berin just shrugs. He tells me the soldiers need something to do—they've been idle for too long.

We move north from our tent, and after just a few minutes, we're outside the area where my brother's soldiers are hard at work setting up for the wedding—the one which will never take place.

It's a good six-hour hike from here to Berin's house. I'm dying to know what Granel told Berin, but that'll have to wait for now. There are enough soldiers around that I don't dare talk about anything too important.

I smile. There is a question, however, that I think I can ask, one I've be wanting to know about… "So… Berin… the cobbler…"

Berin's speed picks up, and he starts pointing out the occasional plant that can be eaten.

I can see he doesn't want to talk about this, which makes me want to ask all the more.

"Berin?"

"Yes, Trip?"

"The cobbler. We didn't go see her."

"No time."

Well, he's right about that. We did run out of time.

"Yeah, but you didn't even try."

"No time."

"What's her name?"

"No time." At that, Berin picks up speed again, and I have to move nearly at a jog to keep up with him.

## 8

## The Black River

I scramble up the side of our little dip in the ground and peer out through the ferns. Someone's coming. So far, we've had over a dozen patrols move past our area, and none have come close to finding us, but I still keep an eye out.

Besides, who I'm really looking for is Ellcia. She and Berin were supposed to be back last night, but it's already past mid-day.

Hanging out in the forest with Hemot this whole time has been both wonderful and horrible. It's been a lot of fun just to chat and joke around and have nothing to do. We've solved all sorts of problems—and likely created new ones—and worked through so much.

It's also been intensely irritating. Hemot, now and then, falls into a slump over the situation with Marleet. When that happens, nothing seems to pick him up. Not even the thought of rescuing her.

At times, he's a lot of fun to be around. At others, he's so very annoying.

The two people approaching our hiding spot are coming directly toward us. At first, I'm a little unsure who they are, but then I catch sight of a bald head—Ellcia—and recognize her cloak.

I stick my head up just enough to catch Berin's eye, and he nods at me before they turn around and head back to the cottage.

We look around in case there's a patrol, and then sneak through the woods until we find the cottage and slip inside.

When I see Ellcia, I'm shocked again by the bald head—even though I saw it just moments ago. It'll take me a while to get used to it.

She's smiling, though.

"Did you see him?"

She nods. "It was weird. We had to pretend we all hated each other, but we got to talk, and he's okay."

"I'm hungry!" Berin says and wanders to the kitchen area. In seconds, he's pulling out supplies and putting together ingredients for a stew.

We sit down while Berin works away, and Ellcia brings us up to speed. She tells us about the journey there, the run-in with the Captain, the issue with Traltor and Nareesa.

I'm surprised to find out that both Rulf and Lirnal are choosing to stay in prison. I don't know if the guards are treating them poorly, but I would think it would not be a nice place. The bit of time I spent in a cell in the mountain was far longer than I would ever want. To choose to stay in there for weeks or months… wow.

When she gets to the part about how many are working to see me get to the throne, my mouth drops open. I kind of thought Ellcia and I were the only ones thinking that kind of thing. Well, maybe Hemot, too, when he's not joking around. I don't quite understand why I can't just lay a claim on the throne right now to get this over, but Ellcia lets me know the problem. Most people don't know I'm out here right now, and if I reveal myself at the wrong time, I likely won't survive long enough to reach the castle.

Berin drops down in his chair at that point. "And Trip's brother… I mean… Lady Ellcia's brother, he's in a tough spot. They've got him on construction, which means they're trying to make everyone think he's useless as a soldier. If they keep doing that kind of thing, soldiers will start to avoid him—thinking if they get too close, they'll be put on construction duty."

I think when I take the throne, I'm going to undo that. I'll make sure people see Granel for the hero that he is. And Lirnal. And Rulf. And even Tilbur. Hmm… Tilbur. I still have trouble seeing him as a good guy. He's always treated me so horribly. But I know he did it to protect me and his position. Uhhggg… it's all so complicated.

At this point, Ellcia turns to Berin. "So, what did Granel tell you?"

A smile grows on Berin's face, and he shrugs. "Maybe we should chat about that after we eat. The stew should be ready within a couple hours. Then we can chat this evening."

Ellcia frowns, but then says, "You wouldn't tell me till we got back here. Now, you're just being difficult. Would you rather talk about the cobbler?"

Berin leans forward quickly, and his smile disappears. "No, maybe now's a good time after all."

I don't know what that's all about, but I'm just as happy that we can dive in right away.

He frowns at Ellcia, who returns a satisfied smile, but then turns to me. "Well, Your Highness, it looks like we have a way to sneak you into your own castle."

My stomach turns over. All these things are weird for me. I guess I'm just getting used to the idea that I have to be King, but to think that it's my castle…

I give him a nod, hoping he'll continue.

"So, Captain Granel can't give us permission to go through the gates, and neither can Captain Tilbur. Both have the authority, but it'll gain us far more attention than we want. There are a few other ways to enter, such as through the guardhouses, but those ways won't work. To use a guardhouse, Tilbur would have to arrange a time when all the guards present are loyal and somehow ensure none talk. Guardhouses in the city are busy places. Too great a risk of a disloyal soldier showing up."

I nod again. "So, that's some of the ways we can't get into the castle."

"Yes."

"I'm kind of more interested in how we *can* get into the castle than how we *can't*," I say.

Berin gives a little smirk, like he's still trying to be difficult. He's doing a good job. This whole thing stresses me out. I don't want to joke around.

Berin leans back in his chair and nods. "Very well. I guess that is why we went into the city."

I nod. I know he wanted to see his brother as well, but there are lives on the line here.

"Captain Granel didn't give an awful lot of information—there wasn't much time for it. He told us what he worked out with Tilbur. He says we are to enter tomorrow night, by the second hour of the watch, through the Black River."

I nod again. Unfortunately, I really have no idea what any of that means. So instead, I shake my head. "Berin. We've lived in the castle all our lives, but we were servants. We have no idea where this Black River is, nor do we know what the second hour of the watch is."

Berin appears genuinely surprised, but then he focuses. "I'm sorry, Draydon. Some of this is such familiar knowledge to me as both a soldier and from my time as a guard that I forget. The Black River is a stream of fresh water that runs into the city. It provides a lot of the water the common people drink. It's called the Black River because when the city was first founded, a blacksmith used it, and the water from his smithy often flowed black. As for the second hour, the first watch of the night begins at the ninth hour. The second hour of the watch is at ten o'clock."

Hemot shakes his head now. "Why wouldn't he just say ten?"

"Because, Hemot, when a soldier uses times like that, he means the time is precise. You cannot be early. You cannot be late. Imagine planning an attack for the second hour of the morning, and some soldiers charge fifteen minutes early, while others show up late. Military time is considered precise by soldiers like Tilbur and Granel."

I smile. Despite how stressed it makes me to think about sneaking into the castle, it's good to have a plan. "So, we have until tomorrow. We'll need to leave around noon to make it there with some time to spare."

Berin shakes his head. "No, it's just under a six-hour hike. We cannot be seen wandering around with no purpose. We need to leave around the fourth hour of the afternoon. We will have to cut it really close."

I turn to Ellcia and nearly scream, "What happened to your hair?" Once again, I forgot that she'd shaved her head. When I calm down, I examine her face. I don't mind cutting it close like that—with the schedule and all—but that kind of thing is really annoying to her. I can see that's the case this time as well.

My mind starts to spin with some of the details and decisions. "How will we get in? I assume there are bars or something. Otherwise, enemy soldiers could walk—or wade—right in."

Berin nods. "I haven't been in that area since I was in my late teens. The memory is fuzzy, but if I recall correctly, solid steel bars block the way into the city, along with a guard of upwards of twenty soldiers."

Ellcia nods. "And getting in…"

"That, I don't know." He turns back to me. "Prince Draydon, I can tell you what I know. I can't tell you what I don't know. The river flows in under the wall. I think it's pretty deep, so I hope you're all strong swimmers. It's also pretty rough as a lot of water flows in and quickly. Once the river passes the wall, there is a short section—maybe around ten feet, I think—where the river runs under a solid wood bridge. At the end of that bridge are the metal bars. I think, if I remember right, there's a wooden door just above the metal grating which allows soldiers to access the area in order to remove objects that flow down the river. I expect Tilbur will have a way to get us up through there."

"And the guards?" I ask.

"Again, Draydon. I can only speak to what I know. We're going to have to count on Tilbur to get us the rest of the way."

"You're right, Berin." I'm reminded that I need to be more "kingly," so I add in, "Thank you. You have done well."

As soon as I say it, it sounds rude to me, like I'm speaking down to him, but Berin smiles. "Thank you, your Majesty. You must know I am, as always, your servant."

I don't really know how to respond to that, so I give a quick nod. He seems to think that's okay and gets up. A moment later, he's humming to himself by the stove as he stirs the stew.

I keep my head down, as Berin suggested.

It's late—already dark—but a lot of soldiers still move around. Seeing as we're right in the middle of a large camp of men and women constructing what appears to be the stands for Marleet and Roran's wedding, a lot's going on.

But most soldiers are either done work for the day or are packing up and heading to their tents for the night, so the busyness of it all will only last so long.

I see Granel from a distance. I'm pretty sure he sees us, but he's pretending he doesn't. He's ordering men to carry lumber back to the east. I think he's moving people out of the way so we can get through without trouble.

"Down here!" Berin hisses, and we follow without question.

Berin leads us around a large tent. It doesn't smell good. As we walk by the entrance, the light of a lantern shows dozens of bunks inside. The smell of sweat pours out, and Ellcia and Hemot gag.

We come to the corner of the tent, and Berin hesitates, peeking around to see.

"What is it?" I ask.

"Frindor." He shakes his head in disgust. "What horrible timing." His hand comes up, signaling for us to wait for just a second, then he waves us on, and we rush to the cover of the next tent.

As I run, I catch sight of two of the men who tried to kidnap Roran. It seems so long ago, but I still feel anger toward them.

Berin comes to another halt—again at the corner of a tent. He peeks around, then looks toward the city.

We're not far from the walls, and I see the river. I don't ever remember using the main gate in or out of Sevord, so this river seems totally new to me.

The good news is, it's not guarded at all.

The bad news is, Frindor's men are heading this way.

Berin sees it too. The advantage we have is how dark it is. But that won't count for much if they decide they want to question us. I have no idea what they're up to.

"Come on," Berin says as he steps out and walks toward the river.

We follow him as if we're just out for a stroll. Berin is actually leading us away from the wall of the city just a little. We're heading toward a stone bridge, and we'll be there in under a minute.

"You there! Halt!"

Berin doesn't stop. Instead, he just keeps plodding along. I think he's pretending he didn't hear them. He whispers to us, "Whatever happens, you keep walking."

"Hey! You! Old man! Stop!"

Berin slows down and just casually waves us on. Turning around, he hollers, "Eh? You say somethin'?"

"Yeah! Hold up. We have some questions for you. The others too."

I hear Berin laugh, and I keep up the pace. We're almost at the bridge. Unfortunately, even if we run now, I don't think we'll get away.

In the darkness, I see the forest on the other side of the bridge. We could hide there for a bit, but I'm guessing soldiers patrol that area as well. We might be able to duck under the bridge and make it into the castle, but Berin will be arrested. I don't think they have any reason to arrest him, but I also don't think they need a reason.

"What do you need them for?" Berin asks in a strange voice. I think he's trying to sound… I don't know… not smart. His voice is kind of silly and… simple.

"None of your business!" the men shout. "Just hold up!"

They're running now. We reach the edge of the bridge, walk up and over. I hear Berin hollering at the men, and I glance back. They've reached him and one's stopped to hold him. The others come after us.

It's dark on the far side of the bridge—quite dark. I duck down, and the others follow. Slipping around and under the bridge, we reach the river's edge and quietly slide into the water.

The river is bitter cold. I almost cry out, and I hear Ellcia and Hemot gasp. I knew it would be cold—it's winter, afterall—but I had no idea it would be like this.

The men reach the bridge and run across. As we wade deeper into the river, I see a movement around where we ducked down. Someone's coming the same way we came. On the city side of the bridge, I see someone else's feet moving down.

"Crouch!" I hiss.

The water's up to our chests here, but we drop down really low. It's dark, so we keep just our faces above water, doing our best to keep the rushing water out of our mouths.

My breaths come in ragged gasps. At first, I think it's fear, but it's the cold. It's like I can't get a full breath.

With my ears under water, I can no longer hear the men. I just hope they don't catch sight of us. The darkness, at the moment, is our friend.

We push on toward the castle wall. At the rate we're going, it'll take around five minutes to get there. It's hard walking like this, and I keep feeling someone bump into me.

My breathing speeds up, and I nearly yell when I see the glow of torches. I raise my head just a bit to see. The torches will be here in seconds.

Berin's gone—they've got him. No doubt about it. The city—we just can't rush in. If we're seen entering under the wall, the men on the inside will have to account for three people. We have to enter undetected.

I raise my head some more and grab Hemot and Ellcia. They come up just a bit, and I pull them close. I think we're far enough from the bridge that we won't be noticed unless someone looks right at us.

"Torches coming. We have to move fast. If they get too close, swim under the water. Don't come up unless you think you'll drown!"

We push forward, keeping low. We're moving with the current, which helps, but it's still tricky to move without noise. After a few seconds, I think I have a good flow. I kick with my feet and use my hands to keep my head up. The water is still about the same depth—likely up to my chest—but I'm managing to keep low.

It's all going well until I catch my foot on a stone and trip. When I try to kick my other foot down to stabilize myself, I hit nothing. There's a drop off.

I go right down and pull myself up. At the speed the water's rushing along, it's hard to keep my face above water. I can't even see the others until one of them—I think Ellcia—crashes into me.

The torches grow bright, and I suck in some air before dipping below the surface. It's too dark, and the water is too rough to know if the others have gone down as well.

I swim forward, pushing myself along. I see a faint glow ahead—I think. I feel like my lungs are about to burst. My hands feel numb. My face aches. I'm not sure what my lower legs are doing, but my thighs feel like they're on fire.

I can't hold my breath much longer. My chest starts to heave like I'm about to suck in a new breath whether I want to or not, so I push up. My head breaks the surface, and I'm moving so fast, I can't make sense of what I see.

I slam into something hard, and water fills my mouth. I grab hold of it and pull myself up. Hemot crashes next to me, and Ellcia gets a gentler experience as both Hemot and I cushion her stop.

I gasp for air and try my best to be quiet. It takes me a moment, but I'm up against a steel grating. We've made it.

I want to scream for help, for someone to pull us out, but I can't be foolish.

I stare through the bars, doing my best to focus. I see my hand firmly gripping the steel bars, but that's the only proof I have that my fingers are even still there.

I see feet. Soldiers. And... a cloak. Not a soldier.

I clench my teeth together to try to keep them from chattering, but my whole jaw shakes. I feel heavy. It's hard to breathe.

My brain's sluggish. It's difficult to make sense of what's going on. Hemot looks like he's passed out next to me, but he's still holding the bars. Ellcia... where's Ellcia.

I'm almost too cold to panic. I don't see her anywhere! But then I realize what the weight is. Ellcia has her arm around me. She's behind me—holding on.

I lower myself a bit so I can get a better view through the bars. I feel Ellcia adjust. I think I might have dipped her head below the water.

I see the men. They're on a walkway that runs next to the water. Soldiers. I don't recognize most of them. They have their backs to me. But I do recognize Tilbur.

Once again, I almost call out, but I hold my tongue. I'm not sure if I can make a sound anyway.

The man with the cloak. It's wrapped around him. He's cold too—not like me, no... so cold... I recognize him. Brain sluggish. The man I see... he's a friend. He's always been nice to me... no... he's not a friend. It's Parthun! It's the man who murdered my father. He only pretended to be nice. I was nothing but a joke to him.

The anger warms me a little, but not enough. I begin to make noise—involuntarily. I can't stop it. It just comes out. A low grunt... moan. With each breath. I hope it's not louder than the rush of the water.

Parthun nods. Turns. Walks away. He walks to a set of stairs and slowly moves up it. A man stands at the top of the stairs. A guard. Waiting for him. Red sash.

The door closes.

There's more light. I think it's above me.

Arms reaching down. Someone trying to pry my fingers from the bars. I'll die. I cling with all my strength. No… I have no control over my fingers. Or anything.

My hands come loose. I'm out of the water.

My body convulses. Can't hear much. Just "Get it off…"

Someone's pulling my clothes off. I hear another voice. "That one's the girl—the one with the shaved head—be respectful. Get her to the other room now."

I'm not a girl. I can't… wait… he's talking about Ellcia. I… I pass out.

# 9

## The Way In

I come to, sitting on the floor in front of a fire.

At first, I don't quite know what's going on. Then I realize I'm naked, except for the towel hanging loosely over my shoulders.

I try to pull it around myself, but everything hurts. Nothing moves well. It just aches.

A face comes down close to me. "This one's awake!"

Footsteps… someone rushing toward me. I think I should react, but I can't bring myself to. Out of the corner of my eye, I see Hemot next to me. He's got a blanket around his shoulders too, but he's still out cold.

A man comes around in front. Tilbur. My first reaction is to pull back. He's always been nothing but cruel to me.

But this time, he pulls me into a hug. "Draydon. Oh, Draydon. I can't believe… Draydon…" He's crying. I feel like I should react, but I can't.

He pulls back and shakes his head, wipes a few tears away and says, "I'm sorry. I just had to treat you that way. All these years… I'm sorry… You… you were a target, but I… if I treated you harshly, your uncle treated you well. I'm… sorry."

I shake my head. I think I understand, but my brain is sluggish. And… I'm still naked. Not pleased about that part.

Someone shoves a steaming mug of something in front of me. I try to take it, but my hands grip the blanket too tightly. I don't think I have control of them yet. Even if I did, I think I'd lose the blanket. Considering the lack of clothing underneath, that's not an option for me.

The soldier comes around. It's Berin… no… it's Hob.

He lifts the cup up to my mouth. I take a sip. Hot chocolate. It's good. Makes me feel better, and my head starts to clear.

"Where's Ellcia?"

Tilbur drops back onto his butt beside me. He smiles. "Don't worry. She's okay. The Lady Ellcia is with the Lady Aldora. They're in another room. The Lady Ellcia's in the same situation as you, so we thought we'd give them some privacy." As he says that, he glances down at the blanket.

Probably best if she has her privacy. That was a horrible ordeal. No need to add more embarrassment to it all. Now… Lady Aldora… yes… that's Marleet's mom. That's good…

I take another sip and the warmth goes right down my throat. Hob moves over to Hemot and gives him a shake. A moment later, a grumpy Hemot is drinking his own hot chocolate.

Tilbur puts his hand on my shoulder. "Where's Berin?"

I shake my head. "He didn't make it."

Tilbur's eyes grow wide, and Hob chokes and collapses on the floor. Tilbur lowers his head and whispers, "He served his future king well."

"Wait, no!" I shake my head as fast as I can, which isn't very fast. "Not dead. He just didn't make it to the river. Frindor's men got him. I think he's likely arrested." My brain's a little foggy still. I need to be careful about my choice of words.

Hob calms right down, and so does Tibur. I actually see a smile. I don't know if I've ever seen him smile before today. His face is so different with a grin that I don't think I'd recognize him if I didn't already know it was him.

"Parthun was here." I don't think I have the energy to form a question or anything. I just throw it out there.

Tilbur nods. "I was here to receive you, and the guards I stationed down here are loyal. Parthun wanted to speak to me about the upcoming wedding, so he tracked me down. I'm not sure he's ever been in this area of the city before." He smiles again. "Terrible timing."

I feel suspicion grow inside, but I try to push it down. I've hated this man for years. It's hard to trust him now.

"When is the wedding?"

He glances over at Hob. The man has a crazed look in his eye. I have to be careful around him. Tilbur turns back to me and says, "It's not supposed to be for another few weeks, but Parthun is planning it for four days from now."

"So, we have to get Marleet out before then."

He looks at me a little funny. I'm missing something.

"Not just Marleet. Prince Roran." He leans forward. "Both of them, Draydon. They're both going to be murdered. You need to rescue them both."

My mouth drops open. What was I thinking? Or not thinking? If I had found another way into the castle, I might have left Roran here. He'd be killed.

"Of course," I say as quickly as I can. "Yes, both of them. So… how do we rescue them?"

"It's going to be hard. We'll get you to the castle tonight, but once there, you'll have to hide. At first, you'll need to take everything slow. We don't have much time, but we have enough to move carefully. However, when we get the Lady Marleet and Prince Roran safely to you, you'll have to get out of the city within the hour, or you'll never get out." He stands up. "We're going to have to move. I can't justify my presence here for much longer. Do you think you can ride?"

"A horse? I don't think I've ever ridden one."

His face fills with shock, then he calms down. "Yes, I suppose that's true."

I glance down. "I also don't really want to ride a horse through Sevord while naked."

Tilbur laughs. "I don't suppose you do. We'll get you some dry clothes, boots, and a cloak. I'll also see that your clothes, armor, and packs get to the castle so you can have them when it's time to move." He smiles at me. "It's good to see you again, Draydon. I... I know I treated you horribly, but..." His eyes drop to the floor before he looks back at me. "You won't remember this, but your father was... well... your grandfather, the King, wasn't around much when I was young. Your father, Geran, was like... he more or less raised me. You were always more than a nephew to me... I..."

I don't know what to say to all that, so I just give a nod. He returns the nod and a moment later, Hob hands me a pile of clothes. My leather armor is with it, and it's dry. That's a bit of a surprise, but I wonder if it's another part of the enchantment. I've never really noticed if it gets wet. Never seemed to cross my mind to check.

I stand up and try to get my clothes on. It's only Tilbur, Hob, Hemot, and me in the room, and none of them are looking, but it feels awkward. A moment later, Hemot slowly starts to work on getting himself dressed. I still ache all over.

When I'm fully dressed and have strapped on my sword and knife, I start to feel better. Tilbur leads us out of the room and down a hall. As I move, my brain clears a bit more, and I realize Hemot hasn't spoken for a while. The swim must have really affected him.

We meet up with Ellcia and Lady Aldora. Ellcia seems just as shaken as I feel, but she smiles at me. Neither she nor Hemot have their own armor. I gather mine's the only one that's waterproof.

A few minutes later, Lady Aldora, Hob, Ellcia, Hemot, and I are all mounted on horses and moving through the city. Tilbur has left us. Something about it not being wise to be seen traveling with others at the moment. Then, a short distance into the city, two other men join us on horseback. They nod, then just come up beside us and ride along. Each man carries a sword and moves and acts like he's watching everything. I assume they are Lady Aldora's personal guard.

"Denner," Lady Aldora whispers. Although it's late, and the streets are empty, there's no benefit to giving more away through raised voices.

"Yes, my Lady?"

"Is everything in place?"

"Yes, my Lady."

I don't know what that's about, but we carry on. I'm not comfortable in the saddle. My butt hurts already, and my back aches. I can't imagine riding for any length of time.

We zigzag through the city, moving south and west. The castle sits directly west from the eastern gate—not far from where we entered. But I'm guessing the southern gate to the castle grounds is the one we want.

When we get to that area, however, we continue to zigzag a little more and end up moving right past the gate. After a bit more, we zigzag north and west. I wonder if we're going to try to enter from the ocean side. That side is toward the harbor. I've used it many times when heading down to the beach, but it seems like an odd choice.

Just when I expect to zigzag west again, the guard—the one Lady Aldora called Denner—turns to the north. We move right up to the wall, and I see a small, but solid looking door that I didn't know existed.

We dismount, still making as little noise as possible. When I step close to Hob, I hear him hum to himself. It's a bit of a tuneless melody, and I don't think he even knows he's humming it.

My heart goes out to him. Knowing what I know of why he went insane… it's hard to see him like this. I hope when I take the throne that I can help him to see that he's a hero—and that he should never blame himself for what happened.

The Lady Aldora knocks on the door in a weird pattern that I don't think I could copy if I had to. When she's done, she steps back and waits.

I hear what I think is about a dozen latches slide open on the inside of the door. A moment later, it swings inward.

Through the door, I see only blackness—not even the shape of a person—but Lady Aldora merely walks in without a moment's hesitation. Hob goes in next, giggling quietly to himself, followed by the guard who hasn't yet spoken, then the three of us, then Denner.

When we're in, the door closes. I'm not sure what will happen to our horses, but I get the impression that Lady Aldora probably has that figured out.

Another door opens, and light pours in, but not enough to see at first. Then the lantern light is slowly brought up, and I see four men. I glance back and see another dozen—soldiers. I assume they're stationed here as guards, which means they must be loyal to Marleet's mom.

I get the impression that there are two kingdoms in Sevord. There is Parthun's, and there is Lord Yune and Lady Aldora's. Which raises the question for me—which kingdom will I inherit? Will I have Parthun's men, and will they remain my enemies? Or will I receive Lord Yune and Lady Aldora's kingdom? If so, will I ever truly rule?

I push that thought aside for the moment as we move through another room or two. I've never been here before. This area is not actually part of the castle. It's part of the wall surrounding the castle grounds. The walk from here to the castle is long and well-guarded. I'm not sure how we'll do it without being spotted.

We reach the outside door—I know it's the outside because I see the torches in the gardens through a barred window—but instead of going through that door, we turn to a cabinet filled with old weapons. Each one has a little sign below it. A few are missing, but in the end, it just looks like a trophy case.

"Billot, give me a hand," Denner orders.

Denner grabs one side of the cabinet, and the other guard—obviously named Billot—grabs the other. They give a shove, and the cabinet slides over to reveal a set of stone steps.

Moist air wafts up from the dark, and Denner takes the lantern while Billot lights another one. Denner leads the way down, and Lady Aldora turns to me. She waves me forward with a simple, "Your Majesty."

I head down the steps, and Lady Aldora follows directly behind me. At the bottom, there's a sharp turn to the right, and before us is a long, dark tunnel with stone block walls. It's shaped like a triangle with the ceiling meeting above my head.

I smile. Smart design. Something like this shouldn't collapse, short of an earthquake. Maybe not even then.

As we walk, Lady Aldora comes up next to me and takes my arm. "Here we go, your Majesty. We can speak a little more freely in here. Few know of this tunnel. It's something typically only the King and his select guards will know of."

I feel irritated by that. I assume this is the King's escape route in case the castle is overrun. I understand that he'd want to get out, but what about everyone else?

"There are four such tunnels as this," the Lady Aldora continues. "They are used for different purposes. One is an escape route—this is not it. The escape route is larger and allows for more people to move through. In case of a siege, the designers intended for the entire city to remain safe in the castle grounds, so the escape route is large enough for thousands to move through."

I feel better about that, but I can't imagine how a tunnel such as that could exist and not be known by many.

"One is a tunnel that leads to an underground water source so those in the keep may survive. It also is a place where food stores are kept."

That makes sense to me. It sounds like the castle was built in order to care for the people, not just protect the King. I think this is why Parthun cannot be allowed to rule. In the end, he thinks the kingdom is here for him. But a King sits on the throne for his people. I think he's like the first servant. That's what I think King Hartor was, anyway.

"The other two are like this. They are a means to travel in and out of the castle unseen. They are intended for two purposes. One is to move small or large forces in or out of the castle in time of need. For instance, if we were to lose the castle, we could potentially regain control of it using these hidden passages. The other purpose is to run messages in or out. One day, we will need to show you each of the tunnels. But for now, this is the one to focus on."

I like the way she speaks. She has a kind, calm, compassionate voice, but is also strong and confident. I get the impression that she's done a lot of teaching and explaining over the years.

"When we enter the castle," she continues, "we will lead you to a small room where you can rest. You will need your energy. Your task is to rescue my daughter, the Lady Marleet, and His Majesty, Prince Roran. However, if you see them or meet them in any circumstance prior to the moment at which is arranged for you to rescue them, you must not show any indication that you know them at all. They will each do the same for you."

I nod. I do that a lot. Nodding. I guess I just spend a lot of time being told stuff.

"Any questions so far, Your Majesty?"

I try to put some of what Nordin taught me into practice. "Thank you, Lady Aldora, for all you've done and continue to do. May I ask how I will know when we have reached the point at which it will be time to rescue the Lady Marleet and Prince Roran?"

She smiles at me. "I'm impressed, Prince Draydon. You have learned much in the last two months. But you are going to have to leave old habits behind. You are no longer a servant. If you wish for me to tell you something, ask me to tell you. Do not ask if you are allowed to ask."

"My apologies, Lady Aldora. It is the way I have lived for most of my life. It is sometimes more comfortable."

She stops, and since she's still holding my arm, I stop too. "Your Majesty, there are two kinds of Kings: those who seek comfort, and those who seek what is best for their nation. You will do well to reflect upon which one you wish to be."

That kind of leaves me speechless. I just stand there and stare at her.

A smile creeps up on her face. "Are you, Your Majesty, hoping to catch flies with that mouth? If not, I recommend you close it."

I close my mouth, and I feel my cheeks grow hot.

"Don't be embarrassed, Prince Draydon. I have spent a great deal of time teaching young people the ways of the Nobility. It is a bit of a hobby of mine. Come now, we must continue."

She begins to walk again, and I keep in step with her. I feel like she's both a kind, caring woman, and a dangerous woman. I will have to be careful around her.

I hate to admit it, but she's right. I have to leave my old habits behind. I always have a lot of reasons I've come up with as to why I should dance around issues and try to just be nice, but I have to lead.

If I'm a King, I have to give up comfort for my people. And the woman beside me, she's my people. So are her two guards. So are Ellcia and Hemot. So is Tilbur, General Lirnal, Hob, Berin… so many others.

I have to manage all this for them. For all of them. Lord Hillbin, Phil the innkeeper, and even those boys who tried to rob me. They're all my responsibility—or at least they will be when I take the throne.

"Any more questions, Your Majesty?"

"Yes, Lady Aldora. You still have not yet answered my question. When will I know it is time to rescue Lady Marleet and Prince Roran?"

She laughs. "You will know because the Lady Marleet will turn to you. The moment she acknowledges your presence is the moment you need to run."

"And where will we go?"

"You do not have a place yet? A place already worked out to take Lady Marleet and the Prince?"

Truthfully, I hadn't really thought that far ahead. But now that I think about it, Nimville is the place to go.

"I'll be taking them up the coast to Nimville."

She nods. "That might be a problem, but I will confer with my husband and then the Lady Marleet will give you further counsel."

I don't really know what to say to that, so I hold my tongue.

We reach a turn, and there's another set of narrow stone steps—this time going up. When we reach the half-way point to the top, Denner motions for all of us to be quiet, and he and Billot dim their lights. At the top, there's a wooden barrier. I suspect it's another cabinet.

Denner puts his ear up to the cabinet and listens for a long time while we stand on the steps leading down. When he seems satisfied, he takes his fingernail and slowly scratches along the back of the wood panels—making a sound like a mouse in a wooden wall.

He then steps back and waits. A few minutes later, he does the same thing again, then waits. Then again, a few minutes after that.

When he's just about to do it again, I near a light tap coming from the other side, and then Denner mimics the tap back. The cabinet then slides open, and we move out into a hallway.

Captain Tilbur is there with a soldier I don't recognize. The man looks mean and entirely untrustworthy. I'm getting the impression that everything this bunch of Nobles does is intentional, so I'm guessing the man's mean and untrustworthy look is not an accident. Once Captain Tilbur lays eyes on all of us, he nods at me, and then quietly slips away with the other man as if he was just here to confirm that we've made it this far.

No one says a word as we move down the hallway. Denner and Billot have left their lanterns in the secret passage, which is now sealed up again. We don't need any more light along here as the castle hallways are always well lit.

I glance back. Ellcia has her intense and serious expression on her face. Hemot... he looks excited, like he always does when there's danger and risk. But there's something else. I think it has to do with Marleet. He looks... determined.

"In here," Denner says quietly.

He leads us through a small door. I recognize this area of the castle. I've cleaned all over the palace. This was never my primary area, but I've actually been in this room before. I think there was a fire or something here, and I helped to clean up some of the mess before the painters came.

"Hey!" Hemot whispers, "I remember this room. I once accidentally lit a fire in here by testing the curtains to see if they were flammable!"

I frown. Yes, that was it. I remember now.

I glance over at Lady Aldora. She does not look impressed. I wonder if she knows how much Marleet and Hemot like each other.

At the back of the room, another cabinet sits. I remember it. It was solid. The fire burnt it a bit, but there was some kind of legacy rule on that cabinet that it was never to be moved.

I smile. I'm beginning to understand the castle in a different way.

Denner steps up to it, clears off one of the shelves, releases a latch at the bottom, turns the shelf until there's the sound of a click, then rolls the cabinet out from the wall.

On the other side is a large room with bunks. It's clearly made for soldiers and even includes a small armory. Denner and Billot move inside, check out the room, then we all go in. Once inside, Hob brings up the light on a pre-lit lantern as Denner and Billot swing the door shut.

In a low voice and with a smile on her face, the Lady Aldora explains a bit more. "You will need to stay here for the next two days. At that point, Denner or Billot will return and take you to where you will meet with the Lady Marleet and attempt to rescue the Prince." She puts her hands up before we can say anything. "I understand that it will be difficult and inconvenient to stay in here for two days. There is enough food and water in here, and there is a room off to the side where you can change and find privacy when needed. I would recommend you keep that door closed, as the smell can be somewhat… distasteful." She gives us a look filled with compassion. "I know it will be difficult, but you must remain as silent as possible while in here. Guards patrol this area of the castle regularly."

She pauses while we take all that in. I had assumed we'd move a little faster on things—maybe even get Marleet out of here before sunrise today. I glance at Hemot. He doesn't look happy. Neither does Ellcia. That's not surprising.

When Lady Aldora and her guards leave, Hob goes with her. I'm kind of relieved at that. He's a little awkward to be around and very unpredictable.

Once they're gone and the cabinet back in place, we settle down in the bunks. They're not comfortable, but they don't squeak when we climb in. This room really was made for secrecy.

Unfortunately, it hasn't been cleaned in what looks like eighty years. We have to turn the mattresses over and use our own bedrolls as the dust is too thick if we don't.

# 18

## The Ways of Nobility

My head hurts, and everything looks funny. I'm so tired. Can't make sense of what's going on.

I'm moving. Shaking, I think. Someone's doing this to me. I want to yell at whoever it is. I don't think I want to move. Colors in front of my eyes.

"Ow!"

"Draydon! I need you to move! Now!"

I shake my head and sit up as I rub my shoulder. "Marleet?"

"We've gotta move, Draydon!"

I swing my legs off the bunk and wrap my arms around her. I feel like crying. I had no idea how much I missed her.

She squeezes me back, but then pushes me away. "I'm sorry Draydon, we have to move. I can't wake the others. Ellcia just pushes me away, and Hemot just smiles and tells me he wants a buttertart."

I stumble over to Ellcia. I can't get her to move, either. At first, I don't know why we're so tired, but then I remember the lack of sleep and that whole river thing. That's gotta take a lot out of someone.

I shake Ellcia again, but she still doesn't move. She pushes me away, so I wrap an arm around her shoulder and pull her up to a sitting position.

That does it, but she's not happy. I think she's about to growl at me, but then she sees Marleet, and her mouth drops open. "No time," I say. "We have to move. Now!"

She jumps off her bunk and goes for her boots, but she stumbles. I leave Marleet to help her, and I grab Hemot. Shaking him doesn't work. Sitting him up doesn't work. In the end, Denner, who's also here, comes over and slaps Hemot in the face.

That does it.

I step in and say, "Hemot! I don't know how much time we have, but we have to move. Now!" To save him doing what I did, I say, "Marleet's here, but there's no time. We have to get her to safety."

His face flashes with joy, then concern, then focus. It's strange… I've never seen that kind of focus on Hemot's face before. He smiles at Marleet, who smiles back, and in less than a minute, we're all out the door.

I see Billot in the hall. I guess he stood guard outside the room, along with another two soldiers who stand not far away.

Denner leads as we rush through the corridors, pausing at every corner to peer around, keeping an eye out for anyone. We move through the castle for about five minutes, I think, until we reach a spot near one of the ballrooms—one which was used for unimportant visitors to the castle.

Denner stops about half-way along the corridor while Billot runs ahead. The other two guards stay back at the last corner. Once they and Billot give a signal—I assume that means there's no one in sight—Denner turns to Marleet.

She points at a spot on the wall and says, "There."

Denner turns and slams his shoulder into that area of the stone wall, and a section moves. I almost laugh. It's like what Rulf did when he led us into that secret passage. I've been in this corridor countless times. I had no idea that was there.

Denner gives another shove, and it opens wide enough for us to go through.

Marleet turns to us and whispers, "Inside! Quickly!"

Hemot goes in first, followed by Ellcia. I slip in next and turn back. Marleet hasn't moved. Instead, she stands before Denner, who appears to be… crying.

"My Lady. Please… be safe."

He then takes her hand and kisses it. I find that a little weird to watch, but then she slips in through the door and says, "Close it, Draydon."

I swing it shut, and she pushes past me to a small hole in the wall. I can just make out the shape of her head in the small amount of light coming through until she puts her eye up to the hole to look out.

When she pulls away, she whispers, "Give me your hand, Draydon."

I put out my hand, and I feel her grasp it. I take Ellcia's hand behind me, and she takes Hemots hand. I only know that because she whispers, "Eww… your hand's all sweaty, Hemot." To which he replies, "I'm… nervous."

We move through the corridors for a long time, doing our best to be quiet. When any of us say anything, Marleet shooshes us.

I'm starting to be able to see her a bit better. I think at first it's just my eyes adjusting to the dark, but that's not it. There's more light coming in, and it's a different light.

The sun is rising, and light's coming through windows… shining through the holes into our corridor.

I'm glad we're still holding hands, though, because otherwise we'd bump into each other every time Marleet slows down—which is a lot. We move fast, then slow, then fast.

I notice when we move slowly, I also hear people talking. I'm guessing we're being careful at those times because we're in areas with more traffic.

Finally, I feel her slow down again, then come to a stop.

It's really dark here. She comes in close and whispers, "We have to be quiet in this area. Too many people. There's a ladder in front of us. We're all going to climb it. I'll go first. Climb to the top and get off on the right-hand side."

I nod. Then remember she can't see me. "Okay."

I turn back to Ellcia and relay the same message. While she relays it to Hemot, I turn back and move forward. I hear Marleet already on the ladder. She's moving fast.

I begin to climb. I guess I had assumed it would only be a short way, but the ladder just keeps going. We were on the first floor of the castle before. I'd say we're heading to the third floor now, at least.

When I get to the top of the ladder, I'm scared, at first, because there are no more rungs, but then I remember that's exactly what I'm after.

Swinging my arm over to the right, I feel out, and then down. There's a floor there—something solid, anyway. I scramble onto it and hear Ellcia come up after me. I whisper quietly, "This way," and she moves up beside me. A moment later, Hemot joins us.

I feel along in the direction I think we're supposed to go and find a solid wall there. In fact, it's solid in every direction except for the way we just came. And… there's no Marleet.

"Hey!" That's Marleet's whisper, I think. "Up here!"

I raise my hand up, and I nearly yell as someone grabs my wrist. "Yep, up here," Marleet whispers.

I slowly stand, hoping not to bang my head on anything and trying not to bump Ellcia or Hemot. We're kind of still on the edge of a drop that likely goes down a couple floors.

I feel Marleet pull me in the direction away from the ladder, and I climb onto another ledge. There's some light here, coming from above. I can just barely make out her shape.

Ellcia and Hemot scramble up next to us, and Marleet leads us down a small corridor, around a corner, and into a small room.

The light in this new room is far too much to bear at first. I squint and cover my eyes. So do Ellcia and Hemot.

But Hemot doesn't have any time to adjust as Marleet grabs hold of him. He hugs her back and a moment later, they're both crying. I'm not surprised that Marleet's crying. But Hemot… that's not normal for him. But I get the impression that he doesn't care about that kind of thing right now.

When they're done, Marleet pulls back.

"Are you okay?" Hemot whispers.

She nods. "I've missed you."

His smile grows. "I have something to tell you."

"I have something to tell you, too."

"Well, I really have something to tell you," Hemot says with a large grin.

"Well, I also really have something to tell you!" Marleet replies with a giggle.

I roll my eyes. This could go on for a while.

I turn around as they continue back and forth, and Ellcia and I look around the room. It's quite large, actually. There seems to be only one way in or out—aside from the windows. I see a dozen or more beds in here, but, unlike the room we slept in, this room is clean. The floor and ceiling are built of stone blocks, and a few pillars set here and there hold up the ceiling.

There's also a small armory, which is actually still quite dusty. It doesn't look like anyone's touched that in a while—nor do I think Marleet expects we'll be using it. I think there's enough armor and weapons for about a dozen soldiers. The same number as there are beds.

It's interesting to me that I've now seen two such rooms in the castle. I wonder how many there are. This is a great way to retake the castle if it is lost, but if the wrong person knows about this kind of thing, it's also a major security threat.

Ellcia opens a large cabinet. Inside are dozens of shelves which are currently being used as a pantry. I think there's enough food in here for the four of us to last a week. Beside the cabinet are two barrels. I expect that's water. There's a trough coming down from the outside wall and another one leading away. I think it's collecting rainwater and dispersing it when the barrels get too full.

There's also a small library—and by "small" I mean about fifteen books. I know Marleet likes to read, although Hemot never did.

We pull off our boots and set them down by the bunks. It feels good to be without them for a bit. I smile as I see our packs with our weapons and Ellcia and Hemot's armor have been brought here. I guess this was planned as our next stop.

Marleet and Hemot appear to be winding down, and Ellcia and I sit on a bunk to wait it out.

"Okay, I'll go first," Hemot says.

Marleet giggles. "No, I'll go first. You went first to tell me that you wanted to go first. So, I should go first."

Hemot laughs. "No, that doesn't count. I want to go first because I've been waiting months."

Marleet shakes her head with a big smile. "No, I've been waiting just as long as you!"

Ellcia clears her throat, and the two glance our way. That seems to have pulled them out. Unfortunately, they both say at the same time, "Okay, you go first!"

That sends them both into a giggle fit, until Ellcia clears her throat again, at which point, they settle down.

Hemot just charges forward. His face grows serious, and I see sadness there. "I've never told you how I feel about you. I... like you. A lot. More than a lot. And when I heard that you were going to marry Roran... well... I felt sick about that. I know you can do what you want... but I don't want you to marry him."

Marleet blushes. "I don't want to marry Roran."

"You don't? But... you'd be a princess?"

She shrugs. "I don't really care about that kind of thing. To be honest, I'm almost a princess already."

Hemot frowns. "What do you mean?"

"Well, my papa is actually related to the royal line. In fact, I'm kind of like a cousin to Draydon. I didn't know that. I'm not close. My papa is something like fourteenth from the throne, so there'd have to be a lot of... you know... dying... before any of us became King or Queen, but I don't want it, anyway. I want something else."

"What?"

She frowns at him. "You don't know?"

He blushes, and a weird look comes over his face.

Ellcia and I decide to have a chat. For one thing, this is shaping up for a long conversation. I can recognize when they're not planning on being direct, and this is that time.

We chat through our next steps. It's hard to know what to do until we talk to Tilbur or someone. I'm not sure who's supposed to give us direction, but at the moment, I don't see any way to rescue Roran without some extra information or options.

Ellcia is of the same mind. We're about to leave the matter when Hemot and Marleet step in front of us. They're both smiling and holding hands. I can't help but smile back. They look happy. I don't know what all they talked about—I find listening to them go back and forth irritates me, and I've learned to ignore it—but they seemed to have settled the issues of each other and Roran.

"I need to bring the three of you up to speed."

I stare at Marleet in shock. I've never heard her speak like that. I mean, she's used all those words before, I assume. But… her voice is different. It's strong. And carries authority with it. It's like she knows what she's talking about—which is not very… Marleet.

I examine her eyes, her posture, her outfit, everything.

I think the young woman standing in front of me, despite how silly she was with Hemot a moment ago, is not the same girl I knew two months ago. This is… this is not Marleet. This is the Lady Marleet.

She looks strong, smart, and beautiful. She was always pretty, but this is altogether different. I suddenly get the impression that when it comes to Nobles in my court when I am King, Marleet is going to be one of the greatest.

I shake my head. Wow! This is not at all what I expected.

"Okay, Lady Marleet, please bring us up to speed."

She looks at me and cocks her head to the side. "Draydon. Your voice. You're speaking like you are no longer the boy servant in the castle. You speak like a Prince."

Ellcia takes my hand and squeezes it. Now I'm grinning like a fool.

Marleet smiles at me again, then makes eye contact with Ellcia, then Hemot, before turning back to me.

"Draydon, I'm sure you know by now that you are the future King of Sevord. The Lords and Ladies have been trying to find some means to work through Roran's abdication, but they have not found a way. At best, he could come forward and put a claim on the throne, but we are fully aware that Parthun will discredit him due to his previous abdication."

I nod. I'm not really sure how to take this new Marleet. I like it, but it's a real shock.

"That means, Draydon, you are the future King. If you don't take the throne, Parthun will rule. In addition to that, it has become clear that Parthun will kill Roran and me. The wedding is not scheduled for weeks yet, but the Nobles have mostly arrived, and Captain Granel will finish the preparations for the wedding within a day or two. We fully expect it to be announced that the wedding will take place within a matter of days."

She pulls up a chair from one of the tables in the room. It's at this point that I notice we have not whispered at all since we came into this area. I gather that means Marleet knows it's quite secret and far from those who might overhear.

Once she's seated, she leans forward, then sits back as if she's remembering something, positioning herself like I've seen the noblewomen sit.

"Draydon, we do not believe it is to Parthun's advantage for the wedding to go forward. At this point, the people are still upset over Roran's abdication. They are happy for the wedding, but wish for matters to be different. The attention of the people is on Parthun, and it's not good. They all suspect Parthun on one level or another for his involvement in the rebellion and for the Prince's abdication. The people wish for General Lirnal to be released and for him to take the throne. The only way we see for Parthun to secure his role is to take the eyes of the people off Lirnal and make Parthun the hero."

I nod. I had already known most of that, but she makes it sound both more complicated and much simpler.

"Everything we see suggests that Parthun is going to kill both Roran and me, and possibly my parents. He will then declare to the people that the murderers will be found, and he'll likely blame Captain Granel, and maybe even General Lirnal—suggesting that he orchestrated it from within prison. They will both be hung, and Parthun will establish his rule, and the people will support him as he is the one who made the supposed murderers pay."

She frowns. "This has all been quite difficult for me to learn and work through. The ways of the Nobility are strange, and I have had to spend a great deal of time studying this."

"You've done well," I say, earning me an appreciative smile. "Now, before we move on, we were told that we would need to spend quite some time in that room down on the first floor. But now, things have changed. I don't think we were there for more than a few hours. What happened?"

Marleet frowns. "My papa's friends in the court noticed many soldiers have been reassigned. It is a strange situation, but those soldiers and guards who are less trustworthy are being stationed closer to the Prince's quarters and closer to my parent's quarters."

I nod my head. I don't understand how things in the castle work, but that sounds like a bad sign.

"We decided in the middle of the night, shortly after my mama returned, that we would need to move quickly if we were to keep everyone alive. We expect the Prince to be murdered by early afternoon."

My eyes bulge, and I glance at the others. They look shocked as well. "Why didn't you start with that, Marleet?"

She shakes her head. "It is all important information, Draydon. We have to have it all laid out before decisions can be made."

I open my mouth to respond to that, but she's right. We have to be thorough.

"So, priority number one, I believe," Marleet continues, "is to rescue Prince Roran. That won't be easy, but we can do it. If Roran and I are missing, then my parents will not likely be harmed, and without our bodies, General Lirnal will not be arrested, nor will Captain Granel. Priority number two is to get the five of us out of the castle. Priority number three is to return and present you, Draydon, as next in line for the throne."

Hemot leans forward. "I still don't understand why Draydon shouldn't put his claim forward now. If we can find a way to keep him safe, shouldn't we move forward today?"

Marleet shakes her head. "I struggled with that as well. It's because of General Lirnal. Right now, Parthun is terrified of General Lirnal. He believes the General is his only challenger for the throne, and he also believes the General has enough support to escape from prison anytime he wishes." She looks intently at me. "He fears that General Lirnal will suddenly walk into the throne room at any moment and lay claim to the throne."

"Okay," Hemot says, "I get that. So, why can't Draydon step forward now and claim the throne?"

"Because, since Parthun is afraid of General's Lirnal's possible claim, he has placed soldiers all through the castle, especially near the throne room. These men are not much more than assassins. They're job is simply to kill General Lirnal—no matter the cost. If you are seen, they will kill you. We can't see any way to keep you alive if you make a move for the throne."

"Then we need Rulf!" Hemot declares.

Marleet shakes her head. "Rulf is under constant guard. No one can get close to him—not even Captain Tilbur. Parthun recognizes Rulf as a true threat. The King has found an enchanted crossbow that was designed to harm giants." She laughs. "I'm sorry; it's not funny. It's just that King Parthun is extremely paranoid. He covers every possibility. The only thing we know for certain is that he will do all he can to remain in power. If Rulf steps out of prison, he'll be shot with the enchanted crossbow—and we don't even know if it'll kill him or what it will do. If he stays in his pit, the King cannot justify shooting him."

"So, what will leaving the castle do for us?" I ask.

"It will allow us to leave for a time while things here in the city settle. It will also shift Parthun's focus away from Lirnal and toward Roran. Parthun will know that Roran can no longer properly lay a claim to the throne, but he will fear the possibility."

"And how will that benefit us?"

"That's the great part, Draydon," Marleet says. "Once Roran is out of Parthun's grasp, he will fear that the enchantment will somehow be canceled. He will fear what Roran might do and what support Roran might find among the people and Nobles." She smiles. "And for us, that's good news. We can use that fear to distract the King. My papa believes security here in the city will be loosened while Parthun seeks Roran elsewhere. And that is the point at which we should return, and you should lay claim to the throne."

"Wow!" I say. That sure is a lot to take in.

She nods at me. It feels a little awkward that she's really only talking to me, but then again, I guess I'm the future King. I know that in my head, but I'm still not used to it.

"So, Prince Draydon," she says with a smile, "what are your orders?"

A laugh escapes me before I can catch myself. "What are my orders? I thought you already said what we needed to do."

She shakes her head. "No, I gave you counsel based on what the Lords who are loyal to the throne suggest. It is up to you to make the decision. Prince Roran was making similar decisions while he moved toward the throne."

"So, Roran is still under the enchantment?"

She nods. "He is, but we have found a ring which cancels the enchantment as long as he wears it—although the enchantment is slowly breaking through. The only way to fully cancel the enchantment is to find the Spellcaster and have him cancel it… or kill the Spellcaster."

"If we kill him, the enchantment will be canceled?"

"Yes. Any enchantments placed upon people are canceled upon the death of the spellcaster."

"Then, we will rescue Roran and take him to Nimville. In time, we will track down that Spellcaster, but for now, we will hide in the fishing village."

Marleet shakes her head. "That's where you stayed the last two months, is it not?"

I nod.

"Then Parthun will look there for Roran right away. He will quickly find out that Ellcia and Hemot are still alive, as he believes you are most definitely dead. He'll assume they took part in my 'kidnapping' and search each of the fishing villages."

"Ah, this is so complicated!" Hemot says.

I see the old Marleet shine through as she breaks into a giggle. "It is."

"Then we can't go back to Nimville," I say. "We can't put them in danger—at least any more danger than we've already put them in. We will head to Haner."

"Why Haner?"

"There are many people in that city who are loyal to the throne."

"Like Phil and Laana," she says.

That shocks me. "How do you know about them?"

"I traveled through there, actually," she says. "Just after you." Marleet smiles and again I see the old Marleet shining through. I think I like both Marleets, and I hope we don't lose either. "When we get out of all this mess, we can tell each other about everything that's happened with us." She turns to Ellcia. "And... you can help me to understand what drove you to shave your head. I mean... you loved your hair."

Ellcia laughs. "Yes, I look forward to telling you about that and everything else."

"So, what is this place?" I ask.

Marleet stands up and spins around. With a big smile, she says, "This is my secret hideout. I found it shortly after Rulf was arrested. I decided I would familiarize myself with the secret tunnels throughout the castle. I've memorized my way around and can travel through much of the castle unseen. When I found this room, I cleaned it and began to stock it with supplies in case we needed it. In fact, I suggest we eat something and get moving."

We lay out a meal and eat. We chat a bit about some of our experiences over the recent months, but not too much. Much of what Marleet tells us is what we need to know about rescuing the Prince.

We also chat about Berin. I'm quite worried about him, but Marleet just shakes her head and tells me to leave it with Tilbur. She explains that we all play our part, and our part has nothing to do with Berin at the moment.

When we finish eating, I focus us on our task. I'm tired and would love to sleep, but it sounds like we have to get the Prince out of here within hours. "So, how do you think we can rescue Roran?"

Marleet smiles. "Well, the easiest way would be for me to simply walk up to Roran's room and ask him to go for a walk. Then we could slip into one of the secret passageways and work our way out of the castle."

"But that's not going to work?" I ask. Something about her tone suggests we have to find a different way.

"It won't. Everything is changing right now. There's nothing definite. We are having to make a lot of guesses, but we think that the King's guards around the palace are keeping an eye on Roran's movements. If we walk through the castle, they will follow us. I'm under suspicion by the King as working against him—he's quite paranoid right now—so if I show up at Roran's quarters, the King's guards will pay extra close attention to us. It would be better to get Roran out of his quarters without my involvement."

"How will we do that?" Ellcia asks. She hasn't spoken up much since we started discussing all this. Neither has Hemot. I think they're letting me lead. I know Nordin and Hella encouraged them to do that kind of thing.

"Well," she says, "my plan was to have you, Ellcia, dress as a servant and deliver the message. But... the whole shaved head thing..." Marleet looks awkwardly at the floor, then smiles at Ellcia. "No servants shave their heads. So... you're not going to work out for that."

Hemot nods. "Then it'll be me."

A pained expression passes over Marleet's face. I get it too. Hemot is great. Really great. And I know he means well. He's just... well... you know... not the most reliable. He's likely to get distracted.

Marleet's expression turns to a frown. "Hemot, do you think you can focus and do this? You would need to deliver a note to Roran's personal guard. They are loyal to him. But you would have to move quickly, keep your head down, and not talk to anyone."

Hemot stands up. "What? Of course I can focus. I might swing by the kitchens quickly to get a snack, and maybe go check out my old room, but I'll get right on it and be back in less than half an hour! If I get into a conversation with someone, it might take longer, but not too much. Maybe an hour, tops."

"No, Hemot!" I shake my head. "You can't do any of that. You would have to go straight to his room and deliver the message, then come right back."

Hemot nods at me and gives me a look like he thinks I'm saying crazy things. "Of course! I would do exactly that. The trip to the kitchen won't take long at all. I'll try to keep any chatting with Tereese down to a minimum, but she'll likely be quite curious about how things are going. She'll want an update, and I think it's only proper to give it to her."

Marleet turns back to me. "So, that just leaves you, Draydon. I didn't want you to have to go out there since you're likely the most recognizable of the three. If you are identified, it not only puts you and Roran at risk, but could expose Tilbur."

"Exactly," Hemot says. "So, I'll go."

Marleet's face fills with a slight panic, but then she smiles. "Hemot. I just got you back! Can you just stay with me?"

Hemot's mouth drops open, and he jumps forward and wraps his arms around Marleet. "Of course!"

She pushes him back a bit. "Good. For now, we'll need to focus. The sun is just up, and I believe it's about four hours until noon. We suspect the King is going to move against Roran just after lunch." She turns to me. "Now is the time."

"What do I do?"

She waves me over to a pile of clothes. "Put these on."

I slip behind the small armory and change. It actually feels a little weird to be putting on a servant's outfit again. It's been so long. But then again, it's comforting. I leave my sword behind, of course—servants don't carry swords—but I keep my knife. It's a little uncomfortable, but I strap it to my chest under my shirt. I'm not sure how I'll get it out if I need it, but… I'll figure out a way.

I come out, and Marleet asks me to sit down. A moment later, she's working on my hair while she gives me the details of our plan.

The people of Nimville don't cut their hair very often, and I've gotten shaggy. I can't help but think that'll help, and it does. When Marleet's done, my hair hangs down over my eyes, and she asks me to do something weird with my lips. I try moving my mouth a few different ways until we find one that helps to disguise me enough.

She hands me a note and explains what I'm to do, then we head to a wall that has no windows.

She gives a push on one of the stones, and a section swings in quite easily. Marleet's never been all that big, so I'm guessing the hinges in this area are well oiled or at least in great condition.

We move down a ladder, then through some corridors, then down another couple ladders. Then up another one. I'm amazed at how well Marleet knows her way around.

When we come to a stop, she signals in the dim light of the corridor that this is the place. We all peer out through the small spy holes until we're satisfied there's no one in the room.

We pull on the stone doorway which swings noiselessly inward. Before me is a hanging tapestry. I think a lot of these secret doors must be behind tapestries.

I give a quick nod to the others and push the tapestry aside, stepping out into the room. I'm about to walk out, when I nearly scream. Off to the side of the room is a man, polishing the wood of a cabinet.

I know who he is. His name is Frelt. He's an okay guy and all, but he's definitely a grumpy man, and if he sees me, he'll tell all the servants.

I move for the door, but duck behind a table as I see him turn.

"Who's there?"

I wait a bit, watching his legs from under the table. When he turns back to his work, I slip to the door and out into the hallway.

Roran's room is not far from here. A guard ahead of me slowly walks the halls, but he doesn't look back. It's possible any one of the guards could question me, causing all sorts of trouble. Soldiers rarely bothered with us in the past, but nothing's the same now.

I round the corner and see Roran's personal guard. I'm told they're loyal to Roran and loyal to the throne. As I walk up, they watch me closely, although I don't make eye contact. Instead, I shift the note in my hand the way Marleet showed me, holding it in such a way that one of the men can easily slip it out of my hand.

I walk by the first man, and he does nothing. I don't want to have to make a second pass, so I hold it out a little more obviously. The second man takes it with barely a movement, and I walk on.

The note was for Roran to head to an area of the castle where we can easily rescue him. I hope Marleet is right, and the men are loyal.

I round a corner, grateful to see none of the King's guards. I just have to slip into a room up ahead, and Marleet says she'll be ready in there. The exit is behind a tapestry showing a picture of a King from over four hundred years ago as he defeated a band of giants. She says she'll have the secret passage open, and I'll be able to just slide in.

But just before I can reach the door, two soldiers come around the corner. They're not normal soldiers. The red sash across their chests declares them to be royal guards. I'm only two steps from the room, and I consider trying to make it, but servants who try this kind of thing get in a lot of trouble. The risk is too great.

I step to the side of the hallway and bow my head, letting the hair fall down a bit, hoping it will cover enough of my face. A moment later, the Regent walks around the corner. No… not the Regent. The King. The usurper. The man who sits on my throne!

# 11

## The Ones in on It

I get a sudden urge to attack him. I can't really see him all that well. Not only because of my hair but also because my head is bowed. There's someone else with him, too. Not sure who, but he walks behind the King.

"So, as I was saying," the King says, "the people need to know that I am not only their King, but I am a strong King. That I have a firm grip on their lives and their future. They need to know with certainty that I have everything under control." He stops, not far from me, and his voice grows serious. "They will only know this if I show them my true strength. Common-folk only learn one way—the hard way."

It's taking everything I have not to go for my knife, but it would be too difficult to get it out right now. I'm clenching my fists, and I think my hands are shaking, so I focus on calming down as much as I can.

"Take this young man, for example," the King says.

My heart races. I want to run. It's a terrible idea, but if he forces me to raise my head, he'll recognize me.

"Will he serve me faithfully if I am kind to him?"

"It's difficult to know, Your Majesty."

The voice of the other man… it's Tilbur. That gives me hope, but also fear. I can't expose him, but if I'm arrested, he's my only hope.

"Well, I think it's not difficult to know, Tilbur. Take young Caric, for example. I was kind to him, yet he betrayed me. This young man here could be the same. But if I am cruel to him, he will fear me, and know that betrayal is far too costly. Draydon's betrayal was only made possible by my kindness."

My hands shake a little, but I try to relax my muscles. I notice my breathing has quickened. I'm terrified, but I think I'm more angry than scared.

"Ah, just talking about him has an effect, see Tilbur? His hands shake. I see sweat on the back of his neck. And he's breathing like a Talic Wolf is on his tail."

The King is right next to me, examining me well enough that he can see the sweat on the back of my neck, but I can't do anything about it!

"If he did not respect me, he'd walk away. But clearly his fear of me keeps him in place." The King steps back and points at my head. "What if, for instance, I was to cut off one of the boy's ears? He doesn't need both ears to serve me. But then he will know that if I'm willing to cut off one ear to make a point, what will happen if he does not serve me with all his heart? Or worse. What will I do if he betrays me?"

Tilbur doesn't respond. I get that. I have no idea how to react, but I fear that Parthun may try to make an example of me.

"It is the same with all common folk. They are simple, but they understand fear. If I show them my strength, they will never dare rebel." He then points at me, and says to one of his guards, "Soldier, cut off this boy's ear. I don't care which one."

I'm about to run, regardless of the danger, when Tilbur hollers out, "Wait! It's you!"

He grabs me, spins me around, and slams me face first up against the wall. Tilbur has always terrified me. He's a strong man—certainly the biggest of his living brothers—and I know I'd have no chance if I tried to resist.

He grabs my hair and twists my head. At first, I'm angry, but then I notice he's twisted my face away from King Parthun. He comes in close and hisses, "Were you the imbecile who cleaned my quarters yesterday? Did you think I wouldn't notice?"

I find myself half flying, half tumbling down the hallway with a screaming Tilbur behind me. He grabs me again and throws me up against a wall.

I get it. He's gotta hide who I am. But… I'm not sure he has to be this rough with me.

He twists me around and throws me again down a hallway, out of sight of Parthun. "This is your last chance, boy!" he hollers. "Clean my quarters properly, or I'll cut off more than an ear!"

I get up and run. On one hand, loyal to the throne or not, Tilbur terrifies me. On the other hand, this is my chance to get out of here.

I race along the hallways, away from Tilbur and Parthun, but this is a real problem. I have no idea where to meet up with Ellcia and the others. The place we were supposed to meet is on the other side of Parthun. I could go there through an alternate route, but that would take me through the busy areas of the castle. That would be nearly as foolish as walking back toward the King.

I come around the corner and slam into someone. It takes me a second to realize who it is, but before I can cover my face, she sees me.

It's Tereese, the head cook.

We stare at each other for another second before she grabs me and pulls me down a side hallway. In a quiet voice, she hisses, "Walk behind me with your head bowed."

I obey and follow her. I'm not sure where she's taking me, but if I walk like this, my hair covers enough of my face to hide my identity. Besides, people always look at the one in charge, not the one following behind. This is a perfect cover.

When we come around another corner, we bump into a servant who's dressed as a kitchen worker. I don't recognize him, but Tereese stops to talk, and I hold back. Part way through the conversation, she grabs my arm and pulls me close.

"Where are you going?" she whispers.

It takes me a second to realize that she's talking to me because she merely goes on with her conversation with the other man.

The best I can do is hope she can take me in a round-about way back to where I need to meet the others. Keeping my voice low, I hiss, "I need to get to the second floor near the Heathercliffe Banquet Hall." That's not exactly where I need to go, but it's close.

Tereese finishes up her conversation, then whispers, "Don't mention this boy to anyone, Mert."

The man nods and walks on. Before we start back down the hallway, she whispers, "Don't worry, he's loyal. But…"

She stops talking as a woman walks around the corner. Instead, Tereese walks on, and I follow close behind.

We're not heading to the second floor near the banquet hall I mentioned. Instead, we seem to be moving in the direction of the kitchens.

When we get there, Tereese has me stand in a corner just inside the door. No one pays any attention to me. Instead, Tereese keeps them busy with other tasks.

After about five minutes, she comes over and loads my arms up with a fancy dish. It has dried fruit all around the edge, but a large, fern-like plant in the center.

I smile to myself. The fern will cover my face just perfectly.

She waves for me to follow her and as she passes, she says, "I can't get you to the second floor right now. You will be caught. I'll take you somewhere safe."

We weave through a fairly busy area of the castle, but the fern does its job well. No one notices me, but I have to concentrate hard to see where I'm going. I almost bump into a few things and once I nearly collide with a soldier, but for the most part, I can see through the leaves.

We end up going down a long corridor not far from the throne room. I feel terribly exposed, despite the fern in my face. It's hard to be near so many soldiers.

"Tereese!" a man calls out.

We both stop, and Tereese responds with, "Yes, sir."

It's the Head Steward. He's been in the castle forever. I don't mean just a long time. I mean he's old—really old. I know people don't live this long, but we used to say he was well over two hundred years old. I doubt that's true, but he sure looks it.

"I need you to check over your staff in the King's Hall. I don't think they'll be ready in time."

He's not angry. He's never really angry. He's just never happy, either. It's all just decisions and information for him.

She gives a slight bow and says, "Yes, Head Steward." She then turns and hollers, "Mert!"

The man she spoke with earlier comes over. I gather from the amount of people at work, there's a big event happening soon.

When he reaches her, she says, "Take this dish to the waiting room. The boy will carry it."

He gives her a slight bow—similar to what she gave the Head Steward. It's a proper response among servants of slightly different position.

"Follow me!" Mert says with an arrogant tone.

I quickly move after him. I hope Tereese is right about Mert's loyalty.

We move down a side hallway—which is quite busy, but often is when an important banquet is about to take place in the King's Hall.

I'm not sure what this is about. I'm assuming it has something to do with Roran and Marleet.

Oh… I get it… I see it all.

Roran is "scheduled" to be murdered within a few hours—Marleet, too. The banquet will be underway, and the wedding will be announced as happening sooner than expected. Everyone will be happy until the murders are announced. Parthun will use their anger to control them. He'll blame… oh… Captain Granel. He'll suggest Granel was so disillusioned because Roran abdicated that he killed the young Prince.

Three threats removed—Marleet, Roran, and Granel—and a chance for the King to establish his role.

I hope Roran got the note okay and made it to where he needed to be, because I'm not making it to where I'm supposed to be. I'm scared, but I'm also frustrated. I don't want to act all arrogant and all, but I'm kind of the only one who can stop Parthun now. I've gotta get out of here.

We round a corner, then down a short hallway, then round another corner again. The waiting room is a large room between a massive kitchen and the King's Hall. It's where everything goes before it's brought out for those attending the banquet. I know we'll end up in the waiting room along this route, but it's a strange route to take.

We round another corner, and Mert comes to a halt. He checks behind us, then ahead again, then peeks into a room on the left-hand side of the hallway. When he pulls back out, he grabs the dish from me and says, "Quick, inside the room, behind the tapestry. Push on the wall."

He then turns and continues down the hallway.

I duck inside and close the door. If Mert had said that to me a few months ago, I would have thought he was crazy. Now, I'm just crazy enough to trust that there must be a secret passage back here.

I pull back the tapestry and start pushing on the wall. At first, nothing, but then as I continue pushing at various spots, a section of the wall swings in, and I step through, letting the tapestry fall back in place.

It's not a moment too soon, either. I hear the door open to the room, and a couple men enter, chatting about the upcoming games taking place in the coming days. It's common practice for guards to check every room repeatedly for threats prior to and during a large formal banquet. I expect that's what these two men are doing.

I leave my door open, since the opening is covered by the tapestry, hoping not to give myself away by making any noise. Once I hear the door close behind them, I swing the door to the secret passageway closed.

I turn around and find it's not a passageway, but a huge room.

I carefully take a few steps. I see it's a large room from the lamps set around the area, but they're all dimmed to the point of nearly going out, offering little to no light for movement.

I reach the closest one and slowly raise the wick. The light casts around the area, and I shake my head in wonder. The area is filled with chairs and couches, along with a small armory—likely enough for a dozen people. All these secret rooms seem to have an armory.

On the far wall hangs a huge map of the castle, laying out the corridors and passageways, including a section for each floor. I turn up another lamp, this one closer to the map, to get a better look. I recognize most of the areas, but some of them include passageways I can't remember. I wonder if some are secret passages, or if I just don't recognize it all from this angle.

Picking up the nearest lamp, I wander around the room, trying to get a good idea of what this place is. A few cots stand up against the wall in one corner. I assume that means someone might sleep here at some point—or it's a backup in case it's needed. A large chest with traveling food sits near the cots. Traveling food keeps well, and the barrel of water next to it suggests whoever uses this room expects he or she might one day have to stay awhile. The water is fresh, as well, not stagnant.

I look back to the door I entered, and at first, I don't see anything. I move to that area and find the doorway. Spinning around, I don't see any other way in until I move around the room and check each wall, at which point I find a few other exits. Unlike the other secret passages, this area does not have spy holes.

I go to one of the doors—not the one I came in— and slowly open it, swinging it back into this room. As is typical, a tapestry hangs in the way, so I listen carefully for a moment before I peek around. It's a small meeting room, although I don't know which one. Many of them look the same.

The handle on the door turns, and I drop the tapestry back in place. The door made no noise when I swung it open. So I slowly close it, careful not to make a noise or move too fast out of fear that the tapestry will shift with the air movement.

I run my hands over the crack where the door sealed shut. The work, the craftsmanship of these doors, solid stone, swinging silently on hinges… it's impressive.

"It always impresses me, too."

I spin around, nearly dropping the lantern. Standing before me is Captain Tilbur.

He smiles and points at the couches. In a quiet voice, he asks, "If it pleases you, Your Majesty, would you like to have a seat?"

Aside from the two short times we had together after coming through the outer wall, my every experience with Tilbur has been mean and cruel. He viciously pursued me in the castle to torment me, insulting me at every turn.

"It is difficult to see you as a friend, Captain," I say.

He nods as we both sit, and I see the pain in his eyes. "I am sorry. I felt the best way to keep Parthun from harming you was to treat you with hatred. I found the more cruel I was to you, the kinder he was. He never really cared about the Lady Ellcia or young Hemot, but you… at first, he almost threw you from the top of the highest tower." He slowly shakes his head.

"Your father and I, Draydon, were close. Very close. As I mentioned, he was almost like a father to me, as my own father, King Trevolay, was always so busy and died when I was relatively young. I would have raised you myself these last eleven years if circumstances had been different."

I don't know what to think of all that, but I do see the kindness in his eyes at the moment.

"Is that how you were able to use my sword and keep it from cutting through that beam in Nimville. You knew how to use it?"

Despite his sadness, he smiles. "It is. Your father trained me with his sword. I learned things that few others know."

Now, that piques my interest. "Like what?"

At this, Tilbur laughs, just quietly, though. It's a sound I've never heard from him—or at least in the last ten or eleven years. "I trained with that sword for years, any chance I could. I couldn't tell you all that I learned if we had three full days just to chat."

"Then tell me this, how did you keep it from cutting through the beam?"

He leans forward and puts his hands together. "I don't have much time. I shouldn't actually be here, but someone needed to speak with you. I'll explain it quickly. In a way, you can communicate with your sword. The King's sword is similar, but different. With Astamatiti, you can command it not to cut through something, and it will obey. You can do the same in battle, but it takes a lot of concentration, so it's not something you'll likely do quickly without a great deal of practice."

"Can I tell it to do other things?"

He nods. "You can. That's where it gets tricky. It won't work well with just anyone. I'm close enough to the throne that the sword did not turn on me quickly, but even so, your father had to command it to allow me to use it as often as I did. If he hadn't, I'd likely be dead as the sword would turn on me."

"What does that mean?" I ask. I can't imagine how a sword can turn on someone.

"It's difficult to know, Draydon. Enchantments turn on people all the time. They're like that—untrustworthy, and protective of themselves and what they deem as their own. They have a certain… personality. They are rarely kind and compassionate. Yours is an exception. It is kind, at times, but it's also cruel."

"How might my sword turn on someone?"

He shakes his head and shrugs his shoulders. "It might just slip out of your hand, maybe not work at the moment you need it, maybe even bounce back and slice into you. Maybe even slowly, or quickly, turn you insane. It's really hard to say, Draydon." He closes his eyes for a moment, and when he opens them again, he stares intently at me. "But make no mistake, Draydon. Enchantments always have a downside to them. Your sword and your armor are two of the better ones I've ever heard of—and you're quite fortunate there—but most enchantments carry with them a nasty threat. Your friend Marleet, for instance… her sword gives skill and allows training speed to be cut significantly. However, it feeds arrogance. I've seen a man run into extreme danger, simply because he held that sword."

"Did that man make it? Did he survive?"

"He tried to take on a Reber Troll, Draydon."

I don't bother asking more about that. I'm not even sure if my sword can kill one of those things.

"So, what now?"

"Now, we get you out of the castle and keep you alive."

"Tilbur…" I've never just used his name when speaking to him before. It seems kind of disrespectful in a way, but then again, maybe it's time for me to act like I'm a future King. "I get it that security is tight, and Parthun will try to have me killed, but why don't I just come forward right now and announce myself as King?" I know I've asked that a lot, but I'm still hoping we can find a way. If I'm going to do this, I want to get it over with.

Tilbur smiles. He actually smiles and lets out a little laugh. He raises his hands at my shocked look. "I'm not laughing at you, Draydon. I'm not laughing at your suggestion. I'm not laughing because I think this is silly. I'm laughing because the situation is so absurd, it's so ridiculous, and it's so controlled. Pathun has arranged everything perfectly. I really had no idea he was as detailed as he is. He's covered every detail. If, Draydon, you were to walk out in the banquet hall mid-way through the banquet, with dozens of Nobles in the room, and officers and visiting dignitaries and announce who you are and make a claim to the throne, you would never wear the crown."

"Why not?"

"Because, Draydon, before you could finish making your claim, you'd have a crossbow bolt embedded in your neck."

My breath catches in my throat. When I recover, I ask, "But, then Parthun will be accused of murder."

"Will he, Draydon?" He stares at me and waits while I figure it out.

I don't like it when people do this to me, but I have to learn how to think it all through. As I run through the matter in my mind, I keep coming back to Parthun getting arrested for murder. Until… I realize… one problem. There would be nothing to suggest for even a second that he had anything to do with it. "We won't be able to prove he did it."

"That's half the problem, Draydon," Tilbur says with a laugh. This time I think he's laughing at me.

I don't feel like figuring this part out. "And the other half?"

"The other part, the bigger problem, actually, is that regardless of whether Parthun can be blamed… you… will be dead."

My face goes red. Yes, that does seem like a big problem. I can't believe I missed that obvious detail.

Tilbur shakes his head. "I'm sorry, Draydon. I know the security situation. I know what all has been set up. I know Parthun. I know where the assassins are stationed. And I know that even I can't come forward as a witness against Parthun because he will easily suggest that I'm in league with Lirnal. That's part of the reason why I am the one interrogating the General. Parthun knows if I get the information from Lirnal, great. If I turn on Parthun, it will be used against me. I'm afraid we have to wait until a more opportune time."

"Can I ask you a question and get an honest answer?" I ask.

Tilbur looks hurt. "I have lied to you many times over the years, Draydon. I'm not proud of lying, but I am proud of keeping you safe. You don't have to worry about me lying to you again, unless we are in a similar situation where my lies are there to protect you."

"I'm sorry. I didn't mean to hurt you with that question." My eyes drop to the floor for a second, but then I raise them and hold Tilbur's gaze. "Do you want me to be King?"

He breaks out in a large grin. "Ah, that's an easy question to answer! I absolutely do! I kept Roran safe because I wanted him to be King. That doesn't appear to be an option anymore. I also kept you safe because you are my nephew, because I love you, because of your father, and because you are of the royal line. And, because you are… well… you're a person. I didn't want some child killed. You deserve to live."

"And Ellcia and Hemot and Marleet? Why did you keep them safe? Or were they just unimportant?" Somehow, my irritation with Tilbur is growing.

"I kept Ellcia and Hemot safe—you likely don't know the lengths to which I went to keep them alive—because I knew their parents, because I cared about them as well, and, just like with you, I'm not in the habit of letting children and young people suffer and die. For the two of them, I did all I could to ensure that Parthun never really even thought about them. I distracted him from them and made him think they were unimportant. As for Marleet, Tereese kept her safe."

"And Tereese is in on this? She wants me to be King?" My voice is growing hard and getting louder.

"Stop, Draydon," Tilbur whispers.

I sit back. I notice my hands are clenched, and my blood feels like it's about to boil.

"Why are you so angry?" He leans forward. "I'm going to ask you a question, and I'm going to ask that you answer me quickly. Why do you find this all so hard to believe?"

"Because I can't believe that…" I stop, and my mouth drops open.

"What, Draydon. Finish the sentence. Quickly!"

"I can't believe you'd all do this."

"For you?"

I nod.

Tilbur's eyes drop to the floor, and he slowly rubs his hands together. When he speaks, his voice is calm and serious. "You've lived your life as an unimportant person that no one seemed to care for, other than your friends. The one person who did seem to show some interest in you, Parthun, was being false. Perhaps you find it hard to just trust that you might be important to others?"

I sit back. I feel like I want to cry. I can't believe this guy is having this kind of effect on me.

"Draydon, this room is a meeting place for those among us who are planning your return to the throne. We carefully select the right moves, the right times, the right places, and more. We all work together to see you—YOU—come to the throne."

"Who else is in this group?"

He shakes his head. "I can't reveal all their identities at this point. I know I can trust you, but the slightest slip could cost us everything. You know, obviously, that Tereese is part of it. Then, of course, Mert, the man who brought you here, is in on it. I expect you can figure out a few more on your own, but I will not reveal their names."

"I'm sorry." I shake my head. "I find it hard to think that you and others who have treated me so poorly are actually on my side."

A grimace fills his face. "There is no doubt about that. I knew, all these years, that my actions could cost me my head one day. I knew I was treating a possible future King of Sevord like trash—like vermin. I knew you might resent me forever for it. But, Draydon, I would do it all over again. That is my sacrifice for the Kingdom. I will be the one hated by all. I have been Parthun's right-hand man. Even more so than General Corter. I have done disgraceful things—many that the people have seen, but you have not. Your people may one day demand a reckoning. I know my place in this story, and it's not as the hero. I am the villain's right-hand man, the one all good people despise. But I will continue to play my part until you take the throne. That is not in question."

After an explanation like that, I just sit there.

He waits a moment or two, then stands up. "I have to go now. I will be expected to review security for the banquet. I came to speak with you, and to let you know that we will have to keep you here in this room for the time being. We don't know where Lady Marleet is right now. Until she makes contact, we do not know where to take you."

"Do you know how she was planning on getting out of the city?"

He nods. "The harbor. But we can't just take you there. She's likely still in the castle trying to figure out where you've gone." He turns to the section of the wall through which he entered, then turns back to me. In a whisper, he says, "I will see you take the throne, Your Majesty. That I promise you on your father's honor. I will not fail to keep his line alive."

He turns back to the wall, swings open the door, listens quietly, then nods to me before sliding out of sight. Once he's gone, I swing the door shut and settle in.

I like the cheese.

I take another bite of it. I tried some of the bread, but it's really dry. Like… really dry. But the cheese, it's good. Hard and quite strong, but good.

I think, more than anything, I'm bored. I took a long nap. I walked around the room. I found a book and read for a bit. I ate. I napped again. I ate.

The banquet has long since ended. I have no idea if I've been in here for a short time, like five or six hours, or a long time, like a day and a half. I just know that at one point, I heard the noise from the banquet, which was quite hard to hear from this room, quiet down. I also know I've slept twice. Maybe for a little bit. Maybe for many hours. Not sure.

I wish I had my sword. I'd practice commanding it not to cut things. But then again, I'd likely just slice up the room. That wouldn't be good.

No one else has come for me. I feel like I should do something or go somewhere. Maybe I should try to make a break for it. Try to make it to the harbor on my own.

But then again, Ellcia and the others might still be searching the castle.

However, if they think I've been caught and killed, they might see no other choice than to try to escape. And I want them safe.

One of the matters weighing on my mind is the timeline. It was explained to me that we had to be out of the castle within the hour once we found Marleet. But, one thing's for sure, that plan has long since died.

I stand up in frustration and make for the door Tilbur used. I'm going to go out and explore, at least a little. I swing the door open. I don't hear anyone on the other side of the tapestry, so I push it out of the way and peer into the room. It's in total blackness.

In one sense, that's encouraging. It means it's likely the middle of the night, and I might manage to get through the corridors without detection. Then again, to move forward in this situation based on "might" seems quite the risk.

I step back into the room and close the door. I have to wait. I can't risk it. Not for me, but for the kingdom. Boredom is the part I play right now.

When I turn around, I suddenly wonder how it's possible a room like this could go unnoticed. Certainly someone would notice there's a space between the rooms. Someone would have to notice the rooms aren't butting one up against another, right?

But then again, I never noticed how thick the walls were. I never noticed how there was room for secret passageways. Nor did I notice all the holes in the walls allowing light into the passageways and allowing people to spy on those in the castle.

My heart jumps inside my chest as I hear what sounds at first like a ghost. I stay perfectly still, hoping a ghost won't notice me if I don't move. That doesn't make sense, but who said a ghost made sense either?

I hear it again. My heart races, and I want to run out of here.

"Hey!"

That ghost's whisper sounds like it's trying to get my attention.

"Hey! Draydon! Are you in there?"

I frown. "Hemot?"

"He's there!" Hemot laughs quietly and hisses, "We've been looking everywhere for you."

"Where are you?" I get the impression that, in a way, they still haven't found me.

"We're just above you… we think. There's a small hole here. We see a bit of light. Marleet thought this was the room. We're going to try to get you out of there."

"Okay." I feel like I should say more, but I'm… not very wordy right now.

Hemot grunts, then I hear him arguing a bit, then he hisses, "You're going to have to leave this room and run to the place where you're supposed to meet us."

"Okay." Again, that's all I can come up with to say.

I wait for more, but I just hear more grunting and arguing. Finally, I hear Marleet's voice. "Stop it, Hemot! He doesn't know the way to go!"

That's good news. For a moment there, I feared they wouldn't be giving me any more details.

"Hey, Draydon. It's Marleet. I'm up here with Hemot and Ellcia and Roran. We're here to get you… Hemot… stop! I know you told him some of this, but it's proper to give him more information. No! Just let me… Stop!" There's a pause, then, "Thank you, Ellcia." She clears her throat and says, "Sorry, Draydon. Hemot feels that he's in charge when you're not around. I told him we don't need anyone else in charge when you're not here, but he thinks that's my way of taking charge. And now Roran is insisting that he be in charge. And… oh… come on! Ellcia! Not you too…"

I don't bother saying anything. I really just want to get out of here and out of the castle. I don't care who's in charge.

"Okay. So, here's what you have to do. I need you to exit using the door closest to the armory. If you're looking at the armory from the center of the room, it's just to the left. You'll come out in a room that's not much more than a storage room. It should be completely empty at this time of night. Find the door out of the storage room, and head left down the hallway, past the servant's quarters on this level, and up the servant's stairs. When you get to the top, go into the first room on your right. We'll meet you there."

I catch myself from saying "Okay" back to her. I run through the directions. It's a little confusing. I know my way around the castle just fine, but I'm having trouble imagining where I am at the moment—especially when that door takes me out near a servant's quarters. I think I'm all turned around.

"What if I get caught?"

There's silence for a moment. If even Hemot isn't jumping in with some silly remark, we must be in a dangerous spot.

"I don't know, Draydon. I think if you get caught, we won't be able to get to you in time. I…" There's a pause, and I don't like it. "Draydon, I don't want to say this, but I think I have to. You can't get caught. There's no way you can let that happen. If someone looks like they're after you, you have to attack first."

"But I… only have my knife. I don't want to kill anyone. There are some clubs here in the armory. Should I take one?"

There's not much of a pause this time. Marleet's voice comes out sad. "No, Draydon. Use your knife."

The message is clear. I have to survive. For the kingdom, I have to survive.

"Just one more thing, Draydon."

"Yeah?"

"You'll need to wait about ten minutes. We have to get there. We'll be ready for you, but the best thing to do is get there when we're already there, so you can just slip in and join us."

"Okay. I'll wait ten minutes."

"See you in a bit, Draydon."

That's Ellcia's voice. It's good to hear she's okay.

I find some paper and decide to leave a note. At first, I just about write all the details, but then I remember that we're trying to keep things secret. I glance around the room. Even though secrecy is important, a note is going to be necessary. If Tilbur or Tereese come in and find me gone, they might think I've been captured.

I scribble:

I'M OKAY. HAD TO GO. SOMEONE CAME FOR ME.
C.

I hope signing it "C" is clear enough, but not too clear. I guess I should sign it "D" and that might help, but then again, maybe not.

I grab a few mouthfuls to eat, then drink a fair amount—but not so much that I'll be sick when I run.

I wait. And wait.

Okay, I think that's about ten minutes.

I stand in the middle of the room and head toward the wall, just to the left of the small armory. When I get there, I can't find a door anywhere. I start searching back and forth until I find one, but then when I look back, I note that where this door is can't possibly be considered "left of the armory".

I move back and search the wall again. It's great, in one sense, that these secret doors are so secret. But then again… how can you find a door that was built so it couldn't be found?

I lean against the wall and close my eyes. Think, Draydon! It comes out in a storage room. That means it won't have a tapestry on that side of the wall. So, how will they hide it?

It hits me. You hide a door like that by making it small.

I drop to the floor and find four blocks that appear to be separate from the others. I push, but that doesn't work. At the bottom are some small holes. They look like they're perfect for rodents, and I don't want to stick my fingers in there, but I need to figure this out. I think it's past ten minutes now.

My fingers go in, and I find something to grip. I give a pull, and the four blocks slide inward. I mumble to myself, "Might have been a good idea to tell me this door was different, Marleet."

After it comes out, it swings around and to the side. I climb through, finding I have to push a few things—can't tell what they are—out of the way, but then I reach back, grab the door, swing it around, and start to pull it closed.

I remember I didn't dim the lights in that room, but maybe that's okay. I tend to forget at least one detail every time I'm doing something important. Hopefully it won't burn the castle down.

But for me, it's now really, really dark. Aside from a sliver of light coming through from the door leading out into the hallway, I can't see a thing. I decide to stay on my hands and knees, but before I go too far, I do my best to push the things I moved out of the way back into place. I think they're wood crates—just small ones.

Once I reach the door, still on my hands and knees, I put my ear up to it for a moment. I don't hear anything at first, so I reach for the door handle, but then stop. Footsteps. Once they've passed, I reach for the door handle again. When I get the door open, I climb to my feet and peer out.

Nothing and no one. I recognize the area of the castle now. I'm not far from the throne room, but hopefully far enough that security isn't super tight.

I head left. Now that I remember this area, I know where I'm going. Unfortunately, the servant's quarters aren't just a few steps away.

I move down the hallway, doing my best to act like I'm supposed to be wandering these corridors. When I was a servant, I was only out this late once. Hemot had decided we should go steal some cupcakes from the kitchen. We would have gotten away with it too, if Hemot hadn't bragged about it the next day. To Tereese. The very woman we stole the cupcakes from. He bragged about it to Tereese! To this day, he still seems shocked that she would punish us for it.

I reach the servant's quarters. Hemot and I lived in this section at one point—I think when we were about eight or nine. I think Marleet did as well, but Ellcia was down one floor. I remember...

"Halt!"

I nearly jump, but I manage to control myself. Then I realize I likely shouldn't have stopped. My only hope now is they won't question me too much. And that they don't recognize me.

I quickly go through how to get my knife if I need it. The only way I can think of to do it is to pull my shirt right up to my chin. That'll look a little on the weird side at first, but it's what I'll have to do.

But... maybe the night guard won't recognize me.

"Turn around!"

My hair hangs down a bit over my eyes, and I try to do something a little weird with my mouth. Maybe that'll change things enough.

I slowly turn around. Two soldiers. I keep my head low. I don't recognize the one...

The other...

He was one of the men who kidnapped Roran and then accused me of it. I gasp.

"It's him! It's Draydon!"

He charges forward, and Nordin and Relin's training kicks in.

I slip to the side, just enough, but stick my foot out. The man goes down, but the second soldier has just about reached me. His arms come out. I spin around, drop, and slam my elbow into his knee.

He cries out and hits the floor, but I nearly scream as well. Pain shoots from my shoulder right down to my hand from the impact!

I step back as the first man—the traitor from the caves—jumps to his feet and spins around, his face full of rage.

At first, I don't understand why they haven't called out for more guards, but then again, what if the guards who come are loyal to the throne?

They need silence. Maybe I should yell… but then again… I don't know who will come either. Two traitors might be easier to deal with than a four or five.

I pull up my shirt to get my knife, earning me a confused look from the man. The second guy is still on the ground, holding his knee. My arm still aches, so I guess I really hurt him.

The guy on his feet charges toward me, and I knock aside his hands and bring my fist into contact with his jaw. He stumbles back, and I kick him in the side of the head as hard as I can.

I drop to the ground, doing my best not to scream. My foot… how is that guy's head so hard?

The guy I got in the knee is doing his best to stand, but the other guy—the one I kicked in the head—he's out cold. Don't know for how long.

I jump up and approach the one still moving, but he draws his sword and swings it at me. Jumping back, I narrowly avoid the tip of his blade. I don't know how to get past him. The room I need is on the other side.

But then again… even if I do get past him… I can't leave him. He knows I'm alive. That might make Tilbur a target. And it'll change everything!

"You're going to die today, Draydon!" the man growls. "And the King will make me a Lord for it." His smile grows, and he starts forward.

I back up, wondering if I should run, but the man lurches toward me… then drops to the ground. A crossbow bolt sticks out of his back.

Down the hall, Roran kneels, putting another bolt into his crossbow. Beside him is a bald Ellcia—still not used to that. She hisses, "Come on, Draydon!"

I run past the man Roran just killed and the other soldier. He's still alive, though. That's a big problem.

As I reach the others, Roran asks, "Are they both dead?"

I shake my head. "The other guy's knocked out." I glance at the others. "I don't know what to do. We can't leave him alive. But we can't just kill him."

Roran raises his crossbow.

"No!" I hiss. "You can't just kill an unconscious man."

Rage fills his eyes, but he holds back. "What do we do, then?" His voice is filled with spite.

I didn't really expect a response like that. I look back at the man. He's not moving. There's a chance I hit him so hard he won't remember what happened, but it's too great a risk to take.

"Okay," I say, turning back to my friends. "Here's what we'll do. We need to let Tilbur know. He can deal with this. Maybe he can take care of it before everyone wakes up and these guys are found." I turn to the two men. "Let's get them out of the hallway."

We pull the men through a doorway. It's a meeting room, but I know this area. This room is almost never used.

I confirm the name on the door. It's the Officer's Board Room. Strange. I don't think I've ever seen an officer in there.

But no matter. It's perfect for what we need.

With the door to the room closed, and trying not to look at the dead man, I stare at the others, thinking through the obvious problem. I decide I'm not going to pretend I have everything figured out. "Okay, first, I don't know where Tilbur actually lives. I avoided him, for the most part, while in the castle. Second, I assume he has a guard. They'll be hard to get past."

The others all look a little unsure, and they shake their head. They don't know where he lives either. All except… Hemot.

"I know where he lives. And he doesn't have a guard."

I'm about to ask him how, but then drop it. Hemot probably played some prank on him at one point. "Can we get to it?"

"It's on the other side of the throne room from here."

I turn to Marleet. "There's no way that I know of to get there without traveling through the most heavily guarded area of the castle. Or we could take the long way around, which means we'll be set back for far too long."

She nods. "I can get us there."

We turn to leave, but I stop. "Let's tie him up."

We pull off his belt, tie his hands, and gag him with a strip we cut from his shirt. Hemot then points out that he can still walk, and we use the other man's belt to tie his feet securely, even running a piece of material cut from his shirt from the belt on his hands down to his feet, hoping he won't even be able to hop out of here.

No matter what we do, no matter how hard we try, we just can't seem to get out of this castle.

# 12

The Things We Do for Friends

Once out of the boardroom, we make it up the stairs and into the first room on the right. It's dark in here, but we leave the door open while Marleet and Hemot get the secret wall pushed in. Ellcia then closes the door, and we make our way to the secret passage in the dark. Once we're all inside, we seal ourselves inside.

"Draydon, here's your armor and weapons and stuff," I hear Hemot say.

I feel a pack drop at my feet and struggle to put it on in the dark, cramped area. After a few minutes, I think I'm all suited up again, and Marleet leads us forward.

We move in a train, holding one another's hands. I think I have Hemot behind me and Marleet ahead.

We walk for a long way, and it's dark—really dark. Now and then we get a bit of light coming through holes, but not really even enough to see where we're going. I'm glad Marleet has this figured out.

Occasionally, I hear someone on the other side of the wall. It's a stone barrier, so no sound comes through the wall itself, but the holes… the sound comes through there. Occasionally, someone we pass is talking to someone else, and whenever this happens, Marleet looks through the holes. I guess to confirm who it is.

At one point, Marleet stops us, checks through the holes, then swings open a door. We step out into a corridor, then run down a short distance, then enter another secret door and continue on through the dark.

"How far until Tilbur's apartments?"

Marleet stops and turns back to me. "We're on the other side of the throne room now. I was just about to ask… wait."

I hear voices again, and both Marleet and I peer through the holes. I can't believe our luck! It's Tilbur and Tereese. They're arguing loudly about how Tereese really blew the meal on some banquet or something.

I can't get over how Tilbur can move from angry and mean to kind and civil, then back to angry and mean. But then I catch something else. Between their arguing, Tilbur and Tereese are talking about something. They loudly go back and forth, but then carefully slip in quiet words now and then. I hear my name mentioned, but I can't make out the rest.

I push my lips up to the hole and hiss, "Wait!"

They both pause for a second, then continue. I gather they think they're imagining the noise.

"It's me! It's Draydon. I'm with Marleet and the others. We're in the wall."

They continue to argue, but Tilbur gives the slightest nod. I take that as a good sign.

"They got me out of that room. I'm trying to get out of the castle, but we were seen by two soldiers." I move my eye down to the hole again to gauge their reaction. I don't really know if they're even hearing me. "The one is dead.

The other is tied up. We fought them in the hallway, but we moved the bodies into the Officer's Board Room."

I look through the hole again, and I see the slightest nod. Then Tilbur growls at Tereese. "You listen here, and you listen good! I'm going to take care of this now. I'm going to clean up your mess. I'm going to fix it. You just get out of my hair!"

Tereese leans forward and pokes him in the chest. "Funny thing for a man with no hair to say!" And then she storms off down the corridor.

As Tilbur turns to leave, he whispers, "Get out of the castle. Get out now." He then walks down the hall and out of sight.

"I guess that message was for us," I whisper.

Marleet, just visible in the dim light of the tunnel, nods at me.

We continue down the hallway with Marleet in the lead and me right behind her. Ellcia and the others follow behind me, I think, but in the darkness, I can only make out Hemot back there.

Marleet comes to a halt as we hear running. I peer through a hole and see dozens of soldiers run by. They're shouting, but I can't make out what they're saying.

A moment later, another few speed past us.

Marleet turns back to me and whispers, "We were supposed to make it out of the castle before they found the Prince was missing. This will make it much more difficult."

"What will they do?" Getting caught is low down on my list of hopes for the night.

"They'll search every corner of the castle and lock down the entire palace," Marleet explains.

"Can we still get out?" I ask.

She nods. "Yes, but it'll be risky. We'll need to be careful."

"Where to?" I have a moment when I realize how much I'm relying on Marleet and how strange it is that she seems to have it all figured out. That's unlike my entire experience with her for my entire life. She's been acting this way ever since we got to the castle, but… it's still weird.

"We continue with the plan," she says confidently.

I nod. "Let's do it."

We move along a bit farther, ignoring the soldiers rushing back and forth throughout. I notice the stone walls in this area are… nicer. They're like the ones near the throne room. I guess that makes sense. That's exactly where we are.

I bump into Marleet, and she hisses at me to be quiet. We both peer through holes, and I'm shocked to see Marleet's mom and dad. They're being pushed along by soldiers, and since they're moving quickly, I can only catch her mom say something about how they will regret this, and her dad says something like, "… missinnnng a slipperrrr."

When they're gone, Marleet turns back to me. I see her quite clearly now. It must be morning, as I think the lanterns in the hallways have been turned up, and there's more light coming through the windows.

She grabs my arm and shakes her head. She's… oh… I know what's up. She feels she needs to get Roran and me out of the castle, but at the same time… her parents. It sounds like they've been arrested. I don't know what all this new Marleet is capable of, but I do still know who she is. She will stick to the plan because she feels it's the right thing to do, but this is going to tear her apart. And tearing her apart is exactly what's it's doing. Her bottom lip quivers, and even in the dark, I see tears just pouring down her face.

"Is there a way we can spy on the throne room without leaving the secret passageways?"

She nods. "But my job is to get you and Roran out of here. I can't risk the plan."

I smile. Maybe being the future King has its privileges. "Then I'm giving you a new order. First, we go check on your parents. Then, we leave."

She hesitates for only a moment before her face breaks out in a grin. Not just a little grin. A huge one. It's always warmed my heart to see her smile. She means the world to me. Not like Ellcia. I mean… I feel very differently about Ellcia and not at all toward Marleet as I do about Ellcia, but I care a lot about Marleet. She needs this, so we'll do what we can.

She grabs my hand, and I grab Hemot's. A moment later, we're rushing down the secret corridors. The light grows with every step, so it's not long before none of us hold hands. I can now make out Ellcia and Roran following behind. I keep checking on her. I don't want to lose her or Roran in the tunnels.

We come to one of those small passageways. This one's about chest height, and we climb inside. We crawl for a bit until we come out on a larger tunnel level with this one, but still not big enough for us to stand. The throne room itself is actually up a few steps, so maybe this brings us to that level.

Marleet pulls us all close and quietly whispers, "We're right at the throne room, and the King's quarters are all around us. Don't make a sound unless you have to." She heads off to the right, then stands up. I follow close behind and stand up next to her, see a ladder, and before she can start up, I climb.

I'm half-way up the ladder before I realized I just jumped in front of her, but I doubt she minds. She's pretty relaxed about this kind of thing. When I get to the top, I see a landing to my left, and I scramble onto it. A moment later, Hemot pulls up next to me, then Roran, then Ellcia, then Marleet.

We squish into the area. It's a little tight for five people, but none of us are big like Rulf. If he was here, I don't think we'd have any chance.

I peer through one of the many holes, and I'm shocked to find we're looking at the throne room from above and behind the actual throne.

I think when I become King, I'll never be able to trust that any conversation is private.

Below us, I see Parthun's head stick up above the throne. He shifts back and forth, and a hand is visible, gripping the one armrest. He doesn't look like he's holding it lightly.

On the left side of the room stand the Nobles—a lot of them. I'd say somewhere around seventy. On the right stand a few dozen soldiers. Tilbur's not there yet, though. Because of his size, his bald head, and his Captain's armor, he's easy to pick out of a crowd.

In the center of the room, before the throne, are six people—four standing and two bound and on their knees. The two standing in front are Marleet's parents. Her mom wears what appears to be a housecoat, and her dad wears… well… it's… um… it's like pajamas, but then he also has a hat that looks like maybe he sleeps in it, but it hangs down to the one side. On his pjs and hat is a pattern of… it's hard to see, but I think it's happy Reber Trolls.

That's a little on the weird side.

Her parents' faces are filled with sorrow and terror.

Behind them stand two soldiers—the two who traveled with us from the gate to the castle in the middle of the night. I think the one man's name was Denner. The two soldiers have their hands on the hilts of their swords, but it doesn't look like it's to harm Marleet's parents. I kind of get the impression that those two men would die for the Lord Yune and the Lady Aldora.

On the floor, kneeling and bound, not too far from Lord Yune's position, are two soldiers. I can't quite tell because they're bound and gagged, but I think they were the two men guarding the Prince.

No one has said a word since I first peered through the hole, but the tension is thick. I feel like at any moment, the room could erupt into a fight.

Before anyone moves much, the door swings open and Tilbur walks in. His face is twisted with rage—nothing new.

"The castle has been searched, my King. No sign of either."

Parthun stands and takes a step forward. Despite how early it is and though Lord Yune and Lady Aldora are in their sleeping clothes, the King is fully dressed.

"So, we have two problems," the King growls.

"Parthunnnn," Lord Yune says, stepping forward.

I'm a little surprised that he's addressing the King by his first name, but he is a strange one.

"Yes, Lord Yune!" the King barks back.

"Whyyyy are we herrrre? It is earlyyyy, and I have not yet had my morning foot bathhhh."

The King shakes his head and mumbles, "Morning foot bath?" but then stops. "Lord Yune. You are here because you, the Lady Aldora, and your daughter, the Lady Marleet, are suspected to have been involved in the disappearance of Prince Roran. I was going to announce that the wedding will be tomorrow, but… now we will have to postpone it until they are found."

"And whaaaat does my dear Marleeeeteeee have to do with Prince Rorannnn? They are to beeee wed, but they have spent littlllle to no time togetherrrr since we arrived in the castlllle."

"This has to do with her because she's missing too!"

The Lady Aldora lets out a little cry, and the Lord Yune leans forward for a moment, his face filling with confusion, then fear. He slowly… although… he makes it look like he's rushing, but he's barely moving at all… How does he do that? Anyway, he slow-quick turns around. When he finally faces his two soldiers, he orders, "Quiiiick, go to our quarterrrrs and see if the Lady Marleeeeteeee is still in beeeed."

I hear a quiet giggle beside me and glance at Marleet. I'm guessing despite what's going on out there, at least some of this is going according to plan.

Denner and the other man turn and run out of the room. One even yells out dramatically, "We're coming, my Lady!"

Once they've exited, Lord Yune turns and faces the King again, his hands shaking, and his face filled with grief. "If they are missingggg, do weeee suspect foul plaaaay?"

The King shakes his head. "No! There's no evidence of it as yet. There appears to have been a coordinated plan to get them out of the castle! I can only assume they have left. We are guarding every exit and searching in every direction, but I want to know what part you had in this!"

Lady Aldora comes up next to Lord Yune and weeps. She grabs his arm and just hangs on him while she lets out a loud wail and says, "My dear Marleet! I caaaaaaaaaaan't lose her again!"

Now, that's the fakest cry I've ever heard. Either she's a terrible actress, or this is all intentional.

The King seems to think so too and steps forward. He points and shouts, "That's a fake cry!"

As soon as he says it, he realizes his mistake. The Nobles are all clearly shocked, and Lady Aldora's grief-stricken display grows more dramatic… and even less genuine looking than before. The King can't take it back, though. He looks like a real idiot for accusing a Noble of fake-crying. He sounded like a little kid. He starts mumbling, "Well… it sounds fake… doesn't it? It does… right?"

"Our daughterrrr is missingggg, Parthunnnn. This is not a timmmme for accusing my wiffffe of disingenuoussss tearrrrs."

"I…" the King begins. I see him glance toward the Nobles. They don't seem shocked anymore. They're angry. Very angry. "I'm sorry, Lord Yune. That came out… wrong."

Lord Yune turns to his wife and says, "Do not worryyyy, my dearrrr. Our daughterrrr will be founnnnd. Would youuuu like to leeeeave so you don't have to heeeear the King's cruel worrrrds?"

She shakes her head and lets out a loud sob. "No, my dear. I would like to stay. If… if you will protect me from such cruelty?" She lets out a small choke, followed by an extremely dramatic sob.

I glance at Marleet. She's barely controlling her laughter. She's shaking so badly, I'm afraid she's about to tumble down the ladder, and I reach out and hold her arm just in case. Her parents are either really weird, or they are masters at this. Ellcia seems to worry about Marleet's safety as well, and she pulls Marleet a little farther from the edge.

I turn back to the scene below us.

The Nobles shift on their feet, and I hear grumbling, even from this distance. The soldiers look uncomfortable. Tilbur looks annoyed. Lord Yune and Lady Aldora hold each other tightly, and the King has his head in his hands.

I realize that the main accusation—that the Lord Yune, the Lady Aldora, and the Lady Marleet are involved in Roran's disappearance—it's… well… it's clearly not even an option now. We're now onto another matter altogether. At this point, we're only talking about how cruel the King is toward a woman who may have just lost her only daughter, and how much of a victim Lady Aldora is from the King's cruelty.

Oh… they're good.

At that moment, Denner and the other man run into the room. Tilbur draws his sword when they come in, but both men drop to their knees, and Denner cries out in a voice filled with agony, "My Lord! My Lady! We have failed you. She is gone. Our dear Lady Marleet. She's… she's gone. We have failed you. We offer our lives in exchange!"

They both drop face down onto the floor, and I hear their sobs.

Lord Yune merely reaches out and calls to them. They crawl forward, and the next thing I know, the Lord Yune, the Lady Aldora, Denner, and the other soldier, Billot, I think, are all on the floor with their arms wrapped around one another, weeping.

I check Marleet. She's doing her best to keep quiet, but the occasional snort sneaks out. Hopefully, the sound won't reach those below.

The Nobles now look ready to charge the throne. I see some with hands clenched, and others wringing their hands—but not in worry. They're mad! One middle-aged Noble steps forward. I'm shocked. It's Lord Hillbin!

A soldier calls out, "The Portly Lord wishes an audience with the King!"

I smile. The Portly Lord…

"Your Majesty. I'm shocked and horrified not only by what I've seen here in the last few minutes, but also that we are all standing around talking about a missing Prince and Noblewoman, rather than finding them. They have either been kidnapped, or perhaps they have, if your assessment of their intense love for one another is true, eloped."

Marleet calms down a little. She's breathing heavy, but she's not laughing as hard as before.

The King growls and shakes his head, but then seems to remember something. He points at the two soldiers and shouts, "These two men have not protected the Prince. Under their guard, he has, as the Portly Lord declared, either been kidnapped or eloped."

Tilbur steps forward and grabs one of the men, dragging him to his feet. One of Tilbur's right-hand men joins him and grabs the other man. "I'll deal with them, Your Majesty. Perhaps a little drop might help?"

I shiver inside. Tilbur's Drop. It's a pit, somewhere down in the dungeon. It's deep, really deep. They simply throw you in. I've heard that most people die from the fall, but those unfortunate enough to survive break bones and then just lay there for days, groaning and crying out for someone to show mercy to them by killing them.

The story has grown over the years to include a dragon at the bottom, or a large nest of human-eating spiders, or shards of glass, but in the end, I just figured it was simply a hole.

I glance at Marleet and so does everyone else. Tilbur's Drop is feared by all people in the city. Marleet merely shakes her head and gives a look as if to say, "Don't worry about it."

Well, I am worried, but then again… if it's a drop… a deep pit. No one will check to see if anyone's actually been thrown in. Maybe… it's just a good way to sneak people out of the castle. They're dropped in there and then can get out. Or maybe… the pit doesn't even exist. Maybe Tilbur just uses that to rescue people.

Ah! There's just so much I don't know about everything!

The King gives his permission for Tilbur to "Drop" them, although Tilbur didn't really wait. They were half-way to the door before the King ordered their deaths—or their drops.

I'm seeing more and more that Parthun does not rule this kingdom. He only thinks he does.

"Then what of my dearest child?" Lady Aldora screams out.

Parthun glances at the Lords, who all give him a disapproving look before he turns back and, in a compassionate tone, says, "We will find her and return her to you."

"Safely?" the Lady Aldora cries. "Will you, on your honor, promise to return her to me safely?"

The King's shoulders slump, and he nods. "Yes. On my honor."

Lord Yune slowly—very slowly—climbs to his feet and then pulls the weepy Lady Aldora up. She looks like she can barely stand. The soldiers join them on their feet and embrace both Lord Yune and Lady Aldora before they all walk out of the throne room, arms around each other, without Parthun's permission.

I glance back at the Nobles. They too, after pausing for just a moment, turn and walk out.

I didn't think people could do that.

Marleet turns from the hole she'd been looking through and sits down with her back to the wall. It's a lot brighter in this area than in a lot of the tunnels due to the holes into the throne room and the window above us. It's just a small one, but it offers some decent light.

She's smiling. "Okay, I was worried there for a bit. None of us expected that my parents would be arrested or dragged to the throne room in their sleeping clothes. That…" She pauses for a moment, and her eyes drop to the floor. "That scared me."

Ellcia puts her hand on Marleet's shoulder. "It looks like they're okay."

Marleet smiles again. "They are. They figured that if we disappeared, the King would try to make it seem that someone was conspiring against him. That would give him the power he needed to crack down on the people and control them more. So, we wanted to push the idea that we either were kidnapped or eloped. No one believes the kidnap option. Kidnapping someone from the castle is a little on the difficult side—that is, if you don't know about these tunnels and, to the best of our knowledge, Parthun doesn't." Her smile grows. "We knew if we floated the idea that we might have eloped, that would be the one that was believed. My parents and the Nobles pulled it off."

That's something I was wondering about. The Nobles… "How many of the Nobles are working against Parthun?"

"About half," Marleet explains. "The others are either on his side, or they don't care who's on the throne."

That makes sense to me. It always feels so good when I learn of new people who are on our side.

I glance around at the group, and my eyes land on Roran. Shame washes over me, and at first, it surprises me. It was hard enough for me to personally think of claiming the throne, but as I look at him, I remember that the only reason I'm doing this is because he's lost his chance.

I didn't want to take that from him. I really do think he should lead.

"Hey Roran," I say. "I haven't really had a chance to say hi. It's good to see you as you."

He nods and gives a smile. I'm so used to him as Mic, a guy I couldn't really even have a conversation with.

I open my mouth, but then close it again as I realize I want to apologize to him for planning on taking the throne. But that seems weird. And I feel awkward.

"Is something going on here that I don't get?" Hemot asks. "You two are acting all weird. Is it because Roran is next in line for the throne but can't rule now because of the enchantment, and Draydon is now going to take the throne even though he doesn't want it?"

Roran just scowls at Hemot, but Hemot doesn't notice.

I grimace and say, "Thanks, Hemot." I turn back to Roran and give an uncomfortable smile. "I'm… sorry about all that, Roran. I never wanted the throne. I…"

He puts his hand up and frowns at me. "Enough. What were you going to say?"

"Uh, that's it. Just, hi."

He nods and says "hi" back, but I can see he's seething inside.

He turns back to Marleet, and his face softens. I notice, even in the dim light, that Hemot stiffens a bit at that. Now I feel like we're just dealing with drama.

"So," Ellcia says. She's trying to help us focus. I appreciate that. "Since they all likely believe the two of you eloped, does that mean we'll have an easier time getting out of the castle?"

Marleet shakes her head. "No, not at all. The plan was for us to get out before anyone discovered the Prince was gone. Now, things will probably be locked right down."

I smile and decide I'm going to add some hope. "Then we'll just have to work harder and slip past them all!"

It doesn't seem to do anything to relieve the stress for anyone except Hemot. But I think he's just excited about the danger.

"Where to next, Marleet?" I ask.

"We need to get to the west side of the castle. There's a tunnel on that side which will lead us past the walls of the keep and to the port."

"Can we stay in the tunnels the whole time? I mean… will we have to step out into the hallway at all?" I don't really want to run through the halls of the castle while everyone is on alert.

She nods. "As best as we can figure, the tunnels were built with a few purposes in mind. One was obviously to spy on people. That one seems kind of nasty to me. Another was to provide a way for people to move about the castle in secrecy for the sake of escape or retaking of the castle. But the other thing seems to be that the tunnels were designed to make it hard to move through the entire castle without exposing your presence at one point or another. It's like they wanted to make it so people easily could sneak through the castle, but not too easily. So, the tunnels are broken up, and you have to move in and out of them. Between here and the port, I think there are about three spots where we need to run through a small section. It'll be risky."

"And how soon do we have to get there?" I ask.

All of them look at me a little funny. "What do you mean?" Ellcia asks. "We need to get out of the castle. The sooner the better."

I shake my head. One of the things Nordin taught me was if there's something that everyone assumes… ask about it. "No, I mean, we need to know how soon. Someone's obviously waiting at the port for us, right? I assume they won't wait forever. If they receive word that we're captured, I expect they'll leave, but they'll wait a bit. Or are we too late?"

Marleet nods. "Oh, I see. No, we're not in a huge rush. They'll leave when we get there. But there will come a point when Parthun will order all boats searched."

I think that one through. If we aren't in a rush, we should probably take it slow. Right now, security will be extra tight. If we rush too much, we risk slipping up and alerting the soldiers to our presence. We'll also find that security should lessen in time, after they figure we're long gone. So, we can't take too long to get out of the castle, but we can't rush either.

"Okay, everyone, listen up. Here's what we're going to do." When I say that, Ellcia, Hemot, and Marleet all lean forward and wait. I'm seeing more and more that I was always thought to be the leader of our little group, even though I could never bring myself to actually… you know… lead.

Roran, however, leans back, crosses his arms, and scowls at me. I actually lose what I'm going to say for a moment, but I push that aside. I'll deal with Roran next.

"We're going to move to the port, but we're going to take our time. We won't want to risk being seen for any reason, so if it takes us a full day to get out of the castle, that's fine. Marleet's going to lead us through, but…" turning to her I say, "we can't take any risks. Getting all five of us out safely is our number one priority."

She nods, and so do Ellcia and Hemot.

But before they can go for the ladder, I add, "Why don't the three of you go down ahead? I'd like to talk to Roran privately."

Ellcia and Marleet both look a little nervous. Hemot looks confused and… hmm… I think he's feeling left out, or jealous. Like I'm choosing a new best friend. "It's okay. I just want to chat through a few things."

The three head down, and I wait until it sounds like they've reached the bottom of the ladder. Turning back to Roran, I see his arms still crossed, and he looks mad.

"Hey Roran."

He frowns at me. I guess that wasn't the best way to start this conversation.

"We need to talk."

His eyes fill with hatred, and he grinds his teeth for a moment before he answers. "What about?"

"About this. About us. We've never really chatted before. In the city, we never talked. I always thought… well… I didn't know how to talk to you. And Rulf kind of scared me. Then we spent nearly three weeks together, but you were still pretending not to be capable of full conversations. Now you seem pretty upset at me."

"I wonder why," he says with a frown.

I find this annoying. I don't want to just sit here and spar back and forth. I want to punch the guy, but I know that's not the right thing to do. "What do you want, Roran? I didn't know someone was going to enchant you. I didn't know it would cost you the throne. I didn't know I would be expected to take your place. I never wanted to be King. Believe it or not… that's not what I want. So, Roran, what do you want from me?"

"What I want, Draydon, is my throne. I want it back."

"And what can I do about that?"

He opens his mouth to answer, but stops. I see his face fall, and then his shoulders slump. After a moment, he shakes his head. "I don't know. I…" He looks back up at me. "I know it's not your fault, Draydon. I know you didn't plan this. I'm just angry. I spent my entire life believing that I was meant to sit on that throne. Now it's gone because someone else took it from me."

I react to that last part, but he puts up his hands. "No, I don't mean you. I meant the Regent. He took my parents from me. Then he held the throne all these years. Now he's taken the throne completely out of my reach, and… and now he's trying to kill me. And I can't even have Marleet."

I'm not sure what to say to any of that. Especially the part about Marleet. I hadn't realized he was actually interested in her. I thought it was all the enchantment. But… now that I think about it. He did seem to enjoy spending time with her on the trip to the mountains. I just figured it was because she's sweet and kind. But I guess there was more.

"I'm sorry, Roran. I didn't want any of that for you. I wish I could give you back the throne, but I get the impression that such a move can't happen."

He shakes his head. "No, it can't. Lord Yune explained that the people's confidence in me is gone. Even if you took the throne and then offered it back to me, it would hobble me. I'd never be able to truly lead the people. And then you…" He looks at me and shakes his head. The earlier anger and resentment are gone, and I only see pity. "You would be my first General, of course, but no one would trust you because you abdicated to me, a man who abdicated to a tyrant."

"Wow," I say before I can catch myself. "It's all so complicated."

He nods and laughs. "That's true. The only reason I get it is because Tilbur and Rulf have been teaching me since I was little. I gather you had none of that instruction."

I shake my head. "No. Only over the last couple of months."

"So…" Roran begins, but then stops. "I guess… that means… you really are going to be King. And I should stop thinking of it as my throne."

My stomach twists at the thought. But… it's not the first time I've felt that over my future. I just have to come to grips with it all.

"Tell you what," I begin. "I think I do need to take the throne. I don't want it, but I have to do this for the sake of our people. We… both of us… have to walk roads we don't really want to walk, for the sake of our people." I stare at him for a moment, and he nods. That's exactly what we have to do. "When I take the throne, I'll plan to keep you close. You may not be able to sit on the throne, but you will be able to speak into the ruling of the nation."

He smiles at that. "Thanks."

"But," I say, thinking of our friends below. "The others are probably getting worried. So, in the meantime, what do you want? What do you need?"

"I want to see Rulf, and I want to be free of this enchantment."

My eyes drop to the floor. I hate that he's going through this. "Marleet tells me you're still enchanted, but they've been able to do something to hold it back?"

He holds up his left hand. I don't really see anything at first, but then I notice there's a strange… something… on his finger. It's a ring, but it's hard to see. I lean in close and see it's made of glass, or at least it's see-through.

"It cancels enchantments. But if I take it off, the enchantment comes right back. It basically just protects me. It doesn't get rid of it." He drops his hand back down. "So, it's still there—the enchantment. In fact, I can feel it at all times. It's like it's waiting to break out and take over." He closes his eyes and squeezes them tight. "Sometimes, it still pushes its way out again."

My heart goes out to him. I didn't know it was this bad for him. "How do we get rid of the enchantment? If you could draw the King's sword, that would do it, but I can't think of any way we can get that sword."

"I asked Captain Tilbur about it. He says that he's only heard one way. A spellcaster's enchantments on objects last forever. But on people, it's different. The enchantment only lasts until the Spellcaster dies."

Yes, I remember now. Marleet told me that. Before I can think it through, I say, "Then we track down the spellcaster and kill him." As soon as that comes out, I'm filled with horror. I don't know if I can just go kill someone. Even in this circumstance. I think that just seems… wrong.

Roran smiles. "Thanks. But I don't know how to find him, and I don't think you do either. Since we don't know where he is, and you're the only one who will recognize him..." He looks at me like there's no hope.

I nod. He's right, which is really frustrating, but then also good. I feel a little sick about what I just told him we'd do... about killing the spellcaster. So, if we can't kill him, then maybe that's better. "And Rulf. You said you want to see Rulf. I don't know if that's possible."

"I know a way," Roran says. "I know one of the guards. He's loyal to the throne and can get us through. If we can get down there, we can get to Rulf. The guard I know is in the prison until mid-afternoon each day."

I nod. "Then we'll go to the prison and see if we can meet with Rulf."

Roran smiles. I think I prefer him smiling at me rather than the murderous look from earlier. I feel like more needs to be said, but I don't know what it is, so I turn to the ladder.

"Draydon?"

"Yeah?"

"Thanks. I... I've hated you ever since I found out I could no longer take the throne. I think I just needed to chat it through."

I smile back. I feel like I have another friend moving forward. When it comes to taking the throne, I'm going to need all the friends I can get.

At the bottom, I'm just about to announce that we have to make a stop in the prison, when I think of something else. "We need to make two stops on the way out. First, we need to stop by the Forgotten Armory and see Hob. Second, we need to go to the prison and see Rulf."

Marleet shakes her head. "We can't get to the prison. We'll get caught for sure."

"Roran has a contact there. He'll get us in and out."

She doesn't look impressed, but she nods. "I can get us to the area and even to some parts of the prison, but I can only get us into the secret passageways. I'm not sure if there's a way into the prison itself from there."

"Then we'll find out." I hope there is. I'm not willing to walk down the stairs. I was down there once years ago on an errand from the Regent. From what I can remember, there's no way we could manage moving past all the guards.

"But first," I whisper, "we need to see Hob." They all look at me like I'm crazy, but I put up my hands and add, "Roran and I… we need to find the spellcaster. I'm hoping Hob can help us with that."

Ellcia opens her mouth to ask something, but Marleet pipes up. "Okay, that one's easy. We can get to that area of the castle without too much trouble."

We move off down the passage and end up in a small tunnel that leaves us slithering along like snakes—even climbing up some form of stairs on our belly as there's no room to stand. When it levels out, we turn left, then go down a short ladder, walk along a wide passage, then up a ladder that I think must be taking us to the third floor, followed by a thin passageway that feels like it goes on forever.

Eventually, Marleet tells us to wait, and she slips around a corner. I peer around, and she's peeking through a small hole. After a moment, she comes back and says, "It looks clear."

She shows me where the exit is, and I slowly pull it open and push a tapestry out of the way just enough to see down the hall. I peer the other way as well, and then we slip out. Marleet suggests we leave the door open as it's pretty hard to see behind the tapestry, and we move into Hob's armory—which is just around the corner.

We find Hob asleep in his chair, and Marleet waves for us to go into the back room. She joins us, but asks Ellcia to wake him up. I'm a little confused by that—so is Ellcia— but Marleet explains that Ellcia, with her shaved head, is still the least likely to be recognized, and an apprentice in an armory is not entirely unusual.

We wait, peering around the corner, as Ellcia carefully approaches Hob. She shakes his shoulder lightly, then a little harder, then quite hard. After a bit, she's beating him on the arm, hissing, "Hob! Hob! Wake up!"

She turns back to us and whispers, "What if he's dead?"

At that, Hob jumps up and screams, "Who's dead? Are you? Wait, who are you? Oh, I know you. You are…"

"What's going on here?"

We pull back to avoid getting caught. I saw someone come around the corner but didn't see his face. The voice, however… that's unmistakable.

It's Frindor.

# 13

## The Last Place You Want to Go

I spin around and see Marleet examining the walls. I gather she's looking to see if there's an exit here that we can use to escape.

"Frindor, Captain, Captain Fridor, Frindor on Friday, no… it's not Friday!" Hob begins to sing, and I think he might be dancing.

"I don't know why Captain Tilbur keeps you around, Hob. I'd have found a reason to push you off a wall by now."

"Ooooooohhh…" Hob says in a mocking voice. "I'm shaaaaaking."

"Who's this?"

My heart races. I glance back at Marleet. She's given up finding an exit. It's just as well. I wouldn't slip into one and leave Ellcia.

"This?" Hob says in wonder. In a quiet voice, he says, "You can see Trip, too?"

"Trip?"

"Yes, Trip. Trip is Berin's apprentice. Trip is here. Is Berin here?"

"Yes, he's been arrested, remember?" Frindor asks. He sounds like he's smiling. "Which raises the question of his apprentice. As in, what is he doing here? Why didn't he get arrested along with Berin? And how did he get into the city?"

I'm not sure why Ellcia is not answering any of those questions. It sounds like they're kind of directed at her. But… she remains silent.

I glance back at the others. None of them look like they know what to do. I think I saw at least one other soldier with Frindor as I pulled my head back, but then I think I heard a lot of feet out there. We certainly can't jump out and attack.

Although… I could probably explain it away when it came time for me to claim the throne. But if any escaped, they would let Parthun know that I'm still alive.

"I…" Hob shouts in a formal voice as though he's speaking to a crowd, "DO NOT KNOOOOOOOOOOW!"

"Then I think it would be wise for us to take the boy into custody," Frindor growls.

"NOPE!" Berin says.

"What do you mean, 'nope'?"

"What do I mean, 'nope'?" Hob replies. "I think it's simple. You cannot take my apprentice in for questioning if he has not done anything wrong or if I have not been charged."

"Your apprentice?" Frindor shouts. "You just said he was Berin's apprentice."

Hob laughs. "Yes! Oh, yes, I did!" He lets out a loud giggle, then shouts, "Trip! Don't stand there! Sweep the floor! NOW!"

I hear quick footsteps, and Ellcia enters the back room. She doesn't make eye contact with any of us, but instead, searches for a broom. When she finds one, she runs out, and I hear her sweep.

Hob clears his throat and then breaks into song:
Now, to whaaaaaat
Do we owe the honooooooor
Of thine preseeeeeence
My dear Captain Frindoooooor.

Have you come for piiiiiie
Or have you come to chaaaa-aaaat.
Do you have licoriiiiice
Or would you like a caaaa-aaaat.

"I'm just doing rounds!" Frindor barks. "The Prince
has disappeared, and I wanted to personally check to see if
you…"

Hob interrupts him and breaks into song again:
The Prince is here, the Prince is here
He's on my heart, he's in my tears
I have a Prince, he's in my pocket
I want to um…

"Oh! I don't know what rhymes with pocket!" Hob
says with desperation as I hear Ellcia continuing to sweep.
"Oh, locket! It rhymes with locket! Now… where was I?"

I hear Frindor growl and storm out of the room.

A moment later, Hob and Ellcia show up in the
doorway. Hob has a large smile on his face, and Ellcia looks
quite disturbed. Before she can speak, however, Hob clears
his throat at her, and points his chin at the broom. "Um,
Trip, did I tell you that you could stop sweeping?"

Ellcia opens her mouth to say something, but Hob
has a bit of a crazy look in his eye. Instead of challenging
him, she merely returns to the other room, and I hear the
sound of the broom scraping across the floor.

Hob steps right into his small office and examines each of us. First, he starts with Marleet. After a moment, he whispers, "Lady Marleet, it's good to see you again."

She nods. "You as well, Hob."

I don't really know what that's about. I'm guessing they've had contact over the last while.

He examines Hemot next, finally whispering, "The Milterite."

Before he can go on, Hemot whispers back, "What is a Milterite? Everyone keeps saying I'm a Milterite, but I don't know what that means."

Hob gives a confused look—which does not seem unusual for Hob—and then says matter-of-factly, "It's just a name for someone from the town of Milter."

"Oh," Hemot says. He looks disappointed.

Truthfully, I am as well. I just thought it would be more impressive than that. I've never heard of this Milter place, though, so maybe it's really... I don't know... exciting?

Next, he examines Roran. After a moment, he bows and says, "Your Majesty." He then grabs Roran's left hand, holds it up, and examines the ring on his finger.

When he's done, he nods and turns to me. "Your Majesty," he says, but then adds a deep bow. "I served your father for many years. I will serve you as well for many more."

Somehow, I doubt that. Not the serving my father part, but the serving me for many years. Hob, though he is quite spry for his age, he's not, well... young. I can't imagine he has that many years left in him.

With his eyes still on me, he says in a stern voice, "Now, you were supposed to, supposed to, supposed to be out of the castle by now. I assume since you are still here, that you have a good reason to risk the future of the kingdom."

I nod. "We need to find the Spellcaster. We need to free Prince Roran—permanently. The only way to do that is to kill the Spellcaster."

He nods. He's serious now. Like Berin. In fact, he seems almost sane. "You're right, Your Majesty. That is the only way. I can give you an item which you can use to track down the Spellcaster, but the Spellcaster himself can only be killed by a powerfully enchanted item."

"Like what?"

"It has to be an item which is enchanted more powerfully than any protection spell the Spellcaster can place on himself."

"Where do we get something like that?" I ask.

"I can think of three items more powerful than the Spellcaster!" Hob says. His voice is still serious, but there's a wildness in his eyes.

I take a deep breath. This is taking a while. We don't have much time. I hear Ellcia still sweeping in the other room. I know she won't be impressed, but I also know she's willing to do this to keep Hob happy while he answers our questions. "What three items?"

"The first is the King's sword," Hob explains. "But that might be difficult. The second is the ring on the Prince's finger."

I look at Roran in surprise. I can't see how a ring can kill someone.

"But," Hob continues, "a ring is not a very good weapon since it's hard to kill someone with it.

Well, that explains that. "And the third?"

"Your sword, Your Majesty. Your sword will kill a Spellcaster. Quite well, actually."

Okay, so that's good. I'm not sure I really wanted to do the killing part, but at least we don't need to track anything else down. "Where is this item we can use to find the Spellcaster?"

Hob's eyes go wide, and he focuses intensely on me as he slowly reaches for my forehead. At first, I want to jump. I'm afraid there's some spider on there or something really creepy, and he's not moving fast enough for me. When his hand finally does reach me, he simply takes one finger, pushes my head aside, and reaches slowly behind me.

I step out of the way to see he's pulling something off the wall. It's not much, just a small bag. Grabbing my arm and pulling up my hand, he drops the bag into my palm. When I open it, I find a bracelet inside.

"Hold it up!" he orders.

I hold it by the chain, and it just dangles there. He points to Marleet, and I hand it to her. It does the same. Then Hemot. Again, same thing. Nothing. When he points to Roran and Hemot gives it to him, the bracelet nearly jumps out of his hand, like it's trying to get away from him.

"The spellcaster," Hob explains, "is in the direction the bracelet points. It will only react that way with someone who is enchanted."

I nod. "East, then." That makes sense. That's where the Spellcaster was before.

"Wait!" Hemot says. "If it does that for Roran, can we use it to prove that Roran is enchanted to give him back the throne?"

Hob frowns and shakes his head. "No, Milterite. I know what the bracelet does. You do now as well. Even the traitor likely knows what this does. But there's no proof. The false King could claim it has been enchanted merely to point east whenever Roran picks it up. It is nothing which can help Prince Roran reestablish his claim."

"So," Roran says. "There really is no hope for me to take the throne?"

Hob's eyes seem to fill with genuine sadness and concern. "I'm so sorry, Your Majesty. But the false King did his work well. I think even if the false King died, the people would not trust you at this point."

Roran's shoulder's slump. I thought he'd already known that, but maybe he was still holding out hope. I don't know what it would be like to expect to sit on the throne your entire life, only to have it taken away by something out of your control.

"But," Hob says, "that's not what's important right now. Right now, you need to get out of the castle."

"I agree," I reply. "We need to leave. But we have to see Rulf first. He's in a pit in the dungeon."

Hob's face screws up, and he quickly shakes his head. There's the Hob we know coming back. "No, no, no, no, no! You cannot go down there. You have to get out of the castle!"

I nearly step back. Hob is really intense right now.

He moves toward me, and his eyes feel like they're boring into me. "There's no time. You have to leave before they find you. If they find you, the kingdom is lost. You, Your Majesty—you are it! If you die, General Lirnal will be left in the dungeon, and likely be killed there, and the false King will secure his reign!"

I know Hob's right. I also don't know why Roran wants to see Rulf. I look over at Roran. My cousin. Maybe he's my friend. I think he is. He might also be my closest ally as we grow older. I see the look of grief in his eyes. I'm about to tell him we can't go, but then I stop myself.

First, Rulf is almost like a dad to Roran—despite the fact that they're the same age. Second, I think I need to make this happen. I think this is something Roran needs, and I'm the one to bring it about.

I turn back to Hob. "No, we have to see Rulf. It is extremely important. And as the future King of Sevord, I say this is what will happen."

"Whoa," Hemot says, "That's really... Kingly of you."

I glance at Marleet. She's smiling like she's really proud of me, and Roran has the most grateful look on his face I could imagine.

I turn to Marleet. "Are you able to get us right to the pit so Roran can talk to Rulf?"

She shakes her head. "I can only get you down there to the secret passages in the prison. I can't get right to the pit. But Rulf's hearing is good."

"Mine's not good enough to hear his reply, though," Roran says.

"I can get you there," Hob says, "but you're not going to like it."

I don't know what that's all about, but I already don't like it. Roran, however, nods and gives a big smile. "Whatever it is, I'm up for it."

Hob gives a big nod in reply. "Then follow me."

We step out into the main part of the armory. By this point, Ellcia has not only finished the floor, but she's also dusted many of the shelves. I hadn't realized how bad it was, but it's starting to look good in here.

"Trip!" Hob barks. "Finish cleaning the armory, then start on my office. When you're done, deal with that mess behind the trash bin in the storage room. I'm not sure what it is, but I'm pretty sure something's living in there."

Ellcia frowns, and I whisper, "Hob, she's not actually your apprentice."

He turns back to me with shock all over his face, but then calms down. "Oh, right." Turning back to Ellcia, he says, "I'm sorry, my Lady Trip. You can stop that now. Why don't you come with us?"

Ellcia glares at him, but sets the broom aside and follows. Hob leads us to the door, checking the hall before we leave. Not long after, we're all in the secret passageway.

We zigzag through, coming to a halt in an area I don't recognize. Although, truthfully, I don't recognize any of the secret areas, so there's that…

"Where to?" Marleet asks. "Is it… the sewers?"

Hob nods, and Marleet's shoulder's slump. I gather she doesn't want to go there. Of course, neither do I, now that I think of it. I've smelled them many times whenever my job took me to the lower levels. I never thought I'd go there willingly—and I certainly don't want to go right into them.

Hob reaches down and sticks his finger into a hole, pulling out a small door near the floor. It's not that big, but Hob goes in feet first.

I follow next as soon as he whispers that I can, but before I duck fully inside, I see Hemot's face filled with wonder. "A secret passage within a secret passage? Did you know about this, Marleet?"

Marleet shakes her head. Her expression is filled with shock. I gather that means there's probably a lot Marleet doesn't know about the hidden ways of the castle.

Inside the hole into which Hob climbed is a ladder. I climb down and let the next person know I'm out of the way. As we descend, the air grows cooler and more moist. When we finally reach the bottom, I think we've gone down around four or five floors. Which means we're below ground level.

I can't see a thing. In fact, once the last person entered the small tunnel leading down and closed the door, the last of our light disappeared, and we've been in darkness ever since.

Once we're all at the bottom—at least I assume we are, I don't hear anyone else on the ladder—Hob quietly sings to himself as he moves around.

I bump into someone and ask who it is. When I find out it's Ellcia, she takes my hand. I feel like I haven't seen much of her over the last while. I mean, she's been around, but I've been talking with Marleet for the most part.

We all gasp as a flash of light catches our eyes. A few flashes later, the smell of a burning oilcloth fills the air. Soon we have light from a lantern.

Hob looks… creepy and a little more insane in the dark, holding a lantern. I think the others sense it, too, and I suspect Hob does as well. As if to confirm his creepiness, he lets out a quiet giggle.

"It's this way!" and then he waves us to follow.

Before we move, I take a look around the room. It's damp and gross-smelling—not sewer gross, but wet soil and mildew gross. I see two sets of bunk beds, a table, a few chairs, one of which looks broken, and some empty shelves. I expect no one would keep food down here as it would quickly go bad.

But one thing's for sure, someone comes down here often. I can tell from how clean the table and chairs are, and the beds look well-made and cared for. Besides that, Hob found the lantern, flint, and oilcloth without any difficulty. I gather this is his secret hideout.

For a moment, I wonder how many people actually have secret hideouts. I had thought that was something only in books, not something sane people actually had.

Oh, wait… that's right. That's the difference. Sanity. Hob is a little short on that kind of thing.

"Hey!" Hob hisses at us. "It really stinks in there. In fact, the smell kind of sticks to you. I'd recommend you take off your armor and cloak. They'll be the hardest things to clean."

I'm not really comfortable with that. I feel the suspicion grow in me, but Roran just pulls off his armor and cloak, and Marleet doesn't seem suspicious at all, so I follow.

"Through here!" Hob whispers.

He swings open a door, and the smell hits us. We all take a step back, and Hob laughs again. "If you want to speak with Rulf, this is the only way."

"I'm not going in there," Marleet says as she gags.

Ellcia agrees with her, and Hemot merely coughs and hacks and sounds like he's about to die.

"I'll go with you, Roran." I nearly groan as I realize those words came out of my mouth.

We set our packs and cloaks on the bed, but keep our weapons. You never know what you'll face.

Once we're through the door, Hob pulls it closed behind us. We have the lantern and, at first, I think about my friends now standing there in the dark and feel bad for them, but then I think about the smell all around me and feel worse for myself. Standing in the dark for however long we take is better than walking through here.

With my hand over my mouth, we move down the corridor with rats scurrying along at our feet. I had heard the rats were the size of dogs down here, but I'm glad that story was untrue. They seem more like beefy mice.

The walls and ceiling are stone, and so is the floor, but the floor itself has a channel cut into it. I assume that's to allow sewage or water or something to flow along without soiling our boots too much.

Hob moves fast enough that we're nearly at a jog, but I don't dare slow down. If I lose him, I lose the light.

When he finally comes to a halt, it's by a small tunnel that sits at around chest height. He waves us to come in close and whispers, "Crawl through here, and you'll come to a small window with bars over it. On the other side should be Rulf's pit."

Roran nods and moves forward but stops, pulling back with a look of disgust. I lean forward for a moment, but then jump back, too.

There's a spider web woven across the entrance to the small tunnel, and sitting in the center of it is the biggest spider I've ever seen.

I feel like we should be tough enough to just knock it out of the way, but it's about the size of my hand, and it's got big, thick, hairy legs. All I want to do is scream and run away.

Roran steps forward, breathing heavy. I think he's about to just push through, but I stop him. I draw my sword and slice the beastly thing in half.

His shoulders relax, and he smiles at me, offering a grateful look.

Scrambling up into the tunnel, he wiggles along until his feet disappear. With the light of the lantern, we can see his feet, but then he starts kicking and flipping over and around. He pulls back a bit until his feet stick out again, and I hear his panicked voice, "There's another one in here! And it's got babies. They're all over me!"

I glance at Hob and even he has a look of disgust. I hope whatever Roran needs to talk to Rulf about is worth it.

I don't know what to do at first, but then Hob steps forward, grabs Roran's ankles, and shoves with all his might. Roran's feet disappear as he slides into the tunnel, his body making a gross slurping sound as it disappears into the darkness.

"That dealt with that little problem," Hob says with a thoughtful look on his face.

"No, Hob, it didn't!" I step up to the tunnel and peer down it. I don't see any sign of Roran, but I hear a quiet "ow" in the distance. It stinks really bad in there, so I step back.

"If you're not happy with that, do you want to slide in there and check on him?"

I shake my head. That's going a little too far.

We wait. It's hard to believe how long he's in there. Now and then I move up to the hole, and I hear faint sounds of whispering. I can tell one is Roran, and the other is obviously Rulf. He talks with a lot of grunts and just lays it all out bluntly. It's an easy voice to recognize.

When Roran finally does come back, I'm actually leaning against the wall—despite the enormous amount of spiders and other… creatures. All I'm trying to do is block out the smell and pretend I don't hear all sorts of scratching and disturbing crunching noises.

"Ahh… baby spiders!"

"That you, Roran?" I ask.

"Um, yeah. You expecting someone else?"

I feel a little dumb now for asking, but I reach up and help him out of the hole. As I do, I find the smell in the tunnel was nothing compared to the smell of Roran. He stinks.

"You get everything you need?" Hob asks.

"I didn't need to get anything," Roran replies. "I just needed to talk to Rulf. That's the first time I've spoken to him since I put on the ring. I… needed his advice."

"Giant advice?" Hob asks. "Not too many people seek out Giant men for wisdom. Most of the time, Giant men just punch things."

"Yeah, well, Rulf's different." He looks at me a little funny before he adds, "Well, he also punches things. And he's good at it."

"I can testify to that," I say. "But I agree with Roran. He's also really smart. And he's got a lot of wisdom inside him. At times."

Hob nods. In a serious tone, he says to Roran, "I know, Your Majesty. That's why Captain Tilbur was so willing to leave you with him for so many years. Few people could have kept you as safe and continued your education like Rulf." Hob's face twists suddenly, and he adds, "Well!

Time to move!" And off he runs down the tunnel, back toward his little secret hideout.

When we get back, I notice the other three keep their distance. I don't blame them. I don't like my smell either.

"We need to get out of the castle now," I announce as we pick up our packs and cloaks.

"Are you heading to the docks?" Hob asks.

Ellcia frowns. "How did you know?"

"Didn't. Just can't imagine you getting out of the city any other way. All the gates at the castle and leading out of the city will be guarded. The streets will be filled with soldiers. You won't get anywhere heading north, south, or east. The docks will be well guarded too, but once you're on a boat, you should be okay."

"You have a good way to get to the docks?" I ask Marleet.

She smiles and nods. "We just have to get back up out of here, and I can find my way."

"Great!" Hob says. A moment later, he extinguishes the lantern, plunging the entire room into darkness. I hear him hum as he reaches the ladder and begins his climb.

I shake my head. "All right, I guess we're doing this in the dark." To everyone else, I add, "I think it's over this way. Just try to follow my voice."

I hear stumbling in the darkness as I reach the ladder. I continue to call to them so they can find me, and I confirm that Ellcia, then Hemot, then Marleet, then Roran go up. Once Roran's up a short distance, I start on the ladder, and it's not long before I'm out in the main secret passageway up top.

Hob is gone by this point. I would have thought he'd at least say goodbye.

Marleet leads us through the tunnels. She's quick in here, and it's a little hard to keep up. I'm not tired. She's just really fast.

We reach ladders, and she scurries down them. She zips around corners and through tunnels. I can tell she's spent a lot of time in these areas. We have to leave the secret tunnels a few times, but we're only out in the hallways for seconds at a time, and no one catches us.

I sure hope she knows where she's going, though, because I have no idea how to navigate all this without her.

When she comes to a halt, Roran's gasping for air. I guess I didn't think about that part. He's likely just been sitting around a lot the last couple of months.

I step up next to him, and just standing by his side seems to give him a bit more energy. I'm really curious about what he and Rulf spoke about, but that's between them. He may simply have missed his friend.

Marleet leads us into a small room. There's a few of these in the secret tunnels. They're usually odd shaped, as if they're just areas the builders forgot to include in the actual rooms. This one is shaped kind of like a giant foot with four widely spread toes.

"They call this the foot room," Marleet says in a whisper. "I'm not sure why."

"It's because it stinks," Hemot says.

"No, that's Draydon and Roran," Ellcia adds unhelpfully.

"I'd be happy to try to clean up somewhere," I say, but no one listens. I don't like my smell any more than they do.

Marleet turns to me, and I can see it's decision time. I guess I'm no longer just the leader of the group, I'm soon to be the leader of the nation. I'll have to get used to people turning to me.

"From here," she explains, "it's pretty simple to get out of the castle. There's a passage that goes down and leads under the courtyard on the west side of the castle, coming up and out at the wall. I mean, *right* at the wall. It would be easier to get out at nighttime, but we don't want to wait that long. I think it's sometime around mid-afternoon."

"Why is it going to be difficult?" Hemot asks.

"The door actually comes out of the wall. Like, I mean, it opens up to the street. It won't be so bad because there's often a banner hanging there, but it'll still be difficult to get out without being noticed." She glances around at each of us. "We're going to have to be quick. Once we're past the wall, we'll have to move quickly through the west end of the city, reach the docks, and find our ship. It's called the Wavebreaker. I've never met the Captain, but he's a trustworthy man, and his name is Stevrick. The plan is for him to take us north. Even before we knew you wanted to go to Nimville, we knew north up the coast was the best option."

"Is there anything…" Ellcia begins… but stops. She glances at me, and I nearly groan. "Anything we can do about Draydon and Roran's… you know… aroma?"

Marleet giggles. There's the old Marleet. As much as I like this new Marleet, I miss the old Marleet that I've known most of my life. "I think I have an idea to fix that little problem—if they each have a change of clothes. But before we go, remember, the name of the ship is the Wavebreaker, and the Captain's name is Stevrick. You can tell him that Tilbur sent you. Not Captain Tilbur, just Tilbur."

I must look a little confused, so Marleet adds, "It's part of the code. No one will refer to him as Tilbur in regular conversation, nor is there any reason for Tilbur to send people to that ship. If the code was that Lord Yune sent us, that might be figured out as he's suspected of orchestrating a lot of things that work against the King. So, if we get separated, tell Captain Stevrick that Tilbur sent you."

Marleet waves for us to follow. We rush along through the passageways. The floor is stone, so it's easy, if we're careful, to be quiet.

After about ten minutes of twists and turns, we come to a ladder. We climb down, and a few floors down, I hear it. It sounds like the roar of a Reber Troll, but the moisture in the air lets me know we're near the river providing water to the city. I've been down in this area once or twice over the years, but never have I approached from this direction. I always just used the stairs.

We reach what looks like one of those secret stone doorways, and Marleet turns to Roran and me. "Okay, so on the other side of this door is a small area that gets a constant spray of water—it'll be like a shower, but a REALLY cold one. You won't be seen because this area is dark, and no one looks in this direction, but you'll still have to be quiet and move quickly."

We both nod and pull off our armor, cloaks, weapons, and shoes. There's no point in getting them wet. We'll be cold enough as it is outside. It is still winter. We leave our packs with our dry clothes behind, and Marleet pushes open the door.

The others jump back as the cold spray shoots into the passageway. I nearly run back as well, but that's not really an option. I need to get rid of the smell. It bothers me too.

We step out and quickly start to scrub down our clothes. I think it feels kind of silly to scrub since the spray hits us hard enough that it feels like it's cutting into my skin, but I want out of here fast. I can barely breathe because of the cold.

A quick glance at the area lets me know I'm standing at the edge of rapids. Light comes from across the way, and I see some movement, but it's no surprise they can't see us with the spray and how dark it is where we stand.

When we're done, we rush back through the doorway, and Marleet pulls the door closed. I dig in my pack for a dry change of clothes, wishing I had pulled them out before I washed up. My fingers are so cold I can barely move them.

When I get my clothes out, everyone turns around as Roran and I change. It's dark in this area, but enough light comes in to manage to get our clothes on. However, I still put my shirt on backwards. And inside out.

When we're finished, I wrap my wet clothes inside a towel and stuff the bundle in my pack, then pull on my cloak and armor. Now, I think only my shoes stink. Unfortunately, they had to wade through all the grossness. But maybe it won't be so bad.

Marleet leads us back up the ladder and down a corridor. I appreciate the movement. It's warming me up.

Finally, we come to a point where she waves at us to stop. I can see well here. Holes run along the walls leading out into hallways and rooms, letting in plenty of light.

We gather around, and she whispers. "Okay, so we need to be really quiet. We have to slip out of the passageway and move down the hall for about twenty steps. There's a supply closet which we need to enter to find the tunnel leading under the courtyard." She looks around at all of us and adds, "We have to move fast. The castle will be well patrolled at this point. If it's evening, there could be a lot of people around in addition to the soldiers."

"What'll we do if we're seen?" Hemot asks.

Marleet opens her mouth to answer, but then catches herself. "I don't know…"

I'm a little taken aback by that. She's been so well prepared for everything, but then again, no one can work out every detail.

I jump in. "We can't let them see the secret passageway, so we can't just run into the storage room. Our only options are to run or attack. If there are only two, we attack. If there are more, we run. Our goal will be to meet back in the storage room." I turn to Marleet. "How do we get into the secret passageway once in that room?"

She shakes her head. "I don't know that either. I... We didn't talk about that detail. I think we're going to have to search."

I nod. Some of Nordin's training is kicking in. "Okay, so Ellcia and I will be a team. Roran, Marleet, and Hemot will be the other team. If we have to split up, we'll stay in our teams and meet back in the storage room. As soon as you get in there, start looking for the doorway. Check along the floor in case it's low down. If you find it, you enter the passageway and be prepared to open it to let in the others."

Everyone nods, and Marleet moves to the wall. She pulls back on a small handle set in the stone, and then carefully peeks out past the tapestry covering the area. I'm suddenly struck by how many tapestries there are in this castle. None of them are easy to make, so I wonder how many people have spent countless hours, days, weeks, and months making all these simply to hang up on a wall somewhere in the castle.

"Okay, it's time to move," Marleet says, interrupting my thoughts.

She slips out and each of us follows. I'm the last out, so I pull the door closed.

"This way," she whispers, and rushes off down the hallway.

I manage no more than three steps before a loud voice barks, "Halt!"

# 14

## The Docks

I spin around, my hand going straight for the hilt of my sword. Four men stand before us. Too many to fight. We could probably take them, but we could just as easily lose against trained soldiers.

I recognize three of the men right away. The fourth is familiar. The three I recognize have terrorized me for years. The one has even pushed me around a few times. He never leaves a mark, but he's never been gentle, either.

Their mouths drop open, and their eyes bulge. I'm about to call for my friends to run, when the one man turns around and orders, "Secure the area!" He turns back and, as he rushes toward us, he hisses, "Your Majesty, wait here."

I'm kind of thrown by this and find myself just standing there, with my mouth open and my hand on the hilt of my sword. The soldier runs past us and checks around the corner. He quietly confirms with the others that there are no others in sight and comes to me. "Your Majesty. We don't have any time for formalities or politeness. Do you have a plan to get out of here?"

I nod. "We do." I know we don't have time, but I have to ask. "Are you loyal to me?"

"I am loyal to the throne, and to you, my future King," the soldier says as he bows, "But we have no time. The next patrol will be here within seconds."

"Then move on. We'll get out."

His face fills with panic for a moment, but then he gives a quick bow. The four men pass by us and walk on as if they hadn't even seen us.

We slip into the storage room just as we hear some new soldiers call out, "Oy! Any sign of them?"

The man who told us to get moving a moment ago calls back, "All clear. You?"

"Would I be asking you if I had found them?" the other soldier calls back.

At first, I assume the soldiers will just continue on, but the soldier whom we saw out in the hallway yells back at the new soldier, and in a moment, they're screaming at each other. I'm kind of shocked, but it's the perfect cover for us. No one will hear anything we do while that's going on.

We move around the room, pushing on walls, moving things out of the way as quietly as we can. It takes a bit, but Hemot eventually finds a block in the wall that slides in. A quick glance into the hole reveals a lack of light on the other side, but we slither through, one by one.

Standing up, I crack my head on the low ceiling. This tunnel is really small.

When we're all in, whoever came in last slides the block back in place.

I don't think Marleet knows much about this tunnel, so I carefully crawl along, trying not to bang my head again. Unfortunately, I run face first into a wall. It hurts. Not the wall. My head. I'm pretty sure the wall didn't notice the impact at all.

To my left, I feel the top of a ladder and climb onto it. I whisper to the others what I found and start down. When I reach the bottom, I quickly find the walls are close together and the ceiling is high enough to walk. We've reached a tunnel. I assume it's one of the tunnels which runs under the courtyard. It's heading in the right direction, anyway.

Once all of us are down, we make our way through the darkness, walking hand in hand. It's pretty scary because I feel like I'm going to tumble off a ledge at any moment, but each footstep lands on solid stone.

When we reach the end of the tunnel, I've no doubt we've cleared the courtyard. We've walked plenty far enough to get past all the trees and flower beds and paths laid out in that area.

I find a ladder, and when I reach the top, I feel around for a doorway while the others climb up. My hands land upon something a little unusual, and I grab hold of it. It's a handle—a small one, and I give it a pull.

The sight of light… well… the sight of anything, actually, is a huge relief. A banner hangs down in front of the open doorway I've just uncovered. On the port side of the castle, banners run along the wall, facing the ocean. It's apparently some tradition, and each banner represents a family. I assume my family's on there. Actually, all our families should be up there somewhere. I've never really looked at the banners, come to think of it.

The opening I've found runs from about waist height up to about my chin, so I crouch down a little and carefully push the banner out enough to see past it.

The street itself is packed, which means on one hand we might get out without notice, but on the other hand, it means there are a lot of people who might chance a look in our direction. When I push the banner out a bit farther, though, I see we're behind a small stand selling Brussels sprouts.

I drop the banner back into place and turn to the others. In a whisper, I say, "Okay, we're behind a vegetable stand. We should be able to get out of here without being noticed by the people on the street, since none of them would be caught dead buying Brussels sprouts. But we'll have to be careful of the seller."

The others nod their heads, and I slip out as quietly as I can.

The seller sits there with his back to me, facing the crowds of people, all of whom carefully avoid eye contact with him. Once we're all out, we try to slip past him, but Hemot trips over a basket and wakes the man from his stupor.

"Who are…" the man begins, but then his face fills with rage. The next thing I know, he's got me by the arm, and he screams, "Thieves! Thieves! Thieves in the marketplace!"

I wrench my arm free, assuming he had the strength of a normal man, but years of a diet of only Brussels sprouts has left him weak and miserable. The seller flips right over his stand, sending green balls of disgustingness in every direction. Unfortunately, the eyes of everyone turn toward us at that moment.

The majority of the people won't recognize Ellcia, Hemot, or me, but Marleet might be recognized as the daughter of Lord Yune and Lady Aldora, and Roran's almost definitely going to be recognized.

"It's the happy couple!" a woman screams out in joy.

Two soldiers a little way down the street start toward us, and I grab the others and pull them out from behind the stand. It doesn't take much urging to get them running, and a moment later we're racing down a side street.

It's not long before the two soldiers behind us are joined by two others, then another group joins in. After a bit, we're running from about two dozen men. In theory, I suspect we could stop running in the middle of a crowd and use the people around to our advantage. I bet we could explain that Roran and Marleet want some time away, and the people might pressure the soldiers to back off, but there's no guarantee.

"Split up in the teams we spoke about!" I order. "Don't go straight to our destination. Get away from the soldiers, and then we'll all meet in about an hour!"

Ellcia and I run off to the left, while the others disappear down a side alley to the right. I assume Roran knows the area well as he grew up on the streets. The rest of us spent a lot of time on this side of the city—especially in the summers. Whenever we could, we always met down at the beach to swim.

We zigzag through the area, picking up speed whenever we can, and it's not long before we put some distance between ourselves and the soldiers behind us. Once they're out of sight, we pass other soldiers, but they don't yet know what's going on, so they ignore us. We can't backtrack—under any circumstances. Right now, running through new areas is to our advantage.

We slip into a small market that operates out of an old warehouse. The large room only holds about eight stands, but it's a busy place. We thread our way through the people, careful to keep our heads down. We've been here enough times over the years that we could easily be recognized by one of the sellers.

On the other side, we climb onto a large bin, and then help each other up onto the roof. We've been up here many times over the years. It gives a great view of the port—which is only about two hundred yards away—and behind us, the palace sticks up above all the buildings. Although the wind is cold, I know we're safe up here and can hide out for a few minutes while the soldiers search the streets.

"How long do we have?" I ask. Ellcia's always better with time than I am.

"About forty minutes, I think, until we're supposed to meet at the boats."

I nod. I would like to have just gone straight to the port, but then, once there, we'll have nowhere else to run. We're better off letting the soldiers search for a bit. We'd been running somewhat to the south. They might think we kept going that way and move off, so later on it might allow us to head to the port without too much trouble.

We sit down and wait. It feels good to just be with Ellcia. My mind is swimming with all that's gone on.

"Marleet sure has changed," Ellcia says.

I smile. "She has. She's almost like a totally different person."

"But Hemot hasn't."

I laugh. "He's changed a lot, but not as much as she has. He's got some catching up to do. She's now pretty serious and focused. I don't know if Hemot is capable of that kind of thing."

We both laugh at that and pull out some of our food. It's no fun eating up here on the roof with the cold wind coming off the ocean, but it's nice to be outside, and nice not to be running for the time being.

We sit and chat for about half an hour. We talk about just about everything, from Ellcia's short hair to how much we've changed over the last while. It's hard to believe it's been less than five months since we first signed up to be one of the Vanguard.

When we figure that our hour must be almost up, we move over to the edge of the roof and watch the crowd for a moment. We see the odd soldier, but they don't appear to be hunting for us. We move over to another side and see a couple soldiers moving through the alleys. I guess that means walking the streets with the crowds is the better option.

A wave of guilt washes over me. Ellcia and I aren't likely to be recognized, but Marleet and Roran are. That means we have it a lot easier. We might be able to just simply wander down the street with our hoods up. But that's not anyone's fault. It's just the way it is.

"Let's move," I say. "The soldiers have calmed down."

We climb off the roof and, with our hoods up, we join the crowds moving through the city. The key with soldiers is to act like you're supposed to be there. If you try to avoid being seen, they notice you. But if you act just like everyone else, you can walk right by them without notice. As we move, we slow down at the odd vendor, then pause to watch some children play for a moment. No soldiers even glance our way.

We reach the docks in just a few minutes, and it doesn't take long before Ellcia spies the Wavebreaker. It's a larger boat than I would have expected—much larger than the fishing boats Hemot and I worked on. A man stands on deck ordering others around. They look like they're about to set sail.

When we board, the man barely glances at us, instead, just waves for us to approach. When we reach him, I whisper, "Captain Stevrick? Tilbur sent us."

The man nods and swings open a door leading to a steep set of stairs. "Get down below and get to work! We ship out immediately!"

"Yes, Sir!" we each say and climb down into the hold.

When we get to the bottom, someone hisses, "Over here!"

We follow the voice and find the others. They look relieved, and Hemot grabs me and gives me a hug. "We thought you were lost. What took you so long?"

I'm a little embarrassed that we took our time, but I thought that was what we were supposed to do. "Just being cautious," I say.

The door above swings open and a voice carries down. "We're checking the hold! You don't want to be charged with resisting the King, do you?"

"No, Sir." I recognize Captain Stevrick's voice. He sounds quite shaken.

We scramble to the side with all the fishing gear. It's dark down here—dark enough that when we slip under the nets, I'm pretty confident we won't be seen.

Three soldiers come down the stairs and begin to work their way through the hold. The area is full of crates tied down. Stevrick obviously does some fishing, but it looks like shipping goods is his main business.

The men rip open two of the crates. They pull out some small shovels. That makes sense. Far to the north is the large farming community. The shovels won't seem suspicious.

When the soldiers reach the nets, the first two just ignore them, but the third says in a mocking voice, "Anyone hiding under there?"

At first, I think he sees us, but then I realize he's just joking around. He's about to walk on when one of the others says, "If you think someone might be in there, either pull the nets up, or stab the area with your sword."

Neither option sounds good to me, but we don't have a way to stop him. The soldier draws his sword and a moment later, he pulls back and drives it into the piles of nets. The area is over by Hemot. I don't hear him scream, so I'm guessing it's all right.

Next, he moves down a bit and stands over me. I ready myself. I might have to move quickly, one way or another, but I have to do it in a way that doesn't shift the nets. He drives the sword down, and it's heading right for me. I shift just a little to make sure I take it right in the chest. I concentrate hard, reminding myself that the blade can't hurt me. My armor is enchanted to protect me, but I can still feel the pain if I think I'm injured.

I feel a bit of soreness, but nothing too bad. I hope that means I'm getting used to the armor.

He's about to drive the blade in a third time, when one of the other soldiers calls back. "Let's go. We've got a lot of ships to check."

When they reach the deck, I just barely hear one of the soldiers say, "Don't leave port. We might search the boat again."

"But Sir," Stevrick replies, "I have to get these crates up north."

"What does anyone need small shovels for in winter?"

"That's not all I have down there. I have some vegetables for the fishing villages. They need these supplies."

"Stay here!" the soldier orders, and I hear them move off.

We crawl out from under the nets. I'm not pleased with this situation. I don't want to have to risk getting caught every couple hours or whenever the soldiers see fit to search us again. But there's nothing we can do.

We settle in for a bit. Marleet, Hemot, and Roran haven't eaten, so they have a bit of a meal. While they eat, we all just chat until the door swings open.

We scramble under the nets again, but the Captain comes down. "It's all right; you can come out. No soldiers at the moment. I'm sorry, Your Majesties, Ladies, and Hemot." I see Hemot frown at that, but he doesn't actually have an official title. Come to think of it, I don't know how the Captain recognizes us all—especially Ellcia, with her hair cut so short—but I'm guessing Lord Yune has it all worked out. "We can't leave just yet. I'm hoping to slip away in the next hour or so. I think they'll grow bored with watching us and just let us leave."

"What do we do?" Hemot asks.

"For now, you'll have to wait."

The Captain wanders up, and we settle in. Nothing really goes on, other than the Captain standing on deck above us and yelling a lot. When he speaks to us, he's calm and polite. When he's on deck talking to his men, he does nothing but yell.

Nordin could be like that, in a way. For the most part, he was calm and focused. But if anyone—even me—stepped out of line on his boat, he yelled and hollered and threatened to throw us overboard. The difference here, of course, is this Captain is average size. Nordin is a big guy and could probably have picked me and Hemot up and thrown us over with little difficulty.

"So, what's the plan?" Ellcia asks. She struggles to just go with the flow. I don't blame her. We really don't know an awful lot of what's going to happen.

I lean forward and smile. "We're going to have to figure a lot of it out as we go, but for now, we head north. We'll have to wait for things to settle down a bit, then we're going to track down the wizard. If Berin is out of jail by then, maybe he can help us get through Switcher Pass to the Talic Region. Once the wizard is killed, and Roran is free, we'll come back here and figure out how to take back the throne."

Until I said that last part, Roran seemed quite happy—almost smiling. But when I mentioned the throne, his face darkened. Not like before. Before he looked angry. Now he just looks sad. I think he's coming to grips with it all. I wonder what Rulf told him.

"How long will we wait?" Hemot asks. "Will we stay in Nimville?"

I frown and shake my head. "Marleet's right. We can't stay there—at least not like we did before. Enough people travel through the area that Marleet or Roran might be recognized, and soldiers might look for us there. I think if we do stay in that area, we're going to have to keep the two of you out of sight," I say as I point at Marleet and Roran. "But I think we might have to live in some of the caves to the east on the cliffs. That won't be fun, but it might be the best way to wait out the winter."

As I say that, I realize that the last thing I want to do is live in a cave in the winter. I wouldn't mind being there with my friends, but if the tension that pops up now and then between Roran and me keeps up, I think I'll get pretty annoyed. I also don't think it'll be warm, and there's something weird and awkward going on between Marleet and Roran. He keeps looking at her, and frowning at Hemot, and she keeps avoiding him. Even when we sat down, he tried to sit beside her, and she put Ellcia between her and Roran and Hemot on the far side of her, away from Roran.

We spend the next while hearing all about Marleet's journey to the city—all the details she didn't have time to tell us before. It's hard to believe she was just a short distance behind us for part of our journey. If we'd stayed in Haner for just another few days, we'd have met up. But then again, if Marleet hadn't ended up at the castle, we likely wouldn't have been able to save Roran—maybe not even known about the danger he was in.

The part about the Shaloomd, however, is quite disturbing. I remember seeing a woman carried over our heads. I think that was Marleet. I feel sick to my stomach when I think about that. Ellcia looks horrified, and Hemot looks like he's on the verge of tears.

I'm also amazed to hear that there are people on top of the cliffs. I had thought no one lived up there. I find it funny to hear about the guy named Fuzzy. Also, hearing Marleet tell us all about them when she knows they don't want anyone to know they exist is kind of surprising, but I can see she's quite annoyed with them.

When she's done, we all sit back in awe. She's been through a lot. We tell her about our experiences, but it seems like nothing compared to her own.

Finally, while Hemot leans back on the nets and starts to doze off, and Ellcia pulls out a book to read, I begin to pelt Marleet with questions about the castle. I really have so much to learn about how things work there, and I think she's the best one to teach me.

She explains how the Nobles interact, a bit about which ones can be trusted, who definitely can't, and more. I learn that Lord Hillbin is actually one of the most loyal Nobles in the kingdom, and he and Marleet's parents are quite close, although publicly they keep a distance in order not to feed the King's suspicions.

I find it interesting to learn, but then hard to wrap my mind around. Growing up in the palace didn't help me to understand any of this. No one explained it to me, and to add to it, it all seemed so unimportant. Now, I realize the future of the kingdom might depend on if I can work with the ways of the Nobility.

We're pulled away from our conversation by a change in movement on the deck above us. At first, I can't quite put my finger on what's different, but the sound... something's changed.

"They're... quiet..." Roran says. "Why are they so quiet?"

"Under the nets," I order.

We scramble under, which is not overly easy, considering Hemot is sound asleep and doesn't appear to want to wake up.

The gentle rock of the boat with the occasional bump against the dock shifts, and I feel us move. I think this means we're setting sail.

The Captain's voice carries through the deck. He's yelling at someone. "What? Speak louder, son! What? Pardon? You'll have to speak louder!" There's a pause followed by, "What? Whatever you're saying, you'll have to wait until we return to Sevord. We've already logged our departure with the Port Master. You can check. We're scheduled to leave at this time. Thank you. No… I'm sorry, what did you say?"

I can't hear the other person, but I'm guessing we're not supposed to leave yet. Captain Stevrick must have found an excuse to slip away.

I can't imagine this is a good thing. I expect the soldiers will send a ship or two after us. If soldiers board us, there's little chance of not being discovered.

Footsteps pound all along the deck as the Captain hollers out new orders. The hatch swings open, and eight men rush down. We don't move. I'm hoping we're still hard to see under all these nets.

The smell of the nets must be hard on Marleet and Roran. For Ellcia, Hemot, and me, it's not so bad. We've spent two months in a fishing village. But I remember how gross the nets were to me at first.

The men who come down into the hold are sailors, and they run to the oars, sliding them out. There are only four, two on each side, leaving two men to work each paddle. They work well together. One man sets the pace, and the others follow.

I can feel us pick up speed. I've seen ships do this countless times over the years. They use the oars to get away from the harbor before they put up their sails and head off. Once we're clear of the port, we can head north. I don't know what the wind's like right now, but from what it felt like before we came down into the hold, I think it should be favorable to speed us along our journey.

One of the men calls out, "You can come out of hiding. No soldiers on this boat."

We pull ourselves out and move toward the men. Judging from the muscle, they're used to running the oars. They're breathing heavily, but I think I'd be struggling a lot more if I were doing that.

"What's going on?" I ask.

"Captain decided to register his departure for now. We'll try to talk our way through that if we're chased down. But for the moment, we're going to push on ahead fast, so if they chase us, we can pretend we don't know what's going on."

"Will it work?" Marleet asks.

The man shakes his head. "Don't know. But we have royals to protect."

I feel uncomfortable with that, but then again, the kingdom's at stake. I also feel honored. So many people think I'm important enough to… risk their lives for.

The hatch opens, and Stevrick calls down. "Your Highness, you and the others may come up on the deck now, if you please."

We climb the ladder. I wonder at first who he was speaking to—Roran or me—but when we step out on deck, it becomes clear. He bows low to me and says, "Your Majesty. Welcome to the Wavebreaker. The ship, crew, and her Captain are at your service."

"Thank you, Captain. We are grateful. What is the situation?"

The Captain rises and points back to port. I'm surprised at how far we're out already. The first mate calls down to the men below, and they abandon the oars as the sails rise.

"Shortly after you boarded, more than fifty soldiers arrived and spread out across the docks. They searched our boat, as I'm sure you're aware, and searched all the others at port. It was just a matter of time before they swept the boats again, and again. We could not risk remaining where we were. I came up with a plan to get us out, and I expect they'll pursue us."

"What are our options?"

The Captain smiles. "The Wavebreaker is a fast ship. It's one of the reasons why the Lady Marleet's father chose this boat. The fastest of the King's fleet in port at the moment will at best match our speed. Our hope is to get far enough away that we can claim we didn't know we were meant to stop."

I smile. "Good work, Captain. And if they do gain on us?"

The Captain nods. "It's certainly a possibility. If so, we'll push on until nightfall and, under the cover of dark, send the five of you ashore in a lifeboat. Or, if we can stay ahead of them, once we reach our destination, I believe we'll have time to dock, and you will be able to disembark before the King's ships arrive."

"They're coming!" the first mate calls down. I didn't notice him scurry up the mast.

The Captain spins around and pulls out a spyglass. I look back toward port and can't see much, but when the Captain seems satisfied, he hands his spyglass to me.

To be honest, I've never used one before, and I struggle with it a bit. I look through, but everything looks so tiny. I wonder how a spyglass is even useful.

"The other way, Your Majesty," Stevrick whispers.

I spin it around, feeling my face go red. We never used anything like this on Nordin's boats. When I look through properly, it still takes me a bit to figure out where to look and what I'm looking at, but then I see it. A large naval vessel is pulling out. They're not moving fast at the moment, which is going to work to our advantage.

When I'm done, I hand the spyglass back. "Captain, how difficult would it be to drop us off in one of the fishing villages along the way?"

The Captain examines my face for a moment. I can see he's working through a lot. Finally, he nods. "We could, Your Majesty. We are at your command, of course. But the Lord Yune asked that we take you to the farming villages. On top of that, it'll be risky—that is why it is something only planned in case of emergency. If we needed to dock, only Grimmer and Shizzer have docks large enough to accommodate our ship. In addition to that, we'd have to dock at night, which is dangerous at the best of times, let alone during winter." He pauses again and says, "If we send you with the lifeboat, you'd need to hide the boat well, or you could be in the same spot—just trying to escape on land rather than on water."

That makes sense. I don't want to risk Captain Stevrick or his crew. I think if I'm not careful, that's exactly what'll happen. If they're found at the dock at Grimmer without a valid reason, they'll have a tough time explaining their need to leave Sevord so quickly.

"I understand, Captain. We will follow Lord Yune's direction."

The man bows. He then takes a few steps away, but stops. "Your Majesty. I do not wish to speak improperly to you. If it pleases you, I ask you permission to order you below deck if the need arises. I may not have the time for politeness or proper speech to a man of your status."

I smile at him. I like this guy. A lot. "Captain Stevrick, your service to the kingdom is invaluable, and has not gone unnoticed. I give you permission when needed to speak to me as though I were a member of your crew whenever I'm on board, and as a friend at any time—on sea or on land. You will never need to explain your words, nor will you need to apologize for ordering me around."

Captain Stevrick just beams at me. Nordin had taught me to offer informality to those who's loyalty is strong. He explained it was the way to move from service to friendship. If I'm to hold the throne, I'll need a lot of friends.

The five of us try to move out of the way as the crew works. It's a busy place on the deck of a ship like this. It's actually the largest ship I can remember ever being on.

It's cold, though. The wind just cuts through any spot it can. I wrap my cloak around myself, and the five of us huddle close together.

Although I don't want to step away, I signal for Roran to join me over near the railing. "Hey," I say, unsure how to dive into this. "You okay with how all this went down?"

"What do you mean?" he asks. I can see he knows, but doesn't want to admit it. I don't want to keep on the topic, but this is important.

"You know what I mean, Roran. The Captain only spoke with me. I…" Taking a deep breath, I dive in. "I was clearly treated like the one in charge—like the Royal. I know we've talked about this, but this is a big one, I think. Once again, Roran, I really didn't want to take the throne from you."

Roran nods slowly. "I know. Rulf explained that to me. He told me I'd have to accept it. It's the best thing for the kingdom now. He said you…" Roran lets out a small laugh. "He said you are small, weak, and annoying, but you're loyal, you have a strong heart, you're intelligent, and you'll make a great King one day." Roran then turns to me and does something that shocks me. "I pledge myself to you, Draydon… Prince Draydon. I will do all I can to see you take the throne, and I will serve you as your first General, or in any capacity you so wish."

I just stare at him. I don't know what to say. The moment drags on long enough that it gets awkward.

"Yeah, he said you do that kind of thing, too. If something surprises you too much, you kind of go blank. He says you'll have to work on that." Roran smiles. "But you don't have to worry about me. I'm struggling with it all, I'm still angry… and it hurts. But I'm behind you. With everything."

I finally manage to pull myself together and smile back at him. "Thanks, Roran." Without thinking, I give him a hug. At first, he tenses up, but then he just relaxes and squeezes me back. I can't imagine how alone he's felt over the last while—especially after losing Rulf. I also realize at that moment that this is probably one of the few hugs he's had since he was about five years old.

I pull away and my heart goes out to him. He's had a hard life. A very hard life.

When we rejoin the others, I glance back at the ship pursuing us. It's fallen behind some more. Despite the oncoming darkness, I see it now just fine without the telescope. Since it's the only ship not at port, it stands out. I expect once it gets moving, it'll maintain that distance in its attempt to catch up to us.

The Captain wanders up at that point, and I ask something that's on my mind. "What if they fire on us? I assume they have cannons."

He laughs. "They definitely have cannons! But only one that can fire forwards. I expect they'll fire eventually, but my hope is that they'll hold off until we're well away from the city."

"Why's that?"

He laughs. "We're running from the King! They'd be fully within their right to fire on us. However, if we're out of sight of the city and a ship fires on us, we can easily claim we feared they were pirates and push on to get away. Once we're at the farming community, they'll arrest us, but we'll have no trouble getting the charges dropped. Besides, if they fire within sight of the city, people will ask questions. Parthun prefers to keep the people in the dark."

"You're not afraid?"

Captain Stevrick turns to me, his face serious. "Your Majesty. Perhaps you may not be aware of what it has been like over the last eleven, nearly twelve years. Parthun has been cruel. He has controlled everything. We cannot do anything without breaking some rule. The people have lived as slaves, especially those of us in the capital. I certainly am afraid. That usurper will do all he can to punish those he suspects might resist him, but we are also ready to die for our freedom. I expect Lord Yune and Captain Tilbur will manage to free us, but if they cannot, our captivity or even our deaths will be a small price to pay to ensure our children live free. We are all Sevordines or Talics, and all of us live to see you take your throne." He grabs me by the shoulder. He's not a tall man, but he's strong, and his grip almost hurts. "Listen, Your Majesty, you must take the throne. Whatever the cost. Free your people!"

Tears form in his eyes, and he quickly turns and rushes away. He barks out some orders at his men, telling them to do what they're already doing before he rushes into his Captain's quarters and closes the door.

"I think you embarrassed him, Draydon," Roran announces unhelpfully.

# 15

## The Nimville

can barely breathe. I stand at the railing of the ship, staring out at the shore… trying to make sense of what I see. I'm hoping I just don't understand. I'm hoping it's just a trick of the light, or maybe it's a village I didn't know about… one that had been destroyed years ago for some other reason.

"What happened?" I ask Captain Stevrick. "Isn't that Port?"

Port is the first of the fishing villages—the one closest to Sevord. The sun has nearly set, a full day into our journey, and it's a little hard to see, especially at such a distance from shore, but from what I can tell, the place is burnt to the ground.

Captain Stevrick doesn't answer at first. Instead, he just stares at the small town. After a long time, he speaks, his voice cracking with emotion. "Yes, that is Port. It's actually where I grew up. Few people leave Port, or any of the fishing villages, but I wanted to sail a larger boat." He shakes his head. "A rumor went out that Port did not fully support the King. It wasn't true. They supported him as well as anyone else. They didn't like it, but they didn't do anything wrong. I think there might have been a few dissenters, but nothing to threaten Parthun's rule. The King sent four hundred soldiers to, as he put it, 'Squash the rebellion'."

"Did anyone survive?"

Stevrick shakes his head. "Four hundred soldiers against a village like Port is not sent to teach the people a lesson. Those kinds of numbers are intended to wipe everyone out. If anyone survived, they have hidden themselves so well, no one will find them."

"Your family?"

He shakes his head. "My wife and children live in Sevord. They're safe—for now. My parents, my brothers, my sister, aunts, uncles, cousins, nephews… all gone. Everyone I grew up with. Gone." He turns to me, and I see the pain in his eyes, but also the determination. "You understand why we all risk our lives to see that man removed?"

I nod.

"This isn't the only time over the last twelve years that this kind of thing has happened. No one talks about it for fear of bringing down Parthun's wrath. Port isn't the first village to be wiped off the map because of that man's craving for power, or fear of losing it. The only reason I can speak so openly now is because the crew is loyal and we're on the open sea."

I don't want to be uncaring, but I have to ask the next question. "The other villages?"

"They're fine. They all have garrisons in them, but they are fine."

"Garrisons? You mean, Parthun has stationed soldiers in each village?"

"He has. Which is part of why it'll be tricky to drop you anywhere but the farming villages. The Northern Tribes, as a people, appear so placid and uninterested in anything political that the King doesn't bother with them. Last we heard, there was no garrison there."

"Appear?"

He smiles, but it's a sad smile. "Yes, appear. People like Parthun are easily fooled into thinking farmers are no threat. He thinks fishermen are simple folk and farmers are easily controlled." His eyes bore into me as he says, "If the day comes that you call the people to fight, the men and women of the coast will be some of your greatest warriors. As they have been in the past. Farmers and Fishermen don't fight for glory, they fight for what's right, and that is what makes a true warrior. Your father knew that. But Parthun does not. It used to be that Grimmer and Port's loyalties were split between the proper heir and a total lack of concern for who sat on the throne. Now that Port has been destroyed, Grimmer will not hesitate to support you, and the other villages will follow you without question. What he has done to Port will turn any who supported the King up and down the Sevordine coast to your side."

I look back to Port. The small town is behind us now. I can barely see any of it anymore. My heart goes out to them. Or those who used to live there.

"Sir," a man says, coming up to the Captain. "I believe the ship behind us is closing the gap. It's not much, but they are gaining on us."

At that moment, I hear the boom of a cannon in the distance.

The Captain turns and screams out orders. I don't understand anything of what he's saying, but the men rush around. I think we're picking up speed—not much, but a little.

I remember with dread that the soldiers behind us aren't interested in arresting us. They want us dead.

I stand on the deck with Ellcia in the early morning light. We've both been given cups of coffee by the cook. He's a bit of a scary guy. His eyes are wild, he moves in weird, jerking movements, and he looks like he's about to stab anyone who comes too close, but in the end, I think he's a nice guy. At least I hope he is.

Actually, I have no reason to believe he's a nice guy at all, other than the fact that he makes good coffee. Even when he walked away, he kept glancing back at us with that wild, scary look, complete with an insane smile.

"He's like a…" I begin.

"Goblin," Ellcia says, finishing my thought.

She laughs quietly and leans up against me for a moment before pulling away. She's taken to wearing a scarf over her head on the deck of the ship. I think it's partly because she hates her hair so short, but also because of the cold wind. Her scalp must be freezing.

I lean back against her for a moment. I know we should be really scared and tense, but the cannons haven't fired since sunset last night, and it's been pretty peaceful. Captain Stevrick figures we'll reach the farming communities before nightfall this evening.

The others are still asleep downstairs, but Ellcia and I wanted to be up. We're going to be passing Nimville shortly. In the short time we lived there, I'd grown the love the place. So had Ellcia. If we weren't… who we are… I think we might actually want to settle in that community. I'd be happy working on the fishing boats, and Ellcia loved working for Hella.

I also liked the muscle I built. I'm far stronger now than I've ever been in my life. It feels good to be in such great shape.

A bit of mist has moved in over the night, and we can't see the ship tailing us. Now and then the first mate calls down from the crow's nest to let the Captain know he still doesn't see anything. I'm hoping we've lost them.

Ellcia and I begin to reminisce about our time in Nimville again, when the first mate calls down. "Captain, ship sighted on our aft, thirty degrees to port! They're nearly upon us!"

The Captain rushes past, yelling out more orders. Before his men even have time to react, I nearly yell in terror as the cannon booms. It's far louder at such a close distance. As I look back, I think I can make out the silhouette of the pursuing warship in the thinning mist.

A wave of anger rushes over me. That's my ship! That's my crew! Those are my soldiers! That traitor is using my own men to kill me, kill Ellcia, and kill my friends!

Ellcia grips my arm, and I pull her in close. In a way, I want to hide below deck, but I'm staying up here. Maybe the men need to see their future King—to see the man they're fighting for.

We move off to the side as two men rush by. As we do, I catch sight of the shore. Toward land, the mist is lighter, and I recognize the area. We're just south of Nimville. If we're caught, we'll die just offshore of our home.

"Vessel sighted. Two hundred yards off the bow!" The first mate's voice carries well in the stillness of the air in the early morning.

I look forward. I can't believe Parthun's men managed to get someone ahead of us. How's that even possible?

"Fishing vessel!" he calls down.

"Nordin!" I look at Ellcia, and she's as terrified as I am.

Of course they'd be out at this time! If we run into them, or if they get hit by a shot from the cannon, they won't survive.

Another cannon fires and hits just off the starboard side. The Captain screams out more orders, and four men rush below to work the oars. That should give us just enough extra speed to get away—I hope.

We've turned portside just a little, perhaps enough to miss Nordin. I catch sight of his ship, slowly moving to the starboard side, and I race across the deck.

"Nordin!" I yell.

"Ric? Ric, is that ya?" Nordin replies, using the nickname they used for me in Nimville.

"Nordin!" I can see the ship well and make out the crew on board. Relin's at the helm, and Nordin and a couple other men lean against the railing. "You have to get out of here! We're being chased, and they're firing cannons! Get out of here! Protect yourselves!"

There's a pause, but just for a second before Nordin calls back. "Ric, we'll take care of them. When ya see the white flag go up, put down anchor and we'll come join ya."

He turns and ignores me after this, even though I yell repeatedly for him to stay out of it. But it's not long before we're past him and we've passed another two of Nordin's boats. I don't know what he's doing, but he's called to the others and has ordered them to do the Tallia maneuver.

I have no idea what that is, but Tallia was the name of my mom. Nordin served under my dad, General Geran, so I expect this was one of my dad's strategies.

We sail on as another cannon boom disturbs the morning, and a splash showers the hull of the Wavebreaker. They definitely want us dead—there's no doubt in my mind about that—but the fact that they're missing… that's weird. Then it hits me. Not a shot from a cannon. That would be really bad. I finally get it. I get what's going on. They do want me dead, but they want it confirmed. It's not enough to sink the ship. If they do that, there's no way to know if any of us survived. But if they board us and can kill us, they'll have our bodies as proof.

Well… Roran and Marleet, anyway. I guess Parthun still doesn't know I'm alive. But if those soldiers board this ship, he'll find out pretty soon.

"What are they're going to do?" the Captain asks as he runs up. "What's the Tallia maneuver?"

I shake my head. "I don't know. But I do know that the man I just spoke with and many of his men served under my father. They're fishermen, but they're also soldiers."

I see the outline of at least four of Nordin's boats. I think maybe I see a fifth, but I can't be sure. They appear to just be drifting, but I expect at least three of them will end up on one side of the ship behind us, while the other two will end up on the other side.

They're far away, but I can just barely make out Nordin and the other crew members jumping up and down and hollering. Another blast from the cannon pulls me away as this one actually flies right over our heads and takes out the railing on the starboard side of the ship.

My whole body shakes. We were standing right there just a moment ago.

"Get below deck, now!" the Captain screams at us.

I want to refuse—I feel like a coward for going below, but I gave my word to Captain Stevrick. We rush for the door leading down to the hold, but before I set foot on the stairs, I call out. "Captain! The fisherman said to look for the white flag rising on the other ship. When it goes up, we should put down anchor and wait for them to come to us."

Captain Stevrick looks horrified at the thought of dropping anchor, but he nods, and I drop down below, following Ellcia.

"What's going on?" Marleet asks as she rushes up to us. "We heard the cannons and more, but we thought we should stay out of their way."

I nod. "The warship has just about caught up to us. We're at Nimville, and Nordin and his crews are, I think, going after the other ship."

Marleet and Roran look a little surprised, but Hemot just stares at me with his mouth hanging open. He slowly starts to shake his head, and then says, "But… they're not… I mean… they used to be soldiers, but they can't board a warship and take down… actual soldiers! If it's all five of his ships, that's only… twenty-five men. They'll never…"

"I know. I told him to get out of the way, but they wouldn't listen."

We wait below, listening to the sound of feet beat across the deck above us, the shouts of Captain Stevrick and the crew, and the occasional shot from the cannon.

Ellcia and I are holding each other, and I see Hemot holding Marleet. I feel bad for Roran, just standing there alone… and I almost reach out for him, but then I think that'll be really weird. So… I don't.

After about ten minutes, there's a change above us. I can't quite put my finger on what it is, but the sound of the men running across the deck and the tone of the voices are all different.

The hatch above us swings open, and the Captain scrambles half-way down the steps. "Your Majesty, the white flag is up on the warship. Are you sure you can trust this fisherman?"

"I laugh. I trust him more than I trust myself!"

Captain Stevrick frowns, but nods at me. He waves for all of us to follow, and he climbs back up.

"Lower the sails! Drop anchor!"

The men don't look pleased with the order, but they obey.

I watch the warship lower its sails and drift in our direction. When they're close enough to drop their own anchor, I see Nordin at the helm. The rest of the men are either climbing all over the ship, adjusting the lines, or they're working on something in the center of the deck.

I can't see what the men are working on as the deck of the warship sits much higher than the trading vessel I'm on, but I have a pretty good idea.

They pull right up next to us, and within moments, the ships are secured to one another. I call up to Nordin, "Permission to come aboard, Captain Nordin?"

He lets out a large laugh and calls back, "Permission granted, Ric!"

I climb up the ropes on the side of the warship. Hemot scrambles up beside me, but the others didn't just spend two months on fishing boats, and they struggle to maintain their grip on the ropes and keep their footing.

I help Ellcia and Roran, while Hemot helps Marleet, and we scramble over the side onto the deck.

The others immediately turn away from the scene before them, but I force myself to look. The men, despite the fact that they were working for Parthun, were my men. I am their future King. I'm responsible for each soldier.

Before me lies a pile of bodies. Nordin's men work quickly to strip them of their armor and weapons, and then toss the bodies over the side. I want to suggest that we return the bodies to their families, but I know how unrealistic that is.

"Are ya…" Nordin begins.

"I'm Draydon," I say. Nordin and the others had agreed to call me Ric for the months I was here to hide my identity. I expect no one would know what they should call me now. "All these men with us are loyal to the throne." I pause for a moment, then quietly ask, "Are the warship's sailors… are they all dead?"

Nordin nods gravely. "I'm sorry, Yar Highness. They're all dead."

"Did we lose any?"

"No. We caught them by surprise. We had half their number killed before they even knew were on board. It was a good thing they were sparsely crewed. We managed to capture the Captain, but he tried to escape and attacked Relin. He didn't realize Relin is… well… he's Relin. The Captain died before he even got close."

I nod. I do that a lot these days. It's my way of accepting what's been said but having no idea how to respond.

"What is the Tallia maneuver?"

Nordin laughs and comes up to me, slapping me on my back. "It's named after yar mother. Yar father spoke about how yar mother used to play this game with ya where she and yar nursemaid would chase ya around the courtyard, boxing ya in and jumping out on either side of ya. Yar father, whenever he flanked an enemy, called it the Tallia Maneuver."

I feel proud of that. It makes me feel like I'm more a part of all this than I thought, and it's like it's kept a part of my parents alive.

A few minutes later, the last of the bodies goes over the side. I'm not too concerned about the bodies washing up on shore. The ocean takes care of that kind of thing. And there are a few sharks in this area.

"So, Prince Draydon," Nordin says with a smile. "Ya now have your first ship in yar new fleet."

I look around, and my mouth drops open. He's right. I think this is one of the biggest ships in the navy, and I think there's only two of this class of warship in total. This is a significant win.

"I'd like a tour."

Nordin smiles. "I'd love to give ya one, but we have a bit of a problem. Once the mist clears, the garrison in town will see both ships. It'll be harder to take the soldiers by surprise. We need to go deal with them now before they cause trouble."

I nod at him, and he and the other men rush off, climbing over the side and down onto their boats. He leaves three of his men on board, but I send them with him anyway. I don't want him to be shorthanded when he faces the garrison.

I call down to Captain Stevrick and explain the situation. A few minutes later, he's on the other side of the railing. "Permission to come aboard, Captain?"

I laugh. "Come on, Stevrick. But I'm not the Captain of this ship. Nordin is. He'll be back once he deals with the garrison in town."

The man furrows his brow. "Nordin, you say?"

"You know him?"

"I've heard of him. He's a bit of a war hero. I…" He looks back toward the beach with a look of awe on his face. "They call him Nordin Trollslayer. They say he actually killed one, but I have no idea how. I didn't think that kind of thing was possible."

My mouth drops open. A troll? Really? Nordin's actually a pretty humble guy. He'll talk about the war, he'll talk about fishing, he'll talk about others, but he never brags. Never even comes close.

I decide to let that one go and focus on the moment. "I need you to secure the ship. Nordin has gone with all his men to deal with the garrison in Nimville, and I don't know what else needs to be taken care of here. But I'm guessing the ship just can't sit."

Captain Stevrick salutes me, which feels a little weird, and then calls down to four of his men. They scramble up the side and onto the deck, not asking permission to board, which is probably fine. I don't know all the protocols for that kind of thing.

A few minutes later, they've moved through the entire ship, and they give a report to Captain Stevrick. It sounds like the ship is in good condition.

I wander toward the stern. Hemot and the others have gone down below to see the cannons, but I'm curious about the Captain's quarters. The door is unlocked, and I wander in.

I'm a little shocked. On one hand, it's quite elaborate. Beautifully designed and decorated. Decorative swords on the wall. Paintings. Little statues secured to shelves.

But I'm also surprised at how small it is. I guess it makes sense. Maybe they don't want to take up too much space, but I would have thought it would be larger.

In the center is a small table with some maps secured on top. There are no chairs, aside from one near the wall. Above it is a fold-out table, latched to the side wall. The bed is also smaller than the bed I slept in as a servant, although when I push on it, it's far softer.

For a moment, I lose myself in a daydream of what it would be like to stay in this room on a long journey, sailing to far distant lands.

"Whoa!" Hemot says, pulling me back. "Look at this! We could all fit in here!"

The others laugh, but I can see they're impressed. Despite how cramped it is, the Captain's quarters is decorated like some of the finer rooms in the castle.

"You've gotta see down below!" Hemot says.

I glance at the others, and they're all just as excited.

We leave the Captain's quarters and head down some steps, then on the main deck, we take the stairs down into the hold. I'm surprised, at first, at how low the ceiling is in this area. The boat is high enough, I'd think they're be plenty of room, but then Ellcia tells me there are three more decks below this one. They've only peeked down at the next one, but they wanted to come get me.

The deck we're on is the one with the cannons. It's amazing! The area stinks like smoke and gunpowder, but I've never actually seen cannons up this close. I can count six right away, but the area is dark, and dividers and support walls separate the area.

"Hemot counted sixteen cannons altogether. Seven on each side and one on the front, and one on the back!" Marleet says. It's fun to hear her voice return to the less-serious Marleet now and then.

We scramble down below and find storage and crew quarters. By "crew quarters" I mean more of a whack of bunks and hammocks. They're packed in so tightly in spots that if the boat shifted even slightly with a wave, the hammocks would swing into one another.

Below that area is a hold which is largely empty at the moment, then another hold below that. I'm surprised at how much water is in the bottom deck. It stinks down here like mildew, and we don't stay long.

We return to the main deck and explore some more. I find two more officer's quarters, although neither are as nice—or as large—as the Captain's quarters, and then I find a nice, comfortable room that I suspect is for a Noble or… Admiral… or maybe the King. I'm not sure. We also find other rooms, including a kitchen and some we don't know the purpose of.

It strikes me at that moment how large of a crew this ship could hold. Guessing by the bunks below, the officer's quarters, and just the space, I think hundreds could fit on board.

We continue to explore for the next hour before we see Nordin's ships coming back. I'm relieved to see them. I've been nervous about my friend's safety. I don't even know how large the garrison was, so I have no idea if it would have been difficult or simple to deal with them. Nor do I know if the garrison was made up of men loyal to Parthun or loyal to the throne.

When Nordin's boats arrive, I'm surprised to see them packed with people. One of the first up the ropes and over this side is Hella—surprisingly not struggling with the ropes at all. She has a large grin on her face, although I can see sadness in her eyes.

She runs up to Ellcia and wraps her arms around her, holding her tight and whispering in her ear. After a moment, the two begin to weep. Hella, in the short time we stayed in Nimville, became like a mother to Ellcia.

When they part, she comes to me and gives me a hug, puts her hand on my cheek and asks, "Are you eating enough?"

I laugh and give a nod. She then turns to Hemot and does the same, although he shakes his head and says, "No."

I look back toward the side where Hella had climbed onto the ship, and a crowd of people are coming over the railing. Nordin and his men are fast on the ropes and slip up and down, carrying supplies. The people are clearly not here to see the ship—they're moving in.

"What's going on?"

Hella smiles at me and reaches back to pull a child over the railing and onto the deck. I feel embarrassed that I didn't jump in to help. The five of us rush over and assist the people, grabbing their packs and helping them move out of the way. When everyone is on board, Nordin and his crews take the boats back—I assume for another load of people and supplies.

Hella comes up to me and smiles again. "So, I hear you're Prince Draydon now, heir to the throne?"

"I am."

"Good. You must be starving."

"Because I'm Prince Draydon or because I'm heir to the throne?"

"Because you're a seventeen-year-old boy!"

I laugh. "You've got me there."

"All right. Show me to the galley, and I'll make you a meal while I explain all that's going on."

I shake my head. "I have no idea what a galley is."

"Oh, my dear Princeling. You have much to learn about large vessels. The galley is the kitchen. I need to settle in and start preparing meals. It won't be long before we have an entire hungry village to feed!"

I grab one of her packs and hoist it up onto my shoulders. Roran grabs another, Hemot grabs yet another, and Marleet and Ellcia pick up the last one together. I lead Hella back to the kitchen, or the galley, and she immediately begins to unpack. Two of the young ladies who worked in her kitchen at her inn join in, and Ellcia gives a hand. She worked with Hella long enough to figure out what she needs to do.

As Hella sets about to make me a meal—although I can see she's not just prepping for me—she explains.

"Not long after you left, a boat arrived, dropping off a dozen soldiers. They'd been ordered to set up a garrison in Nimville. But they were not there to protect. They were there to keep an eye on us, to harass us, and to terrify us."

I shake my head in shock, and she stops chopping long enough to look me in the eye. "Oh, my dear Prince, you don't think they were successful, do you? Have you ever even met my husband? What about Relin?" She laughs, shakes her head, and returns to her chopping. "Nordin let them do what they want for a day or two. He's quite the thinker, that husband of mine. He watched them closely— even staying on shore rather than going out on the boats. The moment they stepped out of line, he, Relin, and about forty others—all soldiers in another time—approached the garrison and put them in their place. They've been pretty quiet since."

I shake my head and chuckle. I think I can picture Nordin doing that. He and Relin can be scary guys when they want to be.

"But we all knew the moment those soldiers arrived that our time in Nimville was finished. It was just a matter of when. We kept an eye on the situation, and when you showed up today, we knew the day had come. Nordin removed the garrison this morning." She looks at me with a serious expression on her face. "Don't worry. None were loyal men. Scoundrels, each of them. Nordin actually served with the father of one of the men. He was a scoundrel himself. Taught his son well. So, they're all dead, and we're moving our village to the open sea."

She throws some wood into the stove and brings the temperature up a bit. She acts like she's been cooking in here for years. Which is strange, since I know Hella has never even left the village.

"I had figured we'd need to head north on foot once we were forced to deal with the soldiers, but this has turned out well. It'll be far more difficult to track us down, and you now have the first ship for your new navy."

"You were going to head north?" I glance over at Ellcia. I can't imagine the entire town simply packing up and… leaving. Just walking north. In the middle of winter. "That's… huge. Everyone was okay with that?"

Hella nods. "It's the way it is, Prince Draydon. To return the throne to the rightful heir, which is you now that Prince Roran has abdicated, our town will need to sacrifice. We have prepared. We were packed and ready to go. The weapons stores were ready, and the fishing boats were stocked with swords and bows in case the need arose— which it did today. We were prepared. And now our future

King has provided a warship for us. It's more than we expected, and we are grateful."

She lays out five plates of food. She apologizes that the food is cold, but tells us she'll have a hot meal ready soon. This is just to tie us over.

We dig in. I'm surprised at how hungry I am, but then again, Hella is an amazing cook. She can make anything taste good.

When we're finished, Hella tells me I need to go walk among the people. I need to see them and talk with them. They need to see the one they're fighting for. I feel a little awkward with that, but Hella and Nordin tend to know what they're talking about with most things.

We head out, and Marleet pulls the others back a bit. I find myself walking alone with the other four behind me. I want to tell them to come stand with me, but Marleet, like Hella, like Nordin, and like just about everyone else, knows this kind of thing better than me. I do remember seeing Parthun, when he was the Regent, walking with others a step or two behind him. I think it's the way of Royals.

Maybe I'll change it when I take the throne, but I don't think now's the time to try to do that.

We walk along the main deck. Not too many people are still up top. Most appear to have gone down below. We wander and chat with some people. They all either curtsy or bow. Some try to do both at the same time. I'm not sure what to make of that.

Within minutes, I'm glad I'm doing this. Ever since I decided to claim the throne, I've been plagued with doubt. It mainly surrounded the idea that I can't believe that people would actually want to follow me. I mean, I could try to lead, but who would want to follow? Even if they did follow, I figured it would likely only be because I was born into royalty—not because they wanted me.

But as I walk and speak with people, I quickly find that they do actually want... me. It's like I'm actually important to them. They all appear sad to leave their home—most have lived in Nimville their whole lives, going back generations and never intending to leave—but they're all committed to this.

Committed to me.

We head below, and it's not long before I find people settling into the crew quarters. They appear to have found ways to separate areas to keep it private for individual families. They have also taken over part of the hold to use as a small school and play area for the children. Some are even doing a bit of decorating.

But what's most fascinating and encouraging among the people is an unwavering belief that they are doing the right thing.

When we return to the main deck, Nordin's next load is here, and the others and I help as best we can. I notice a lot of weapons come with this load. Nordin had a shed just outside of town where he kept his arsenal. I had thought it was enough to equip around thirty men, but I think it's definitely more than that.

When I consider the weapons and armor taken from the soldiers on the warship, plus what we have from the garrison, I think we're well equipped. Not to fight an entire war, but equipped for the beginnings of such a war.

I just hope it never comes to that.

As Nordin goes back for what he believes to be the final load, I help the new arrivals find their way around the ship. Despite the fact that I lived and worked among them for two months, when I pick up their belongings to carry them below, they look at me with a mixture of shock and admiration.

I see Marleet whispering to the others, and next thing I know, they're all calling me Prince Draydon, or Your

Highness, or Your Majesty. At first, I think they're mocking me, but then I see the sincerity in their eyes.

When Nordin returns again, this time with his final load, I once again help the new arrivals and then join in with taking the stores down below.

When we're done, I smell the meal Hella has made. I highly doubt she could make enough for every person on board. There has to be somewhere around four hundred at the moment, and that's not counting Captain Stevrick's crew.

Before we can dig in, however, Nordin sends word, and everyone comes on deck. I mean everyone. All the adults, elderly, children. All of them.

The children squirm and wiggle while Nordin takes his spot up on a raised part of the deck. I expect I'll have to learn the name of the decks and more at some point, but for now it just seems like a lot of confusing terms.

He begins with some comfort and encouragement for what they've left behind, but then reminds them of what lies ahead. As he speaks, they all listen intently. Even Captain Stevrick. He hasn't tried to push on or anything. He just seems content to be here.

When Nordin finishes, the people clap and cheer. I do too. He's a fantastic public speaker and what a motivator!

But then he turns to me and waves me forward.

Nordin places his large hand on my shoulder. "This young man lived among us for two months. We called him Ric and refused to show him the respect due his station. Not out of stubbornness or rebellion did we treat him as nothing but common, but out of a desire to protect him. But today, he is safe, and he is recognized as a Prince of Sevord, and the man next in line for the throne."

Then Nordin drops to his knees, and I nearly groan. I kind of want the whole "Prince" thing to take a rest for a bit.

"I, Nordin Trollslayer, Lieutenant under General Geran, and leading man of Nimville, along with my wife, Hella…" at that moment, Hella slips in beside him, also dropping to her knees, "now pledge myself to the throne and my future King, Prince Draydon. I declare now our fealty to our King."

Hella nods and then they both rise to their feet. I hear a lot of movement, and turn to see everyone on board, including Captain Stevrick, have dropped to their knees. They all then shout out similar words to what Nordin has just said, all at different times and different speeds. It's a mess, and it's hard to make sense of what they're saying, but I think they all just swore fealty to me.

When they're finished, they rise and wait. I nearly frown. It's one of those times when I'm supposed to say something non-dumb. I don't do non-dumb well.

I hold up both my arms, and then realize that probably looks silly, but it's too late, so I go with it. "My friends. I hear your promise, and I accept it with humility. And I give a promise back to you. I promise that I will serve you and the people of Sevord as your King, with kindness and the same loyalty that you have offered to me."

I don't know if that was good, but the people seem pleased. I meant every word of it, too. Nordin looks like he's about to walk away, but I stop him.

"Nordin, as your future King, I now return your status in the military, but I also promote you to Captain, transfer you to my navy, and offer you this ship as your charge. And I rename this warship the Nimville after the brave people who hold it for their King."

The people begin to scream, and at first I think they're about to attack me, but they're going crazy with excitement. Some of them hug the railings on the boat, while others jump up and down.

I kind of meant it as a small gesture of my gratitude to them, but clearly this is big for them.

Nordin comes up to me with a large grin and tears in his eyes, grabs me and lifts me right off the ground. "Thank ya, thank ya," he whispers in my ear.

I suppress a shudder at the feel of his whiskers on my ear. I do not enjoy that.

He drops me to the ground, and everyone cheers again before they begin to disperse. It's amazing how intense they can be one moment, then just wander off the next.

The people of Nimville are pretty fantastic.

# 16

## The Frippolee

Two hours later, the ship has set sail, heading north. Nordin's fishing boats follow along. They're much, much slower than the Nimville, but they still move at a decent speed. With Nordin's five fishing boats and this warship, I now have a fleet.

It's just as well that we're moving slow. Captain Stevrick took the Wavebreaker on ahead. He has also pledged allegiance to me, but he says we will need to keep separate to protect us from suspicion. Such a move should help to hide the fact that the warship has been taken over—at least for the moment.

Nordin has appointed anyone with any experience in war, fighting, or even travel as a soldier and equipped them with armor in addition to filling out his crew to man the ship. It turns out a ship like this takes a lot of people working really hard to keep it moving.

"I need to get back out on deck in a few minutes, but I believe we have a few things to discuss," Nordin explains as he gestures to the table, and we gather around.

This room is one I didn't find on my tour earlier today. It's not a big room, but it has a table in the center secured to the floor. It's perfect for looking at maps and discussing private matters.

Normally, at what we used to call our Council of Lords, I would start the meeting by inviting everyone to sit. But… no chairs in this room. So, we set aside the plan to sit. Around the room stand Nordin, Hella, Relin, Phimon, Gran, Roran, Hemot, Marleet, and Ellcia. They are, at present, my Lords and Ladies.

I address the group. "I call this meeting to order. The Captain needs to get out of here soon, so we won't discuss much." I turn to Nordin and ask, "What are your hopes for where to go from here?"

"We hope to head north. On the other side of the farming communities, there's some good fishing. I propose to head there while we await yar orders. But that move is dependent on ya, Yar Majesty. If we are going to war, we will need to offload the non-combatants."

I nod. "I have another matter to deal with before we can take back the kingdom. Besides, I have received word from Lord Yune that the timing is not right to take the throne. I will most certainly be killed if I try."

"What is it ya have to do?" Nordin asks. "What are our orders?"

Now, this is the problem. Sailing north is fine and all, but I have to cross the Talic Region. The only way to that area is through Switcher Pass, which is south of here. It's about a week's journey from Nimville, but from the farming communities… I would say it'd be a two-week hike, just to get to the pass. Then another nearly three weeks to cross the Talic. Every mile we sail north is one mile I'll have to walk south again.

"Your orders are to head to that fishing spot, but to send ships back to the farming communities now and then. When I call, I'll need you to come."

"And ya, Your Highness?" Nordin asks.

"We have to cross the Talic. So, we'll head south again from the farming communities."

Nordin looks at me a little funny. "You mean, so ya can cross through Switcher Pass?"

I nod.

He glances over at Relin, who frowns back. Nordin turns to me and pauses for a moment before looking like he just decided to do something foolish. "There is a rumor—just a rumor—that there's a way through the cliffs up north. I have heard tell of it a few times, but no one has been able to find it. If ya'd like, we can track it down. Relin and I believe it does exist."

"But…" I begin. There are many things I've always believed that turned out not to be true. But another path through to the Talic Region? It was always said there was only one way. Well, I mean, you could travel for weeks through a barren wasteland, up and around. But no one considers that an option when you could simply walk through Switcher Pass. "Are you sure it exists?"

Nordin shakes his head. "No, not completely sure, but pretty sure. Relin and I have heard a lot of stories about it. Enough to make us think it's doable." He frowns. "Honestly, I wouldn't even suggest it if I didn't think ya'd be risking your neck by going south. From what ya've told me of all that's happened in recent days, security will only get tighter from here on. I fear, Yar Highness, if ya go anywhere near Sevord, ya'll be captured."

"Then we'd better find this other passage," I say with a smile.

Relin shakes his head. "Yar Majesty…" He purses his lips and shakes his head again before saying, "From what I hear, it's dangerous. Not just a little dangerous. But VERY dangerous. There are gratters in that area, along with some of the big cats, and it's even been suspected that the Talic Wolves originally came from there. Plus, who knows what else is up there?" He glances at Nordin and frowns again before saying, "Personally, I think the reason no one can say for sure that it's there is because no one survives the trip through."

That makes me frown. "How do we find more information about the path? As in exactly where it is and more? And how to get through."

Relin shrugs. "I don't know exactly, Yar Majesty, but I suspect the people in the farming communities will either know a bit more or have more rumors to go on."

I don't like the sound of all this, but I think Nordin's right. We won't likely make it through Switcher Pass again—especially after the escape we just managed. Parthun would know we're on this side of the cliffs and would block off Switcher Pass to keep us contained.

"Orders, Yar Highness?" Nordin asks.

The room goes silent, and everyone watches me. I glance at Ellcia. I'd kind of like to get her advice, but Nordin taught me that certain decisions simply need to be made. The information is before us. Ellcia would speak up if she had additional information. Now, the decision is mine.

"We'll head north and follow Nordin and Relin's lead on making use of this secret passage through to the Talic Region. The details of this journey will be worked out over the coming days, but in the meantime, Nordin needs to return to the deck. We head for the farming communities." I look around at each person on my Council of Lords and Ladies before declaring, "You are dismissed."

They file out. I don't know what lies ahead with Nordin's secret path, but I don't think I like the sound of it. I don't know what a gratter is, or a big cat, but I certainly don't want to come face to face with another Talic Wolf.

But whatever we have to face, I need to fulfill my promise to Roran.

Two days later, we're approaching the farming communities. The area has no official name, although the people here call themselves the Northern Tribe. There's apparently some reason behind that, but no one remembers what it is. Even among the people.

The settlement is made up of over two thousand people. The main industry is, of course, growing crops for the kingdom. The people live well, seeing as they sell food to much of Sevord and the Talic, although shipping takes a large portion of their profits.

It's a strange sight, actually. In Sevord City and Nimville, the cliffs were always close. There's no real room for farmland. But here... here is different. The cliffs have angled toward the east so far that, while I can make them out in the distance, they're certainly not close.

Between here and the cliffs, the fields spread out for miles. There's nothing growing on them at the moment, of course, seeing as it's well into winter. Snow covers much of it, but the brown dirt pokes through in many spots. The fields appear to go on and on forever.

When we reached the mountains where the rebels lived, I remembered looking out over the fields and thinking that was a lot of crops. But that was nothing compared to this.

I wonder to myself what it would be like to be a farmer. I can't help but think it would be hard work but involve fewer people trying to kill me.

The thing that adds to the appeal of farming, in addition to less frequent assassination plots, are the houses. All along the fields, here and there with roads connecting them and connecting it all to the port, are small cottages with smoke drifting up from their chimneys.

It looks so peaceful.

"We'll be docked within half an hour, Yar Highness," Nordin says, coming up behind me. "Are ya sure you want to go through with this?"

"I am. It's time, Nordin."

I feel Nordin's large hand on my shoulder. "The crew and the people of Nimville are behind ya, Yar Majesty."

"Thank you, Captain. I'm counting on it."

Nordin walks away, and I sense someone else has approached. I know it's one of my friends, because everyone else announces themselves.

I feel the person take my arm. Unless it's Hemot trying to be annoying, it's Ellcia.

"I'm nervous."

I put my arm around her and hold her close. "Me too. But I think this is the right move."

She leans in and confidently says, "I know, and I agree. But it's still scary."

"Yup."

She's right. It certainly is scary. I'm not sure how this will go, but it's time to stop hiding. Although I can't yet make a claim on the throne in Sevord and though it might put Tilbur at risk, it's time we all took a stand. It's time that the risk took us to a different place. In the last two days, I've realized it's time to step out of the shadows.

My warship, the Nimville, moves in toward the docks, and I watch as a large procession of people move from the center of the town toward us. Nordin was right. He figured if a warship arrived, the leading people of the Northern Tribe would come out and greet us as they'd assume a dignitary was approaching.

I think they'll be surprised who it is who steps off the boat.

Nordin knows a few of the people in this area. He served with some of them in the Battle of Reber's Gate. It's possible they might recognize my father's armor, and even recognize me as I look a lot like my father.

The Wavebreaker sits at the dock, and I see Captain Stevrick on board. I don't expect he's told them anything, but I assume he knows something's up by this point. Not only am I wearing my armor, but the seamstress from Nimville sewed me a cape and royal garments. I kind of look the part now, although the cape feels like overkill.

Once we're docked, the gangway is set out, and the procession from the town waits patiently at the end of the dock while one man walks forward. I'm guessing that's the Reeve. They don't have a Lord over this area, or a mayor. The man in charge, the Reeve, is elected by a council and oversees all political and judicial matters. Kind of like a Lord, but without the fancy title. He also doesn't receive his title for life. He's appointed by the community and affirmed by the King for a term of ten years.

When he reaches us, he positions himself opposite the gangway and waits. He keeps eyeing me. I would guess he's confused. I'm tall, that's for sure. Taller than the average man. After my time on Nordin's boat and with my armor, I'm certainly broad enough in the shoulders. I mean, I'm not like Nordin, but certainly as broad as the average man. But my face... I'm still only seventeen. I'm clearly the one in charge, but I'm sure my face suggests otherwise.

The soldiers—the men appointed by Nordin—file off the ship onto the dock dressed in the armor from the soldiers who had been on the ship a few days ago. They march just as Nordin taught them, and it's impressive. Aside from a few small slip-ups, they look like they've been doing this their entire lives.

They move down the gangway in twos, splitting apart at the dock and forming a line of soldiers on either side. When they're finished, I watch as Nordin's plan for how my procession advances.

Nordin himself goes down the gangway first, stepping onto the dock, and nodding to the Reeve. They speak for only a moment. Nordin told me he would inform the Reeve that this was a royal visit, but not mention the name.

Next, Relin moves down to the dock. Nordin tells me he has quite the reputation along the coast as "Relin, the Hero of Reber's Gate." Neither man would tell me how the title was attained—I could see it embarrassed Relin somewhat—so I just accepted it and let it go.

Next, Hemot disembarks. He's actually an important figure in the kingdom because of his parents, but since he himself has no legal status, aside from his claim to their personal wealth and land, his actual official status is low. Despite Hemot's protests, Nordin insisted that Hemot keep his mouth closed. I'm pleased to see Hemot offer a slow bow as Nordin introduces him, then he moves off to the side, closest to the land.

Next, Ellcia disembarks, and Nordin introduces her. Since she is an official Lady of the Kingdom, her presence carries a great deal of weight.

Fourth, Marleet steps forward and slowly walks down to the dock. She certainly moves the most gracefully out of everyone. That's quite a change from the awkward girl I grew up with. As the daughter of Lord Yune and Lady Aldora, and as an official Lady of the Court, which I learned was a higher status than Ellcia's status, she could possibly be the most powerful Noble ever to visit the farming communities in the Reeve's lifetime.

The effect such a move has on the Reeve is dramatic. Once Marleet, or the Lady Marleet, steps to the side, he looks up onto the deck of the boat with absolute wonder. Nordin had explained that the Reeve would have high expectations indeed if the Lady Marleet was not the primary dignitary.

Next, Roran disembarks. When the Reeve sees him, his face fills with confusion, but when Nordin introduces him, the former crown Prince of Sevord, the man perks right up. Then, when Roran steps to the side and waits, the man's eyes bulge with shock. Four more soldiers, complete with red sashes across their chests, move down the gangway and stop before stepping onto the dock. One of them calls out, "Make way!" and all the soldiers already on the dock march down another ten steps before the four men acting as my honor guard take up position, hands on the hilts of their swords, watching everyone as if they might be a threat.

It all feels a little too much, but Nordin insisted it was necessary.

So, when I slowly move down the gangway, stopping twice to look around and take in the scenery, the Reeve appears ready to drop to his knees.

When I reach the bottom, I do my best to follow Nordin's instructions. I wait patiently, staring hard at the Reeve, but not with a look of arrogance or in an unkind way. My instructions were to stare at him as if I were trying to understand him.

After a few moments, Nordin speaks. For the others, he spoke in a normal volume, but with me, he calls out, "It is my honor to introduce to the Reeve of the farming communities…"

I put my hand up. Nothing threatening, but just enough to signal Nordin to stop. When I do so, he gives me a slight bow and then steps to the side.

When the Reeve sees this, he looks at me with panic, but I smile at him, and give a respectful bow. "It is good to meet you. May I ask with whom I have the pleasure of speaking?"

The man stammers for a moment, but then catches himself. "My name is Frippolee, Sire… Sir… Your Ma… My Lord. I am the Reeve of this community."

I smile once again and give another bow. "It is an honor to meet you, Reeve Frippolee." I pause for just a moment before asking, "Do you know who I am, my friend?"

"No, My Lord. Please forgive my ignorance."

"There is nothing to forgive, Reeve. May I call you Frippolee?"

"Of course, My Lord."

"Thank you. I mean no disrespect. Are you certain I may speak so informally to you?"

"Absolutely, My Lord." Frippolee looks like he's about to pass out. I hope whatever Nordin has me doing to him with this approach works out.

"Excellent. Then I invite you to call me by my first name. Please, while in private, such as we are now, call me Draydon."

The man furrows his brow, then looks at me with confusion, then recognition fills his eyes. He opens his mouth to say something, but I interrupt him. "Frippolee, is there a place in which we might discuss important matters with more privacy?"

The Reeve opens his mouth, but nothing comes out at first. Nordin suspected there might not be a place in the area worthy of a dignitary, let alone a royal dignitary. "My Lord… Draydon… there is my office, but it is not a place fit for you and your entourage. It is small, only large enough for me and my assistant to have small meetings. There is the town hall. It is… larger. Perhaps that is the best place."

"How about your home?" I hadn't been sure about this, but Nordin had, once again, insisted.

"Oh, My Lord… I mean… Draydon… my home is not fit for visitors of your status."

"Frippolee?"

"Yes, Draydon?"

"Is it fit for you and your honor?"

"Yes, Draydon."

"Is there anyone there who might not be trustworthy for our private conversation?"

"No, Draydon. It is just me and my wife. She is a good woman. She will hold her tongue on all matters of which you wish, as will I."

"Then, if it is a place of confidence, and it is a place which is fit for you and your honor, then it will surpass my own needs by far." I give a smile and step in a little closer. Glancing to the sides, I add in a quiet voice, "I'm not one who needs all this pomp."

"Yar Highness," Nordin says. "This is necessary for the future King of Sevord."

I frown at Nordin but give him a bow. "It is true, I guess. But it is far more than I need. Or desire."

At that, Nordin gives his own bow. "It is one of yar many qualities which inspire loyalty in yar subjects, Yar Highness."

I turn back to Frippolee and give another bow. "Is it possible, my friend, to meet in your home soon? Perhaps with you, your wife, and any trustworthy leaders of the community? Only those you wish to have there, of course."

"Of course, Your Highness, I mean, Draydon. Of course. We will leave at once. If it pleases you, will you follow me?"

We head down the dock, but before we move too far, I take Frippolee by the arm. "My friend, if it is acceptable to you, I wish to keep my identity a secret for the moment from anyone who might not be at this meeting. At least until we work through the matters on my heart."

"Of course." Pointing to those who came with him in his procession, he says, "All those you see before you will be joining us."

Turning back to Nordin, I say, "Please remain with the ship, Captain. My honor guard will be enough."

And with that, we move off, with two of my honor guard leading the way, with me and Frippolee following, with Marleet, Ellcia, Hemot, and Roran behind us, followed by the other two of my honor guard, and finally the men and women from Frippolee's procession.

I think I have managed to follow Nordin's instructions perfectly, so far. We will see if I can continue when he's not around.

I sit on Frippolee's couch.

The walk to the Reeve's house was interesting… to say the least.

Everyone stared, but no one did it openly. We walked past a market selling clothes, thread, gifts, odds and ends, small farming equipment, and more. Everyone more or less continued what they were doing, but I knew they were looking at us.

Countless eyes stared out through windows. Children peered over and around barrels, doing their best to hide their presence. I still prefer to be in the background, but I guess that life is no longer an option for me.

When we reached the Reeve's house, I was impressed. It's nice, but not a mansion. Well kept, clean, and large, but not so large that I get the impression that he's trying to be anything special. It's the kind of house I would love to share with…

I stop that line of thinking. I continually have to remind myself that the option for a simple life is no longer mine.

Frippolee's wife welcomes us in an awkward manner. I don't think she's awkward. I think she just has no idea how to act around us. The look in her eye says she's not even sure this is all happening.

When we enter, she offers us drinks. I'm not sure what to ask for, so I take a risk. "What is a common drink around here? I often enjoy coffee. What is it you drink?"

Frippolee looks at me in shock, but then slowly says, "We have a form of coffee we drink here. It is strong, mixed with sugar, and we add cinnamon and other spices."

I smile. "Then that is what we would like to have. We are your guests, Frippolee."

Frippolee's wife, whom I realize now I didn't learn her name, scurries off into another room to make this particular drink. I see Ellcia nearly get up to help her, but then she hesitates. I know Ellcia would far rather be doing something than sitting here in a meeting.

As we wait, we speak of the farming community, how their system of government works, and more. It turns out, only those who have spent at least ten years working on one of the farms can work in town as an exporter. The Council is then made up of the six primary exporters, and the Reeve is selected by vote of the Council from those six.

When Frippolee's wife returns, we are all given a cup of this coffee mixture. None of the cups match. That's not a problem for me. It just seems odd because it appears that Frippolee's wife used just about any container she could find. I have an actual cup, along with Marleet, Roran, and Ellcia, but Frippolee himself has a bowl, and Hemot has what appears to be an old saltshaker, just without the lid.

I take a sip, and my whole body trembles just a little. I did not expect that. It's good, but it's kind of like a kick in the back of the head. I suspect I may not sleep for a month.

I set down the cup and thank Frippolee and his wife for their hospitality, and then lean forward. The room quiets right down, and everyone focuses on me.

I feel a wave of nervousness come over me, but I do my best to set it aside and remember Nordin's advice.

"Frippolee, and… Mrs. Frippolee…" In response to that, she smiles like I've given her a compliment. I think I'm out of my league here in trying to understand a people I've never met before. "… and members of the Council. I recognize this visit is unusual, but I turn to you in my time of need, and in a time of the Kingdom's need."

I wait, as Nordin told me, to let that sink in. They all look a little confused and a little scared.

"I am not sure what you have heard of all that has happened over the last nearly dozen years, but please bear with me as I cover what you may already know, and some things you most certainly do not."

I launch into a retelling of the rebellion that cost King Hartor and Queen Shalsee their lives. I tell of my father and mother's death, and how Prince Roran fled the castle and lived on the streets for many years, hiding his identity. I speak of my experience, along with Ellcia, Marleet, and Hemot. Then I speak of our escape from the castle, though we were as of yet unaware of our true identities, and my tale takes us through to Roran's enchantment, his abdication, General Lirnal's arrest, and more.

"So, you see, in the last few months, the man next in line to the throne was enchanted to abdicate. The man second in line to the throne, that is me, has had multiple attempts on his life and is currently thought to be dead by Parthun. The man third in line to the throne was arrested and charged with treason but has yet to be tried and likely never will be.

"That leaves Parthun, the man at the center of it all, set to inherit the throne. But he is unaware that I still live. Now, I have captured this warship, and stand with the support of these Lords and Ladies, along with the support of many others in the Kingdom, but I will not speak for them, as they must speak for themselves."

I look around the room. Everyone's face is filled with shock, maybe some fear, and a look that suggests they do not want me to continue.

"I am here for support. As the primary farming communities for the Kingdom, I seek your fealty. I seek your friendship."

I wait. They don't respond at first. Nordin didn't think they would. Reeve Frippolee opens his mouth to say something once or twice, but then closes it again.

When I've waited as long as Nordin suggested, I continue. "This is what I look for. It is time for me to step out of hiding and begin to reveal myself. This will enrage the usurper, King Parthun, but he cannot stand in my way or deny my claim to the throne without declaring himself a traitor. I suspect he will either threaten all those who support me or try to kill me before I can take the throne.

"I have come here for your support, and this is what it looks like. I ask that you offer me and those with me a place of safety during these difficult times. We seek shelter as we coordinate along the Sevordine coast and throughout the Talic. My soldiers will, of course, protect you. We do not ask you to fight, although if you are in danger, we ask that you fight to protect yourself, those whom you love, and to protect that which you own.

"And I ask that you spread the word about me, as long as it is safe and does not jeopardize your people. I ask that you spread the word that I am alive, and that I am preparing to bring forward a claim on the throne."

I pause again, and this is where Nordin says that I will establish myself as a different kind of royal. "But the immediate question that must be answered is obvious. What if you refuse?"

The men of the Council, Frippolee, and his wife all tense up. With the five of us, all dressed as Nobles, but all wearing swords and armor, plus my honor guard standing by the door, we must appear as quite the threat. I expect they believe they have no choice in the matter, as if I might kill them if they don't support me. But that also means the moment Parthun's troops arrive, they will do what he says, instead.

"Let me tell you the answer to that question, so there is no doubt," I begin. "If you refuse, you are still my people, and I will still serve you as the rightful heir to the throne. I will still seek to protect you, and I will not punish you. When I take the throne, and I will take the throne, you can be sure of this, I will not hold your choice today against you. I will not look back. I will only look forward. And you will continue to be my friends, and at that point you will offer me your fealty. If you stand with me today, we will work together and build our friendship now. If you do not, I will still love you as a King should, and you will suffer no consequences from me."

The room is silent. The eyes of the Council members flick toward one another, but no one dares even to turn his head.

I laugh and put my hands up. "Please, Frippolee. Mrs. Frippolee. Members of the Council. You are not in danger here. We come armed not due to a threat, but because we are warriors. We have had to fight far more than we wish. You are certainly under no threat from us. We will leave you now, and you may take the time you need to discuss my request. But hear this. Your safety is my concern. I will not abandon you, even if you do not support me now. If your answer is no, we will spend some time negotiating a means by which we can offer you our protection in case Parthun sends soldiers here. But for you, at this time, please, feel no fear from me. I am your future King. Not your enemy." I turn and smile at Frippolee's wife. "Mrs. Frippolee? Thank you for this coffee. It is something I have never tried before, but I hope to have it once again in your home in the future."

I stand, and everyone stands with me. Frippolee's wife smiles at me and thanks me for the compliment, offering her home as open to hospitality anytime I wish.

We leave and walk back toward the docks. Nordin figured we would not make it the entire way, and he was right. A messenger boy comes running to meet us and is stopped by one of my honor guard. The boy hands a note to the soldier, who hands it to me. The note simply reads, "If it pleases our future King, we ask that he might return to grace us with his presence once again."

"We're going back to the Reeve's house!" I call out, and our procession turns around.

## *17*

———•———

# The Cliffs in Sight

When we return, Frippolee, his wife, and the entire Council stand outside. A crowd has gathered—I suspect at the invitation of the Reeve. I'm not sure how this will go, but I guess this means we're not keeping my presence a secret.

We stop in front of his house, but I take a step forward, give a small respectful bow, and ask, "Have you come to a decision so soon, my friend?"

Frippolee steps forward and asks, "We have." The man glances back at the other members of the council and then turns back to me. Hesitantly, he asks, "Is it true? You will not hold it against us if we refuse?"

My heart goes cold. I had not expected them to refuse.

"It is true, Reeve Frippolee. You have my word. You will be my friend either way, although I prefer your support."

He bows and smiles. "Then you are not like the man who sits on the throne. He is cruel. He is unkind and unforgiving." As he says this, the other members of the council and all the people nod and mumble their agreement. "We have already heard of what he did to Port, the first fishing village this side of Sevord City. If you are the rightful heir, we must support you. But if you are to be a kind King, we wish to support you."

At this, they drop to their knees in front of us, and the people gathered around drop as well. Frippolee then calls out, "We offer you, O Prince Draydon, rightful heir to the throne, our fealty and our love."

Without thinking, I drop to my knees as well. As soon as I do it, I kind of regret it, because I landed on a small stone. It's not a huge stone, but just enough to make me want to scream, cry, fall over, and call out for a doctor. It takes all my willpower to hold it in.

"And I offer you, my friends of the farming community, my love and commitment. I will serve you as your King, faithful to you, and you will always have my ear in my Court."

I stand up quickly, mainly because my knee is in agony, and everyone else stands as well.

From this point, Nordin gave me no advice. And I really wish he had. Because it's just awkward. We all just stand here, staring at one another, hoping someone else will know what to say or do next.

That's when Marleet steps forward. "On behalf of the future King, I would like to invite the Reeve and Council and their spouses to join us on Prince Draydon's flagship, the Nimville. Please come for a meal and a tour of the ship."

I smile at Marleet. I've always cared a great deal about her, but she was so difficult since she and Hemot were so much alike. But now she's become someone who surprises me at every turn!

Everyone's face lights up, and they follow us to the ship. I wish I had someone I could send ahead to warn Hella, but I can't very well send my friends as they are Nobles, and I can't send the honor guard as they're supposed to be here with me. I briefly consider running ahead myself, but then remember I'm supposed to be the heir to the throne. Soooo… I just walk side-by-side with Frippolee.

As we walk, the Reeve grows serious. "Prince Draydon…"

"Please, call me Draydon while we speak informally. You are one of the first to declare your allegiance to me. I will always remember this."

Frippolee smiles and bows slightly toward me as we walk. "I am very aware that your presence could lead to a civil war. You are the proper heir—of that, I have no doubt. I met your father once, years ago, and you look like him. In fact, he was not much older than you when I met him, and if I didn't know better, I would say that I met him once again today, but only that the years had been kinder to him than to me."

I'm thrilled with that. I knew I looked a little like my father, but certainly not that much.

"But I also know King Parthun will not give up the throne easily. He will fight to keep his control. He has been a brutal man, even to the point of punishing our people for a lean harvest. Many of our young men were led away in chains four years ago because we had a dry year with little rain. We did all we could, but I lost my sons that day."

I stop and look at Frippolee. I don't want to say the wrong thing here. I'm just horrified at this. "Are they still alive? Do you know where they were taken?"

He shakes his head. "I suspect they are still alive. We were told when we made up for the poor harvest, our sons would be returned to us. If his soldiers spoke the truth, our sons will be held somewhere."

I shake my head. One more thing in this kingdom, one more horrific act of injustice, and I had no idea it was going on.

"When I take the throne," I say, "come to me in Sevord, and we will do all we can to find them. I do not know where they might be. I did not even know they had been taken, but we will search the records and find them."

The man's eyes fill with hope, and he nods. He doesn't speak, though. I see his bottom lip tremble. I get that. I've been there. I know it's best to remain silent during those moments.

"Come, my friend," I say. "For now, there is little we can do for your sons. The best we can do right now to save them is to remove Parthun."

"But," Frippolee says, stopping again. "I have two reasons for bringing this up. First, I know that your presence could lead to a civil war, and we have just declared which side we will stand on. But second, I fear that those taken from us will be used to sway our position. I fear we will be forced to abandon you to save our sons."

I nod and take his arm. "Listen, my friend. For now, all I ask is that you spread the word that I am alive, and that these four Nobles, along with two of the heroes of the Battle of Reber's Gate, stand with me. This is all I ask. By the time we must all come out in public, I hope to have enough support to keep the sons of the farming community safe."

Frippolee's eyes are filled with sadness, but he nods. "Thank you, Draydon."

I give his arm a squeeze, and we continue on until we reach the boat. Once there, we find Nordin has arranged a concert for us. I assume he saw us coming. Many of the people of Nimville play instruments, and we spend time listening to some of the coastal folk songs as the smells of a meal drift toward us. I don't know what she's cooking, but it's making my mouth water.

The rest of the evening is spent with Frippolee, talking, dreaming, learning, trying to understand one another. I'm not one for this kind of thing, but I guess I need to get used to it. When we're just about finished, I tell him I would like to meet with him privately tomorrow, and I ask him to come to the ship.

He promises to return, and they leave. In the meantime, I have a lot to discuss with Nordin and the others.

I sit across from Frippolee. He's just told me the story of when he met my father. I guess it was a big event in Shizzer, the main fishing village just south of here. He went with his parents to meet the first General of the Armies of Sevord and got to shake his hand.

It turns out Frippolee was the same age as my father, and the two spoke for quite some time about farming, fishing, war, kingdom politics, and personal hobbies.

It also turns out my dad enjoyed carpentry. I didn't know that.

We're meeting in my quarters around the table. There's no one else here. I'm not too concerned about my safety. Even if Frippolee turns out to be lying about his loyalty to me, he's not a big man, and I'm well-armed. I'm also wearing my armor under my cloak.

"I have a question for you, Frippolee." I stare at him for a moment and lean in. "I need you to keep this question and all this information secret—even from the Council and your wife."

He nods. "Of course, Draydon."

"I have to get to the Talic Region, but Parthun controls Switcher Pass, and there is little chance I'll get through without being caught and executed." I smile. "I'd rather avoid that, if I can."

Frippolee laughs. "I expect so. I assume you're wondering about the rumors that there is a secret passage through to the Talic from this area?"

I nod. "Is there?"

"There certainly are rumors! And plenty of them, too!" He looks down at the table and adds, "If there were such a path, you would take it, would you not?"

"Yes."

He shakes his head. "I am sorry. I cannot tell you anything."

I frown at him, and he sits back. As comfortable as he seemed to be with me a moment before, he's certainly afraid now.

"Draydon, please… please understand. There is a way through. It is known to a few of us, and it has been used at times. But we have not allowed anyone to use it in years."

"Why not?"

"Do you know what is in there?"

I shake my head.

"There are many creatures in that pass. It is small, although in spots it widens out. It is home to many beasts and monsters. There is a nest of gratters in there—although I suspect there may be more than one nest. There's talk of the occasional Reber Troll. And…" He looks at me and frowns. "It is the primary den of the Talic Wolves."

I lean back at that. I still don't know what a gratter is, but I'm hoping we can get past them. I know if we're careful, we should be able to deal with the trolls—I mean, avoid them. We can't actually *deal* with a troll. The only thing you can do is try to get past one without annoying it. I know if we don't bother them, trolls are quite passive.

But Talic Wolves. I was afraid that rumor was true. Those beasts are nightmares.

And if a Talic wolf sets its sights on us… again… we won't likely survive the second time.

"Draydon… I am just the Reeve of the farming communities. I'm not a great Lord or Noble of the Kingdom. I don't have any say except over what happens in this region. But those are small things. I cannot presume to stand in your way. But if you go in there, you won't come out again. We do not allow anyone to use it because everyone who goes into that pass dies."

I don't really like the idea of dying. It's not on my to-do list for anytime soon. But… I don't think there's any other way through.

"I have to go. I have to use it. I can't use Switcher Pass. That area is certainly heavily patrolled now. Even people who are not enemies of Parthun are likely questioned." I smile at Frippolee. "But I have a few advantages."

He looks at me and shakes his head. "I can't see how any of your training or experience or anything could get you through."

I nod. I'm not willing to tell him about my armor. Or my sword. Especially my sword. I've kept those things a secret for a reason.

"It's not my experience. I have other ways to keep myself safe."

He frowns. "Draydon. We are living under a tyrant. Even as far as we are from the capital, we experience his cruelty. And what we have experienced is nothing compared to what others have endured. If you risk your life, you risk the Kingdom. Is this what a King does?"

I smile at him and nod. "Frippolee, my life is for the Kingdom. I truly do not wish to be King, but it is the road I am called to walk, and I will walk it with integrity. I will seize the throne back from that usurper and rule with kindness and honor. But I cannot do that if I am not true to my word. And I have given a promise that I must fulfill. It is a risk to my life and to the Kingdom, but I have given my word. If I do not do this, I prove myself to be a liar, which means you will lose one liar on the throne, only to have him replaced by another. And then you will not even know if you can trust my word to show friendship to you. I must do this if I am to rule. So, yes, this is exactly what a King does."

Frippolee's head slump's forward, and he nods. "I think I understand. I do not think it is wise for you to go in there, but I know you must be true to your word, or we will have gained nothing." He looks back at me and says, "I will give you directions to the man to whom you must speak and send a letter giving you permission to enter the pass. There is only one who knows exactly where it is. Even I do not know the exact location. But, we have learned something else about the pass which you must know…"

*Three hours later…*

I've spent the last few hours speaking with Nordin, getting his advice, and fine-tuning our strategy to move forward in our attempt to snatch the Kingdom from Parthun's control.

I'm not comfortable with what I've learned about the pass through the cliffs, but I know I have to act. And I know the others are going to be angry with me. Not that I'm going. They know that already. But they will be angry with what I've decided.

I guess this is the part where I lead in the right direction, even when no one is happy with it.

The only problem I face is… will they follow? If not… I'm not really leading anyone or anything.

I sit down with the others. Nordin isn't here. I've already talked this through with him. He's not pleased, but he agrees with me.

I've sat myself down at the table in my cabin. I've learned there are chairs for the table, and they can be secured to the floor. I have set one of the chairs on one side of the table, and the others are on the other side. Nordin insisted I do it this way. It makes it clear that they are in my office. That I am in charge.

I think it also places a large wooden structure between me and the others, which is probably good, considering Ellcia is likely to leap across the table and gouge out my eyes when she hears what I have to say.

Hemot, Marleet, and Roran smile, but Ellcia does not. She knows something's up.

I stare at her for a moment as she stares back. Her hair's growing in. She still looks beautiful, even with her hair gone. I know she was upset about it earlier, but she seems to be doing well with it now. She still covers it at times, though, but I think that's mainly due to the cold.

Marleet has been chatting with Hemot and Roran, but she suddenly stops and looks at Ellcia and me. "What's wrong? Why is Ellcia upset? And why do you look sad, Draydon?"

I open my mouth to answer, but Hemot gasps. "I know what's going on!" Hemot points at me and says, "You've decided to use the Nimville to attack Sevord! We're going to war!"

"What?" I say, shaking my head. "Are you nuts? We can't attack Sevord with one warship and two hundred soldiers, most of whom are untrained."

"Oh, sorry," Hemot says. "Then why are you both upset?"

I glance back at Ellcia, but her eyes are on the floor, and she's grinding her teeth. Yep, she knows what I'm about to say.

"I've spoken with Frippolee. I've learned about the pass. And he's told me two things." I pause for a moment as I take a deep breath. "The first one is, it's extremely dangerous."

Hemot, Marleet, and Roran all break out in laughter. They laugh, and Hemot and Roran punch each other in their shoulders. It takes them far too long to calm themselves down.

When they do, I ask, "What's going on?"

"I thought you had something to say that might be unusual, or different, or hard to handle," Hemot says.

"Yeah!" Marleet adds with another laugh. "What have we done the last three months that hasn't been dangerous? We've been living on the edge, nearly dying at every single moment." Her face twists, and in a goofy voice she says, "Oh no! We are about to do something dangerous! I think this is something we've never done before! Maybe we will almost die! Oh, wait! We've almost died a hundred times!"

The others laugh again, and even Ellcia has a bit of a chuckle.

I smile and nod, putting up my hands. "Okay, so that was a dumb thing to say. It's just that this is likely going to be more dangerous. This pass is suspected to be the den of the Talic Wolves."

That gets their attention. The eyes of each of my friends bulge, and Ellcia's face goes pale. She shakes her head and quietly whispers, "No... you can't do this, Draydon."

I look down at the floor, taking another deep breath. When I'm ready, I look back up at them. "That's not all. The other part is this. Few people have survived this pass, but those who have... Frippolee tells me no groups have made it through. Only those who have either braved the pass alone or with only one other." I let that sink in for a moment before telling them plainly. "Roran and I are going alone. The rest of you will stay here."

They're silent for a moment, and Hemot and Marleet's mouths hang open. Ellcia looks at me like she really is about to climb over the table and gouge out my eyes. I begin to work through my exit strategy.

"We'll face it together, Draydon." Her tone says that's not up for discussion.

Hemot joins in and says, "We'll be the first group of five to make it through."

Even Marleet nods her head and says, "If we die, we die together."

I glance at Roran. I see he's struggling right now. The look in his eye suggests the ring's power is failing. Every time I see that, I'm reminded of how urgent it is that we find that Spellcaster. And soon.

I turn back to the others and shake my head. It's time to lead. I stand up, but the others remain in their chairs. I see they're a little surprised, and none of them know what to expect. "This is not up for debate. This decision is already made. It may seem foolish, but Roran needs me, and I have given my word. We will be leaving tomorrow morning. I'm not asking for permission or even agreement from any of you. I'm informing you of what's happening."

The others just sit there. I don't know what I expected from them, but they are not happy. Well, Hemot and Marleet seem disappointed, but they accept my words. Ellcia does not. Not at all. But I know she'll support me in this. Perhaps not right away, but she will in time.

Still standing, I continue. "For the rest of you, I need you to work hard for the Kingdom while I am gone. I need you to spread word that I have been found, and that I am putting forward my claim for the throne. I need you to put your names, titles, and influence behind me as you send out word. I need the entire coast to be aware of my claim, and if the names of Nobles are already behind me, then it will strengthen my claim."

I hate having to speak to my friends like this. This has never been the way we've done things, but I'm finding this hard, too. I just want the conversation done.

"Are there any questions?"

Hemot and Marleet shake their heads. I've crushed them, that's obvious to me, and I hate myself for doing that. Roran just looks uncomfortable. But Ellcia. I've wounded her. Deeply. And I don't know what to do about it.

When no one raises a question, I say, "Then I need to be alone for a time." I remain standing while they file out.

And I am reminded, yet again, that I don't want to be King.

I have my pack on, and Roran and I are ready to go. Frippolee is here. He's upset. I know he doesn't want me to go, but I also know he understands.

I had a chat with Hemot and Marleet last night. They're doing okay. They tell me they understand, and Marleet let me know that I will have to do that kind of thing many times when I'm King. I don't like the idea of just declaring my orders, but… I guess she's right.

However… she also said that Ellcia is probably not one of the people to do that with.

Likely ever.

Ellcia showed up on deck a few minutes ago. She came and gave me a quick hug, then backed away and stood with everyone else.

I'm grateful to Roran, because as I'm about to just leave, he stops me and tells me I'd better have a chat with her. I thought she wouldn't want to talk, but she's actually relieved when I ask.

We enter the boardroom and talk for a bit. We go over some of the same stuff a few times, but then she explains that she'll never be a proper Queen for me if I just order her around. "Do you really think that's the way we want our marriage to be? And do you really want to rule this kingdom alone, with me just one of the many people receiving orders?"

I shake my head. "I don't. I… just… I didn't see any other path last night. And I couldn't come up with how to talk to you about it."

She smiles at me, but it's a teasing sort of smile. "Well, then, that was your battle last night. You're not going to know how to get through every step you take when you're King, but you'll still need to face it. You can't just order your way through everything."

I grimace and nod. "I know. I'm sorry."

"I don't want you to go."

I shake my head. "I don't want to either. But…"

"But," she continues for me, "you've given Roran your word. And that is what will have to carry us through."

I smile at her and am reminded again of why I love her.

"How will I know if you've survived?"

My heart goes cold at the question. She's barely keeping it together. I can see that in her eyes. I don't have a good answer for her, so I give her the only answer I have. "You will have to move forward, assuming I'm alive. Assuming I've made it. There will be no other way to communicate for a long time."

She wraps her arms around me, and I hold her tight. Probably longer than I should, considering everyone is still waiting outside for me.

When we let go, she's smiling, but tears stream down her cheeks. We head out and join the others. Everyone seems happy to see Ellcia smile. I'm guessing the way I acted yesterday was not kept secret.

I rub my hand as I join Roran. It aches as I've spent a lot of the last few hours writing letter after letter. Apparently, if Ellcia and the others are to spend their time here calling for support for me, they're going to need declarations written by my hand. I hope they use them all, because it was a lot of work if most of them just sit on a shelf somewhere.

I feel like I should give a speech to everyone before I leave, but I don't know what to say. Besides, I've already spoken with everyone about their roles and about what I'm doing.

I give a nod, and they all smile and cheer. Well, those who don't know much about what I'm doing and how dangerous it is, they smile and cheer. The others just look like they're doing their best to maintain a steady expression.

We walk down to the dock and trudge on through the village. My honor guard is going with us for part of the way, but they'll return to the ship within a few hours. Nordin and Frippolee felt it was improper for Roran and me to walk through town without some formality.

Once we're past most of the farmhouses and more or less out of sight of the people, I send the men back. They don't seem too pleased to let us go. For one thing, they're taking this "honor guard" thing seriously. The other thing is, I've lived and worked beside these men in Nimville. They're good guys. And they care about me.

Once they've gone, the weight of everything lands on my shoulders. I don't know how long this will all take, but if it's anything like my last journey across Sevord, we could easily be close to three weeks. Each way.

I look back and immediately miss Ellcia. I kind of wonder how long her hair will be when I see her again. I'd actually like to be here to see it grow.

That's a weird thought. But I'm a weird guy.

We move along paths and roads leading through and around the fields. We were encouraged not to walk in the actual fields as they are covered in snow and have holes and furrows in them. If we step on one and go down, we might twist an ankle and our whole journey will end. Right in one moment.

These paths also have ruts and holes in them, but since they get a bit more use, it's easier to see what we're walking on.

We spend most of the day like this, slowly zigzagging our way to the east. The cliffs are visible in the distance, but they barely stick up above the horizon. They look just like a small line just out of reach. Almost like they could be dark storm clouds, warning us to take cover.

Roran and I don't talk much. I think he's pretty happy. I see the struggle in him every time I look in his direction, but he's likely so relieved to finally be on the way.

I decide to dive in to start a conversation. "I'm so sorry, Roran, that you're going through this. Hopefully, we can find this Spellcaster and free you in a few weeks."

"You've already said that."

I nod. I think he's probably right. I feel pretty bad about it all. I kind of wish he could still take the throne, but everyone has been clear. There's no hope of that.

He clears his throat and glances at me. "I'm sorry, Draydon. I'm not trying to be rude or mean. I just… this enchantment. I feel like it's sitting just behind my heart, waiting to push out and take over. I can feel it fighting for me. The ring isn't doing anything like what it was at first. It… uh… still works. But it feels brittle. Like the ring's protection is about to shatter. And I can see it."

That catches me by surprise. "What do you mean?"

He holds up his hand and comes to a stop. I take a look, and my mouth drops open. It looks like the ring's spiderwebbed with cracks, but there's something moving in there… a blackness… and a gray… swirling all around.

"It started doing this about a week after I put on the ring. It wasn't bad at that point—I mean, I wasn't feeling the pressure—but I could feel the ring struggle. At first, it was just a little crack, but it's grown a lot over the months, especially the last couple of weeks."

I put my hand on his shoulder. "Then let's pick up our speed."

He smiles, and we push on. He struggles a lot more than I do with the weight of the pack and the hiking along the road, but he's a lot more motivated than I am. Most of what I can think of is how much I don't want to enter that passage. Aside from fulfilling my promise and helping Roran, there's very little pushing me forward.

"According to Frippolee, the guy's farm is not far from here. Supposed to be down in a valley."

We're near the end of our second day of travel. The journey has been pretty uneventful so far. Just fields, paths, more fields, the occasional lone tree. The most exciting thing up until now has been the appearance of a flock of birds intent on digging through the thin layer of snow. We've also barely spoken, but I don't think it's because he's angry. I think we just don't have much to talk about.

It's been boring.

Of course, quiet and boring is better than the last time we moved east across Sevord and the Talic. Back then, it felt like we could barely take three steps before someone or something tried to kill us. Come to think of it, this journey has been nice.

"His name's not Frippolee."

"What? I…" I don't really know at first what he's talking about, but then it comes to me. "What do you mean? He told me that was his name."

"Nope. Not really."

I wait for him to continue, but he doesn't. He just keeps walking. I hate it when people do that.

Finally, I'm about to ignore the issue and pretend I don't care, when he says, "It's kind of like a title. In the Northern Tribes, they have official statuses like Reeve, or Mayor, or Lord, or Duke, or whatever. But if you rise to that position, you get a name as well. Frippolee is an old name that means leader of the people. So, with a title like Reeve Frippolee, it shows his legal status, as Reeve, but also his status among the people, the Frippolee."

"Huh…" I say. I find that kind of interesting, but I'm also now wondering what his actual name is.

"So, Hemot's and Marleet's families have large properties up on the northern side of the Talic. Hemot, as the new landowner and heir to his family's estate, is actually a Frippolee, and Marleet's dad is a Frippolee."

"Are we Frippolees?" I ask with a smile.

He shakes his head. "Nope. Well… I guess I could be. But the King can't be a Frippolee. It's more a position recognized by the people. But the King doesn't really have to be recognized by the people. He's just the King whether you want him to be or not. There's a story of a King many generations ago who was named Frippolee, but he spent a great deal of his time in the north and somehow earned the title."

I don't envy Roran's upbringing—he grew up on the street—but I do envy his education. He knows far more about this nation than I do.

Roran chuckles to himself. "So… um… you know how you called his wife, 'Mrs. Frippolee'?"

I frown and nod. This doesn't sound good. I'm not sure what I've done.

Roran laughs. "Did you see how happy she was when you called her that?"

I nod slowly.

"Imagine if the King came up to you and called you the First General of the Armies."

"Okay…"

"What would that tell you, Draydon?" Roran laughs. "What… um… message would you receive loud and clear?"

I close my eyes and stop in my tracks. "I just declared her the Frippolee of the area."

"Yup!" Roran says with yet another laugh as he halts and turns around. It's good to hear him laugh. I doubt he's done much of that in the last while. But I don't like that he's laughing at me.

"Did I mess things up big time?"

Roran stares at me. "I have no idea, Draydon. I'm guessing this is going to be a confusing one for her since she's not the elected Reeve, but now she's Frippolee. It might take them a while to figure out what it means. I just hope no one goes on a power-trip. If they do, there could be a lot of trouble. The Reeve and his wife seem to get along well, though, so I'm guessing they can work it out."

I shake my head and start up again. I don't know how I could have avoided that one. Well… I could have actually asked her name. I also don't know if it makes much difference.

For the next while, we chat more. He starts to tell me a bit of what it was like growing up on the streets with Rulf. It feels strange to think that I've never known this, but we haven't had much chance to actually talk, considering he pretended to be nearly incapable of regular conversation when we first met.

It turns out they stayed in many different places over the years. Abandoned attics, an old warehouse, a vegetable market. Of course, places like the vegetable market were only available during the winter months, but they managed to find places to stay for just about every night. He did have to spend a few nights on the street, though. Some of them were in the dead of winter.

I feel sad about that. I had it pretty easy compared to him. Though I spent all those years deceived about who I was, I always had a warm bed and plenty to eat.

I tell him a bit about life in the castle. The part he finds hardest to believe, despite the fact that he already knows it, is that Parthun always treated me well and was almost like a father to me. Well… like an interested uncle, anyway. I never suspected he was capable of all he had done.

Our conversation's interrupted as Roran catches sight of a cottage. We've come to the edge of a fairly deep valley. The land slopes down here and around to the other side, and then the valley runs off to the south for quite a long way. It's a large area, and I suspect the level ground at the bottom is all farmland.

Down the side and through the center of the valley is what looks like a large river. A stone bridge runs across it from this side to the other, not far from where the cottage sits.

The wind has just recently picked up, and it's cutting through my cloak, so the sight of the smoke coming up from the chimney looks quite appealing to me.

We start down the hill, and at the bottom, we move along what might be a road. There's more snow down here than up above, so it's hard to tell what we're walking on.

When we reach the bridge, I'm impressed at not only its workmanship but also its size. The river is wide, and I suspect during the spring and times of heavy rain, it likely flows pretty fast and deep.

As we walk through the gate leading to the cottage, I glance at Roran. "I think we should go by our other names while we're here. I'll call you Mic. You call me Caric."

He nods. "That's fine with me, Caric."

We take a few more steps before the front door swings open. I'm about to call out a greeting, when an old, scruffy man with no hair on the top of his head, but a long scraggly white beard hanging down to his belly steps out with a crossbow.

And fires.

# 18

## The Heart of a King

The bolt moves so fast we don't even have a chance to react. It zips by my right shoulder, and I hear the thud as it lodges in the old fence post behind me.

A warning shot… no… wait. From the look on the man's face, that was no warning shot. He just missed.

He pulls out another bolt, drops his crossbow down to the ground, and begins to pull back the bowstring.

Roran and I race forward, but we slow down and then stop. The man's struggling with the bolt. It slips out, then he puts it back in, but can't get it pulled back far enough. A moment later, the crossbow just… falls over.

"Do you need a hand with that?" Roran asks.

"Yes," the man says, "maybe if you could, um… pull the thing… back for me, I could put the, um… pointy thing in it and then… I could shoot these intruders. I think… um…" The man raises his eyes and stares at Roran. "You look familiar. Are you my great-gramma?"

"What?" Roran looks offended at first, but then calms himself. "No, sir, I'm sorry. That I am not. We're guests. We're visitors, sent here by Reeve Frippolee. He said you could help us."

The man slowly nods. "Yes, I think that's probably right. But what about the intruders?"

"They're not a problem, sir," Roran explains.

The man stares at the crossbow, and Roran reaches down, takes it from him, and the three of us move back into the cottage.

What hits me first—even before seeing the mess, hearing the screech of birds, and the incredible heat is the smell. It reeks in here. It smells like… it takes me a moment to place it. In Sevord, now and then, I'd come across someone who hadn't bathed in a long time but was also really dirty. It was a smell like nothing else.

My heart goes out to the man. Here, all alone, and he's clearly struggling with his mind. I don't really know what we can do, though.

I jump as something scurries by my feet. At first, I think it's a small cat, but it looks like a squirrel. As I look around, I spy a couple of them here and there. The poor man must have trouble feeding them and himself over the winter.

He moves to a stove and puts some water in a pot over the heat. A moment later, he drops some tea leaves in.

I don't like tea. I plan on turning it down at first, but then I realize the main reason I don't want to drink it is not because of the tea. It's because of how dirty everything is. I'm disgusted, but then I remember something.

He's mine. This man… he's in my Kingdom. I'm his future King. He's my responsibility. I have to care for this man, just like everyone else.

I spin around and try to figure out what I can do. I see a few chairs and clean them off, along with a table. There's plenty of gross stuff all over the place, but I dive in and start cleaning. If I can't care for this man, how can I care for an entire Kingdom?

By the time the tea is ready, I've actually managed to clear the table and chairs, and started to make a dent on the mess in the place. I mean... a small dent. Very small.

The man gives us each a cup and has one himself. I'm sure the cup wasn't clean before the tea went in, but I drink it anyway.

When we've sat for a bit, the man says, "I don't remember you arriving. Have you been here long?"

I shake my head. "No, we just arrived. What's your name?"

The man focuses on me, but just sits there with his mouth partly open for a long time. When he finally speaks, he simply says, "I don't think I can remember that."

"That's okay. My name is Caric. And this is Mic. We're here to see you."

"Are you here to give me my new orders?" the man asks.

I nod. "Yes. You need to tell us how to find the pass, then when you're done, we need you to leave this place and travel back to the farming community. They will take care of you there."

"Do I need taking care of?"

"Absolutely," I say with a smile. "I'll send a note with you telling them that you are to be welcomed into the community and helped as much as you need it."

"That sounds nice." The man's eyes glaze over. "I don't think I've seen many people for a while. I'm not even sure..." He focuses on me for a moment, then asks, "Are you here now?"

"We are," I say with a smile and put my hand on his forearm. "You're not alone anymore."

My heart breaks for this guy, especially when I consider that he's a man in my Kingdom. I wonder how many others live like him.

"What was the first thing you needed?"

"We need to find the pass."

At that, the man's eyes clear, and he sits up straight. "Oh, that's a dangerous place, Caric. I'm afraid you'll not survive your journey through there."

I glance over at Roran, and the look in his eye is the look he gets when the enchantment is fighting for control. "That's okay. We need to try."

I pull out the letter from Frippolee and show it to the man. He holds it out at arm's length, squinting at the page, but eventually seems satisfied.

"Come with me."

He grabs a cloak, and we walk out the front door. Once he's led us around back, the three of us trudge our way up the hill in the direction of the cliffs. When we reach the top, he points. "See that copse of trees on top of the cliffs?"

"I see them."

"Directly below that and slightly to the right is the opening. It's just a crack. Not much more than the size of you, actually. On the other side, it opens up, but right there, you can climb through. The opening might be covered with bushes or more, so you may have to dig your way through." He turns back to me. It's amazing how lucid he is right now, compared with a few moments before. "What's the other thing?"

"Ah, the other thing," I say. I had told him there were two things—the second being his orders. "I need to write a letter for you, and then I need you to go back to the farming community. When you get there, find Reeve Frippolee and give him the letter."

"But… my farm…"

I shake my head. "That mission is complete. It's time for your next one."

He stares at me for a moment before a large smile breaks out on his face. "That sounds good." He laughs and adds, "You look like your father! General Geran was a good man!"

"How do you…" but I stop. His eyes tell me he's no longer lucid.

"Come with us," I say, and lead the man down the hill.

When we get to his cottage, I ask Roran to pack some supplies for the man. I fear he might not find his way back to the farming communities, but I think he won't survive here much longer on his own. I don't really know what the right thing to do is.

We get him packed, and I write a note to Frippolee, telling him the man needs to be cared for, fed, and provided a place to stay. I wonder to myself who's going to pay for this man's food and lodging, but I just have to let them figure that out.

When he's ready, I confirm that he knows the way to the farming community and what all he's supposed to do. I even write a second note and tie it to his sleeve. It reads, "Go west, back to the farming community. Find Reeve Frippolee."

I watch him go. He moves well, but then again, he has a bit of a limp. At the moment, he seems fine. I frown and say, "I hope he makes it."

Roran lets out a little chuckle. He hasn't spoken much since we arrived, and he doesn't say anything, other than to head back into the cottage to extinguish the fire. I don't know what to do about the animals, so we just chase them outside. I think they should survive. They usually do, when they don't have a cottage to hide from the cold.

When we're half-way up the hill heading east again, I ask, "So, what's so funny?"

"You."

"And what's funny about me?"

Roran just climbs for a bit longer, grinning the whole way. I wait it out. He has a harder time on hills than I do. When we get to the top, I ask again. "What's funny?"

"It's not so much that you're funny," Roran says. "It's just that it makes me laugh because I realized something."

"What's that?"

"Rulf told me when I met with him that I have to give up on the idea of being King. As much as I knew that, and regardless of how many people have told me that, I still couldn't let it go. I actually went to Rulf to ask him to help me take the throne. He told me the only way I could take it now was by force, and that would make me a tyrant."

We walk in silence for a bit. I appreciate Rulf saying that, although it scares me a bit, what Roran was thinking.

After a couple minutes, Roran continues. "Rulf told me that despite the fact that you complain a lot, he respects you and thinks you'll be a good King. He says you'll likely be as good a King as my father was. And he told me just to get behind you. Be your greatest support, and that's how I can love the Kingdom."

I nod. I don't know how to respond to that. I don't think I'm a complainer, but anything I say about that right now will sound like complaining, so I just hold it in.

"I trust Rulf, and I've been working on giving it up. And I think I have, Draydon." He stops, grabs my arm, and looks intently at me. "I really have. But I was still worried about the Kingdom, until I saw you with that man. I think if you can love a man who stinks like that and who's clearly not in his right mind, you're going to be a good King."

I feel my face go all hot. I've never been one for compliments. I always feel like I don't deserve them.

His eyes drop for a moment before he looks me in the eye again. "When I was growing up and had to... you know... pretend to be like that man," Roran says slowly, "I saw you a lot in the city. I knew you were my cousin. I knew you had been my friend, but you didn't remember me. And…" He takes a deep breath and smiles uncomfortably. "You always treated me well, but I felt you looked down on me."

I nod. I don't think there's anything else I can say or do. He's right. We both know it.

"You've changed, Drayon. You're not that guy anymore."

I nod again. There's not much about me that's the same person I was a year ago.

"Promise me something, Draydon."

"What?"

"Promise me you'll love all of Sevord like you love that man right there."

I smile and bow my head slightly. I feel my eyes watering a bit, and I kind of want to cry. "I promise, Roran. I promise to try to love everyone like that. But I want you there by my side to hold me to my promise. I need you."

Roran surprises me with a big hug. I hear a muffled, "I promise, Draydon."

When he lets go, I feel awkward. He obviously does, too. I'm not a huggy kind of guy, although I do it now and then. On top of that, tears stream down my cheeks, and he's crying too. I don't like showing too much emotion, and I don't think he does either. Without another word, we turn and walk forward.

And I think today, I gained a brother.

We've walked along the edge of the cliffs for about ten minutes now. We're a little south of where we need to be, I think. So far, we haven't seen any openings or even areas which might be camouflaging a hole or passage.

I had wanted to approach the passage from the south of where the man said so we could make sure we didn't miss it, but I hope to see something soon. So far, the area has just been solid rock.

The cliffs in this area are not as high as they are farther south. It's interesting to see how low they are, and it makes me wonder if they are even lower the farther you go north. I get a brief image of the cliffs actually flattening out so we can walk up them, but that wouldn't make sense. Everyone always says there's no way up or down. The only way is the one Marleet spoke about, which no one knows about. I think I had read that the cliffs actually curve around the Talic region, closing that area off until nearly the mountain range.

"What's that up there?" Roran asks, pointing ahead.

We pick up speed, and in a moment, I see it. It's a series of bushes and trees that grow up the side of the cliff. It doesn't look out of place or anything, except for the fact that we've been told the opening is here somewhere.

When we get close, I notice the plants. Although they're dormant as it's still winter, they all grow toward the center. "I think this is it."

The ground slopes up somewhat at this point in the cliffs. We scramble up, and as we get closer to the center, I hear something. Can't quite make it out, but it's there. It's a roar... but it's also words.

Despite the freezing wind, I feel myself begin to sweat. I'm not even sure what it is, but something sounds familiar.

We pull back the branches, and sure enough, there's an opening, and the two of us immediately start to squeeze through, but then we stop, and my heart goes cold.

I hear it clearly now. The anger, the rage, the hatred. The insatiable hunger. The desire. The evil. My hands begin to shake, but not from the cold.

I haven't heard that voice since we first fled Haner months ago, but it screams the same thing it did back then. It's the same four words over and over again, a voice I had hoped never to hear again.

"Give me the princeling! Give me the princeling!"

I look over at Roran, and his face has drained of all color. The only way forward now is a path that leads us straight to the Talic Wolf. The Talic Wolf that only wants one thing.

Me.

# Continued in The Long Battle
## Book Five of the Sevordine Chronicles.

# Pronunciation Guide

Now, you might think that I have tried to create a proper
pronunciation guide, but I don't know how to do that. I
could look it up, but not only do I not understand
diacritical markings, but I think most people don't. So… I
made a pronunciation guide that makes sense to me with
the capital letters pointing out the emphasis.
And here it is.

| | |
|---|---|
| Berin | BARE-rinn |
| Caric | CARE-ick |
| Corter | CORE-ter |
| Draydon | DRAY-dunn |
| Ellcia | ell-CEE-ah |
| Farnum | FAR-num |
| Frindor | FRIN-door |
| Frippolee | FRIPP-oh-lee |
| Granel | GRA-nell |
| Gratter | GRA-terr |
| Haner | HAY-ner |
| Hartor | HAR-terr |
| Hella | HELL-ah |
| Hemot | HEM-mot |
| Hillbin | HILL-binn |
| Leito | LAY-toh |
| Lirnal | LIR-nall |
| Marleet | mar-LEET |
| Morgin | MOR-ginn |

| Nordin | NOR-dinn |
| Parthun | PAR-thunn |
| Rainer | RAY-nerr |
| Reber | REE-berr |
| Relin | RELL-linn |
| Shaloomd | sha-LOOM-d |
| Shalsee | SHALL-see |
| Shawn | AWE-some |
| Talic | TAL-ick |
| Tallia | TAL-lee-ah |
| Tilbur | TILL-burr |
| Trevolay | TREV-oh-lay |

# CHECK OUT THESE BOOKS BY
## Shawn P. B. Robinson

## Adult Fiction (Sci-fi & Fantasy)

The Ridge Series (3 books)
ADA: An Anthology of Short Stories

## YA Fiction (Fantasy)

The Sevordine Chronicles (5 Books)

## Books for Younger Readers

Annalynn the Canadian Spy Series (6 Books)
Jerry the Squirrel (4 Books)
Arestana Series (3 Books)
Activity Books (2 Books)

www.shawnpbrobinson.com/books

9 781989 296622